P.I.E.C.E.S.
A Booster's Story

P.I.E.C.E.S.
A Booster's Story

TAMMY FOURNIER

Urban Books
1199 Straight Path
West Babylon, NY 11704

P.I.E.C.E.S. A Booster's Story copyright © 2008 Tammy Fournier

ISBN- 13: 978-1-60162-035-4
ISBN- 10: 1-60162-035-7

First Printing November 2008
Printed in the United States of America

10 9 8 7 6 5 4 3 2 1

This is a work of fiction. Any references or similarities to actual events, real people, living, or dead, or to real locales are intended to give the novel a sense of reality. Any similarity in other names, characters, places, and incidents is entirely coincidental.

Distributed by Kensington Publishing Corp.
Submit Wholesale Orders to:
Kensington Publishing Corp.
C/O Penguin Group (USA) Inc.
Attention: Order Processing
405 Murray Hill Parkway
East Rutherford, NJ 07073-2316
Phone: 1-800-526-0275
Fax: 1-800-227-9604

This book is dedicated to the strong women in my life who helped mold me into the woman that I have become. To my grandmother, Mama Grace, who taught me the love of God and family. To my mother, Minnie Morgan, who taught me about class and style, and to my sister, Kim Castaneda, who taught me that knowledge is our future.
I love you all!

ACKNOWLEDGMENTS

What I know for sure is that life is a journey. There are people you meet along the way who come into your life for a purpose. They come to teach you something, to show you something, to give you something. I have been blessed to meet angels along my journey, and for them I am truly grateful.

To my dearest friends, Kim Hairston, Donna Hayden, and Leonard Hall, you have been my rocks. Kim, you taught me how to grow into a woman. Donna, you taught me how to have a real relationship with God. Lenny, you've taught me how to be a true friend.

To my sisters, Tei Street, Tamela Collins, W. Shawn Gibbs, Fran Frazier, Tamera Moore, Joyce Beatty, Yvette McGee Brown, Earth Jallow, Joylynn Jossel, Diana Lee, Lela Boykin, Marisa Starks, Ashley Price, Brandy West, Jonna Hayden, Warden Tracy Parker, and my aunt, Nancy Winfield; you all have shown me what it means to give of yourself in service. I pray I become the women you all are. Do it, my sisters.

To my Langford cousins, you have shown me how to value and support each other as family. Patricia Ann, your lessons have molded me into a strong, proud black woman.

To Rev. Gary Sims, Tei Street, Pastor Victor Davis, Tamela Collins, Revival Development Corporation, Bishop Roger Hairston, Temple of Faith, the Girl Scouts Seal of Ohio Chapter, Warden Tracy Parker, Franklin Pre-Release Center, Exodus Marion Correctional, Bonds Beyond Bars, Flintridge Development Board, Ray of Hope, Juvenile Justice Planning Committee, Citizen Advisory Board, and my agent, Joylynn Jossel—I am forever grateful to all of you for believing in me and blessing me with opportunity.

Some people live a lifetime searching for true love. I have been blessed to know true love three times in my life, so to Larry Donnell Price, Melvin Jesus Fournier, and Kerry Scott Mitchell, I say thank you for loving me.

To the heirs to my throne, my reasons for living, and all that is good in me: Beau, Deone, and Ashley. All that I am, and will ever be, is because of you three. To Ashley, who is the wisdom, kindness, and patience in me. To Deone, who is the leader, strength, and gentleness in me. And to my firstborn son, Beau, the thug, fighter, and giver in me, I am honored to be your mother. I worship God for blessing me with all of you.

To my grandchildren Emmanuel, Heaven, Jaden, and my Maggie (Precious), you are our future. Know that it is knowledge that sets us all free.

And to all my brothers and sisters on lockdown, your life has a purpose and God has a plan for us all.

P.I.E.C.E.S.
A Booster's Story

Prologue

Mama's House

The Christmas of 1984 was much anticipated, just as every other Christmas before. Seven-year-old Tara lay on the living room floor on Christmas eve, enjoying every sight, sound, and smell of the season. The house was dressed up for the occasion. Every nook and cranny was adorned in some sort of Christmas trinket. There was a mixture of religious holiday decor and secular retail holiday themes. The air was filled with the smell of spices and baking meat. Tara could hear in the distance the collard greens boiling rapidly in the oversized steel pot.

Christmas held a special place in Tara's heart. It was the one time of year when she felt special and all was right with the crazy world she'd been forced to live in. The warm, special feelings came few and far between. It was not because she wasn't loved; it was because it was so hard for her grandparents to focus on just her alone when there were so many other mouths to feed, clothes to wash, and beds to make.

"Tara? Tara? Girl, do you hear me talking to you?"

Mama Grace yelled as she entered the living room with her hands on her hips and a look of annoyance on her face.

Mama Grace was Tara's maternal grandmother. She was a kind, loving, and stern woman. There was nothing not to love about Mama Grace, which is why she held such a special place in Tara's heart. Tara always said when she grew up, she wanted to be just like Mama Grace, especially since that was the only mama she knew to be like, with her biological mother gone and all.

"Gal, didn't you hear me calling you?" Mama Grace continued. "If you hurry up and get your narrow tail in the kitchen, you may be able to lick the bowl with the last of the caramel cake batter Mama Minnie is putting in the oven," Mama Grace instructed.

"Ooh, ooooh, Mama Grace, I want some," Tara said as she leaped up from the worn carpet and ran for the kitchen.

"You know I done told you about running in this house, gal," Mama Grace yelled behind her to no avail, as Tara kept on running, breaking house rule number one: no running through the house.

Mama Grace stood in the narrow doorway that separated the small living room from the dining room and wondered how she had made it through the last three years raising five young children and holding down a full-time job. It seemed like only yesterday she sat before the angry-faced, elderly judge and overworked social worker, pleading for the chance to spare her grandchildren from the iron jaws of the system.

The children, all a year apart in age—Michael, the oldest at twelve years; Benny, the second oldest; Karen, the prissy girl; Reggie, the curious boy; and Tara, the baby—all sat in the sparsely-lit courtroom in the large wooden chairs that seemed to swallow them whole. Mama Grace had come to the courtroom that day to save her grandchildren from "the man"—the white man. They were trying to send them off to different foster homes; some even run by white folks. But Mama Grace was not about to have that. She was going to do everything she knew how to prevent such a travesty.

She knew it would be a struggle adding five more mouths to her overstretched budget; however, she could not let the man raise her grandchildren. She'd seen nothing but pain from Mr. Charlie, the so-called men with the fancy degrees and all the opportunity. Even though they did their best to try to convince Mama Grace that the bleachy-clean foster home was the best place for the children, if she could help it, her babies were going home with her.

"Sir, I know y'all feel we too old to be raising these small children," Mama Grace sang, looking over at Ernest, her husband and the children's grandfather. "But I been raising children all my life. If it ain't been my own, it's been somebody else's. I think every somebody who ever grew up in my neighborhood has lived with me at one time or another. Raising children is what I do. It ain't fittin' that black children not be raised by black folks. And they need to be raised together for that matter; under the same roof. Now I know it's gon' be tough, but that's what family is for. I got my daughter and my son with me today, and they both willing to say they able to pitch in if need be. With that said, I'm gon' return to my seat, sir," she said, smoothing out the wrinkle in her eyelet two-piece spring suit with the matching pillbox hat.

"Thank you, Mrs. Moore. You may step down," Judge Shoemaker instructed.

Mama Grace glided across the creaky buffed wooden

floor with elegance as she smiled at her family seated in the chairs behind the divider.

"If there are no further arguments, I am ready to announce my decision," the judge said, looking down over his glasses at a paper in front of him. "I find that it is fitting that the minor children be placed in the custody of Mr. and Mrs. Ernest Moore until review in December of 1968. This court is dismissed." Judge Shoemaker banged the heavy gavel on his large, antique desk. And from that day on, Tara and her brothers and sisters had been Mama Grace's responsibility.

Tara entered the kitchen and glanced around to see where she could squeeze in between her brothers, sister, and two cousins, Bruce and Rick. The kitchen sat at the back of the house. It was a modern-day miracle that all the children—along with two refrigerators, pots, pans, mix-matched chairs, two china cabinets, and the large, overworked stove— fit in the small space.

"Karen, save me some. I want some," Tara whined.

"You've been in there playing while you should have been in here," Karen shot back.

Karen was Tara's big sister by two years, and Tara looked to her sister for everything in her world filled with boys. Karen took one final swoop of the bowl with her skinny fingers and then passed the bowl to Tara.

"Oh! Thanks, Karenba," Tara snorted as she grabbed the bowl from her sister and squeezed between her cousin Rick and her youngest brother, Reggie.

"Move, Tootsie," Reggie said, using the nickname they often called Tara.

"Hey, let's see who can make theirs last the longest," Rick offered as his eyes shot across the room to his older cousins.

"Don't start that playing in my kitchen," Mama Minnie scolded, while placing oversized cake pans in the oven.

Mama Minnie, who was Mama Grace's mother, was the matriarch of the family. As long as Tara could remember, Mama Minnie lived with Mama Grace and Granddaddy and provided much-needed assistance with the care of the children.

Every occasion had an added elegant touch if Mama Minnie had a hand in it. She had a way of making a little go a long way. She could stretch a few groceries into a feast that would feed everyone who just happened to stop by.

"Whew, that was good," Tara offered, licking the last of the batter off of her fingers and then handing the bowl that had been licked clean to Mama Minnie.

"Wow, girl, I can put this dish in the cabinet. It doesn't even need washing." Mama Minnie laughed.

"Can we have some cake when it's done?" Tara begged Mama Minnie.

"No, gal, you know these cakes are for Christmas dinner," Mama Minnie said. "You'll just have to wait 'til tomorrow."

Tara glanced at the large three-leaf table in the small dining room; it was filled with an assortment of holiday treats. Mama Minnie looked forward to the holidays. She would start baking a week before Christmas. Tara's eyes soaked in all the treats. She could almost taste the sweet, sticky icing of the three-layer caramel cake. Fresh-baked chocolate and oatmeal cookies were piled high on shiny silver trays, sitting next to her favorite dessert, coconut and pineapple six-layer cake. The lovely prepared goodies spread across the old wooden table could hold up in the best of households. The Moore family was poor by most standards, but the abundance of love and attention that went into the holidays was rich.

"Who's the bull of the woods?" Tara could hear her grand-father saying as he entered the front door with his drink-ing buddy, Preacher Morgan. Granddaddy was a medium build, bronze-colored, handsome elderly man. He had what would be called good hair in the ghetto, and keen white features. It was no secret to anyone who knew him that he was part Indian and very proud of it. He made everyone aware that he came from a family of proud black folks. He instilled in his children, as well as his grandchildren, that being a Moore was a badge of honor.

He often shared stories of how his great-grandparents were some of the first to own land after slavery and how there was a town in Tennessee that was named Promise Land by his ancestors. He would tell stories of how the land still belonged to the family and how they were rich in history.

"Tara, go get ya granddaddy a shot glass," he demanded, getting comfortable in his favorite chair by the front door.

Tara ran into the kitchen and pushed the step stool to-ward the cabinet. "Get away from there before you break your neck," Mama Grace yelled as she reached in the yel-low metal cabinet, removing two small shot glasses. "Here, take these to that old fool before he gets started." She handed the glasses to Tara.

"Mind your own business, old woman," Granddaddy spat, walking into the kitchen and sucking his teeth.

There was a love-hate relationship between the dedi-cated married couple. They both stayed clear of the other, each respecting the power the other held over the house-hold.

Tara loved her granddaddy. He made every one of the grandchildren feel like they were his favorite. And what Tara loved about him most was that he was much easier to get stuff out of than Mama Grace.

"Granddaddy," Tara whined, figuring she'd try her luck at getting a piece of cake. "Can we have some cake?" she asked in her sweetest voice.

"Tara, didn't Mama tell you those cakes are for Christmas dinner?" Mama Grace cut in. "Come over here and help me plug in the lights for the tree."

Tara made her way to the tall, silver, overly decorated tree. With her small hand guided by Mama Grace's, they plugged a string of lights into the wall. The tree sprang to life as the lights began to warm up.

"Mama Grace, can I plug in the color wheel too?" Tara begged

"Go ahead, but be careful. You know that old thing overheats," Mama Grace cautioned.

The color wheel was a bulky, weird-shaped wheel with a lightbulb and three primary colors that spun around, causing the tree to change colors. After plugging the most nostalgic decoration of them all into the wall outlet, Tara lay on the floor, enjoying the rainbow of color the wheel gave off.

She became lost in her thoughts, imagining what surprises the brightly wrapped packages underneath the tree held. Tara decided to find one with her name on it and give it a shake to see if she could try to guess its contents. Just as she got up from the floor, the front door flung open. Tara saw three large shadows enter the living room. As she tried to focus her eyes, she heard a voice say to her, "Come here, baby."

Tara looked into the beautiful woman's face that looked hauntingly like her mother. But this couldn't be her mother, Tara reasoned. Her mother was dead.

One

The Workhouse

"Trraaays!" Creeper yelled, startling Tara from her daydream. She looked around the overcrowded cell and thought, *Damn, another day in this bitch.* Tara could not believe she was spending Christmas eve in this motherfucka—the workhouse.

Tara had been confined to the overcrowded, sweaty, stinky concrete box for ten days now. There were thirty-two women crammed in what was laughingly called a dorm. The room was designed to house fifteen inmates, but the county was known for rackin' and stackin' as many bodies as possible in each holding tank.

Rumor had it that the Franklin County Correctional Center located in the south end of Columbus, Ohio used to allow the women to leave the dorms each day. They were made to work in the gardens that used to be located in the fields out back. The women were forced to work "from see to can't see" each day, so the center was given the name "workhouse."

"What's for lunch?" Creeper demanded to know from no one in particular.

"Vegetable lasagna," an inmate named Shorty offered, hoping to gain some unknown points from Creeper.

It was a known fact that Creeper was the chick in charge. Reputation was everything in the belly of the beast. Creeper was infamous behind the walls and on the street for beating a bitch down in a New York minute. Hell, Creeper could even hang with some of the best nigga toe-to-toe. She even held weight with the deputies. Everyone who worked the dorms was filled in on the dangers of Creeper. She was known for putting motherfuckers in the hospital when they dared to try her.

Creeper walked from the sleeping area into the dayroom, looking around for a victim. "Hey, crackhead hoes, I'm getting some extras from y'all worthless bitches," she spat.

The intimidated women continued to focus their eyes elsewhere, hoping not to gain attention from Creeper. She swept the room with her eyes and then made her way over to the newest victim in the dorm. The poor crackhead had just arrived the night before. She hadn't even fully awakened from her crack coma when Creeper attacked.

"Trick bitch, I'm taking yo' shit," Creeper boasted. "And yours too," she added, staring down Two Tall, a six-foot hooker who was sitting beside the new girl and somebody's grandmother who was bought in on a drunk-driving charge two days ago.

Tara entered the dayroom and yelled, "Creeper, leave those girls alone. You ain't taking shit. Quit fucking with everybody. You are just one miserable bitch; plain and simple."

Creeper looked over at Tara and settled down. "Damn,

Tara, you always blocking a bitch's actions," she complained.

Creeper and Tara knew each other from the streets. Tara, just like Creeper, held an unspoken respect in the dorm. But it had nothing to do with her going to blows with a chick or being violent, period. But instead, it had everything to do with her bloodline. Everybody knew what family Tara came from, a family of straight hustlers. And that alone earned her the utmost respect.

Legend had it that her father was Wendy Anderson, one of Columbus's infamous pimps; and her mother was M&M, given name Mary Moore, who was credited with putting the *B* in boosting, as well as the *i-n-g*.

Legend had it that the court system labeled girdles criminal tools thanks to the skills of M&M. She was famous for being able to pack twenty to thirty pieces (which was the simple term boosters used to refer to their boosted merchandise) into her girdle on one trip into a store. When M&M hit a store, it was hit. She would make several trips into one store if she caught them slippin'. A day's work for M&M could retire a person for a year.

M&M would tell a person in a minute that she had expensive taste and it took a lot to maintain her lifestyle. Everyone in her inner circle knew she required a lot because she gave a lot. It was a known fact that she supported every member of her family in one way or another. She would often provide school clothes for every child in her entire family: daughters, sons, nieces, cousins, and grandchildren. Whenever anyone saw a member of her family, they were draped head to toe in the best pieces.

Another tale that had given M&M a name in the streets was the incident in which she was involved in a shoot-out with the police that left a state trooper dead. The state initially tried to pin the murder on her, which would pretty much have been an automatic life sentence, but after a forensic investigation, it was determined that the officer was killed in the crossfire of his fellow troopers, and that M&M never even fired the gun they had found on her. As a result, she was only sentenced to three years at the Marysville Ohio Reformatory for Women on a grand theft charge for stolen goods.

That's right; M&M played for keeps. The Game was her life and she protected it with all she had in her. She was ride or die. She believed completely in holding 'em down by any means necessary. M&M was a female gangsta. You had better come correct in her presence or not come at all.

Tara had learned from the best, so not a chick up in the workhouse was a threat to her.

After passing through the dayroom, Tara walked into the sleeping area where the bathrooms were housed. She made her way over to one of the sinks and turned on the water. "Damn," she mumbled quietly to herself as she looked into the cracked, poor excuse for a mirror, while splashing water on her face. "I look pretty good for a stripped-down bitch."

The deputies had made Tara remove her signature hair weave when she was booked in. Thank God she had just come from getting a fresh perm from Trey, her gay stylist, on the morning of her arrest. *Wow,* Tara thought while observing herself in the mirror. *I look just like Mom with my hair short.* Although everyone always said that she was the spitting image of her mother, Tara never saw it . . . until now. She didn't know if it was because of her features that she seemed to look more and more like her mother, or if it was because she was finding herself in the same predicament as her mother once had—locked up.

Tara's mind drifted back to the day her mother came home from serving three years in Marysville at the Ohio

Reformatory for Women. It was that Christmas eve way back in 1968.

During the shoot-out with police, M&M had been arrested. The state troopers took photos that day of what they estimated to be more than $150,000 worth of stolen mink coats, which had been taken from fur shops in cities from Atlanta to Canada.

I don't know how Mom served three years confined in one of these hellholes, Tara thought, shaking her head as she thought to herself how frightened she had been all those years ago on Christmas eve when her mother had walked through Mama Grace's front door after serving that bid.

That day, she just knew that she had to have been seeing a ghost or that her mind was playing tricks on her. Her grandparents had called themselves sparing their grandchildren the truth of where their mother was for three years. Nothing was ever spoken to them about the situation, so Tara was left, at seven years old, to form her own conclusion from the bits and pieces that she had overheard as a child, and the words that mostly stuck with her were *shooting* and *dead.* Tara had just assumed that her mother was involved in a shooting and had died, and no one had bothered telling her otherwise. Nevertheless, that reality was shattered when her mother, along with her dad and Aunt Bootsie, walked into the cramped living room that had been her world. Tara didn't know whether or not to be glad that her mother was alive, or angry at everyone else for allowing her to think that she was dead.

All these years later, Tara adored and respected her mother. She hung onto every word and lesson her mother offered. Tara learned at an early age that the "po-po" were not there to protect and serve, but instead were the family's archenemy. She recalled the many times her dad and his partners would hide in the basement when her mom's parole officer would drop by unannounced.

"Tara, get the door and stall her while your dad hides," M&M would direct. Being on parole, M&M wasn't about to be seen by her probation officer with street people.

Tara always felt proud to be given such an important task, and she always carried it out to perfection. She would then be rewarded for her skills with crisp dollar bills from her dad and his friends.

"Tara, you eating?" Creeper walked into the bathroom and asked, snapping Tara out of her thoughts.

"Girl, you know I don't play about my vegetable lasagna," Tara shouted. "Matter fact, I got six nutty bars for whoever don't want their tray," Tara added before she turned off the water and then headed for lunch with Creeper.

After lunch had been eaten and the trays collected, Tara surveyed the telephones to see what the waiting lines were looking like. The phones and televisions were valued commodities in the dorm. There was an unspoken code that the new girls were given first dibs on the phones in hopes that they could call somebody to help them make bail.

Another inmate named Rosie noticed Tara watching the phones and offered the one she was using. Tara reached for the phone and thanked Rosie.

"Girl, I got you later. You good for whatever snacks you want," Tara told Rosie. Tara was set with stationery, snacks, and personal items from the moment she hit the door. It paid to know people. She didn't even have to call in a favor; a bitch was set up from jump.

The lines between the haves and have-nots were well defined. If inmates had someone on the streets holding them down while they were on lock, then their time went a lot easier. They could purchase badly needed items and snacks from the jail's commissary.

The items on commissary were designed to provide the women with essential things to get by. There were toiletries, writing materials, and an assortment of snacks. The items purchased were exchanged for every favor known to man. Inmates were able to exchange sex, cleaning duties, phone calls, and drugs for the coveted items.

Tara dialed the number to M&M's house and prayed someone was home. She was anxious to hear word from her attorney, and knew that if anyone had been on the case with him, it was M&M.

Tara was being detained on a probation hold. She was already out on bond on a punk-ass petty-theft case when she got popped. If her judge wanted to be a bitch, Tara could be held up to thirty days before going to court. She'd need a good attorney to get the hold lifted.

"Hello, hello," Tara screamed into the phone receiver. She could hear M&M's voice through the annoying automated recording.

"I hate this county shit," M&M said, annoyed after following the prompts that enabled her to speak to her daughter.

"Hey, Ma, what's up?" Tara shouted, trying to be heard over the noise in the background.

"Nothing much, baby, just sitting here with Dirty Harold, trying to fence some pieces off to him," M&M shared.

Dirty Harold was a fence man, someone who would buy all the stolen pieces a booster would bring him at a third of the ticket price. A good fence was a booster's dream. M&M was known for breaking many a fence man's wallet. She often said that their money would run out long before her pieces ever did.

"Those are Jones of New York slacks suits, Harold. They showing a lot of green in the stores for spring," M&M stated to him while stacking twelve different lime green pantsuits onto the bed. "You know I only feature the latest fashions," she offered with a sly grin on her face.

"M, I don't know if my customers are ready for these wild colors," Harold said, examining the bright green suits with a look of doubt spread across his face.

"You better get with the program or get left," M&M schooled. She then turned her conversation back to Tara. "Baby, baby, Mama sorry. I'm trying to chase this dollar. What's going on with you?" M&M inquired.

"Nothing, Ma, just trying to find out what's up. I really don't want to spend Christmas in this joint," Tara moaned.

"I know, baby," M&M replied. "Slim talked to Attorney Watson about your hold. He has to try to get you before a cool judge to sign a bond for you. He's waiting on Judge Crawford to return." M&M had referred to Tara's father by his nickname of Slim.

"Ma, did Daddy say he was going to send someone to put some money on my books?" Tara asked.

"Yeah, he told me that he's sending one of those strawberries down there to put two hundred on your books tonight. James left a hundred dollars over here for you, and he said to tell you to keep your head up and he will holler at you next week," M&M said to her daughter and then began adding up the pieces, in a whispering count, that Dirty Harold had selected.

"That's three-hun, then? That's cool," Tara said, thinking how cool it was for James to throw her some ends as well.

James was a famous pimp from New York that didn't like motherfuckas knowing he was in town. He held so much weight in the streets that even the police banned him from the city. It was rumored that he had hoes in all fifty states. He was labeled a danger to the public in three different counties. He was so smooth with his pimping game that women were known to have one conversation with him and just walk off from their whole lives. Before they knew what hit them, they were hoeing out both pant legs and giving him all their money. He could turn a saint into a sinner before God got the news.

"Yeah, and like I said," M&M said after counting up the pieces, "Slim sending ol' girl down there with another two."

Tara could only smile at what her mother was saying. It amazed her how her mother would mention her father's other women, referring to them as strawberries, as if it were nothing. Tara did not know how M&M did it: sharing her man.

M&M often told Tara, "That nigga ain't going anywhere. He knows what he got. I'm the best moneymaker in the game. And I'm fine as hell too, and I can cook. He knows another pimp would swoop me up before God got the news."

M&M had been with Slim since the beginning. She was his bottom bitch. She was proud of her position. She trusted that when the hustle was over, they would retire together. She came hard for her man and her family. Everybody who knew M&M respected that in her.

After a couple seconds of silence on the phone, Tara sighed, "Okay, Ma, I'm gonna let you make that money. Merry Christmas. I'll call you the day after Christmas, if I don't get out by then," Tara explained.

She wasn't even gonna try to fight the long lines for the phone on Christmas day. Every ho, gold digger, and crackhead would be trying to use the day to her advantage on the telephones on Christmas day because they knew al-

most all of their family would be gathered in one place
and they could talk to everybody. Tara knew she would be
gathered with her family at Mama Grace's house if she was
out. But she wasn't; Tara was confident, though, that her
family was handling her business in order to get her out
there just as soon as they could.

"All right, now, baby, but make it late. You know I got to
get that taking-back money."

Getting taking-back money was a tradition for M&M.
She would take her leftover pieces that she hadn't sold before the holiday back to the stores she had boosted them
from for cash. This was before the amateur boosters wore
that good hustle out by being lazy and not even trying to
get rid of their pieces on the street, but taking them
straight back to the store they had stolen them from on a
constant basis. Once the stores realized they were buying
their own shit back, they all created new return policies
that included exchanges, due bills, and gift cards only on
returns without a receipt.

"Talk to you later, baby. I love you," M&M said in her
warm, loving voice.

Tara hung up the phone and thought about calling her
dad, but then thought against it. She knew he wouldn't be
home. It was Christmas eve, and Slim had more stops to
make than Santa Claus. He had to collect from all his hoes
and boosters. So Tara just chilled out until it was dinner-
time.

After dinner, Tara headed to the dayroom. She sighed
and glanced around the room. Some of the women who
had been in the dorm the longest were beginning to put
up homemade Christmas decorations. Christmas cards
that came in the mail were hanging festively around the
dorm. There were Christmas trees made from old *Ebony*
magazines placed on both tables in the dayroom. Each

page of the magazine was folded into the center of the magazine toward the spine to create the shape of a tree.

Several women sat in front of the television singing Christmas carols. Tara could still smell the turkey and dressing that had been served for dinner. It wasn't anything like Christmastime at Mama Grace's house, but Tara decided to make do.

"Hey, it's Christmas eve. Let's get this place jumpin'," Tara said as she danced her way over to Creeper and a group of cool-in-the-game sisters. "Hey, y'all, let's stay up late and try to celebrate the holiday. I'll share my snacks with the dorm and y'all do the same." Tara had a smile on her face.

"Fuck, Tara, I ain't trying to give my shit away to these nothin' bitches in here," Rosie spat.

"Rosie, the only reason yo' sorry ass got shit is because somebody looked out for you," Tara hissed.

Tara and some of the other women had collected a bagful of snacks and personal items from women who had purchased items from the commissary that week. They would then divide them up among women who didn't have any money to shop with. One time, Rosie had been one of those women who they had to share with.

Rosie thought for a moment. "Yeah, you right. I just can't stand some of these sorry hoes in here. Look at them over there telling them shoulda, coulda, woulda stories." She pointed to a few of the women who were sitting around talking. "Half the time they lying," Rosie explained.

Just then, a forty-seven-year-old ho named Mercedes could be heard telling Too Tall that her man, Fast Black, was buying her a home in Dublin, a suburb of Columbus, and she planned on retiring once she got out. Everyone knew she'd been in the dorm with a $250 bond. If a bitch couldn't raise $250, then there was some shit in the game.

The women in the dorm were laughing and giving each other dap. Spending Christmas in jail with a bunch of inmates was nothing compared to the Christmases spent with Mama Grace and her family; however, the choices Tara had made in her life had left her without any other choices at all this Christmas.

Christmas day had come and gone. The day after, Tara awoke from a restless sleep and cleared her thoughts while positioning herself more comfortably on the narrow steel slab that was covered with a thin green plastic mattress. This was comically called a bed. The smell of misery, disappointment, fear, and stale, stank breath filled the air.

Tara sprang to her feet and quickly crossed the overcrowded cell to the bathroom area, careful not to disturb the other women. She wanted to take advantage of the moment of make-believe privacy. She wanted to take a quick shower before the dorm came to life, invading the atmosphere with the annoying sounds of the morning; miserable bitches. She also appreciated the luxury of not being eaten alive by the stares of the dyke bitches in the dorm.

Tara had always had a bangin' body. From the time she was nine years old, she was turning heads with what she was working with. She had a fat-ass, ghetto booty that was complemented by a small waist. Standing five feet six, her chocolate, flawless skin added to her exotic beauty.

Tara tiptoed behind what was supposed to be a privacy wall and swiftly began to undress. Once in the shower, the warm water felt good against her skin. She massaged the sticky, creamy soap onto her body. Tara's hands drifted to her thick thighs as she began to play with her private place. Her hands moved slowly in circular motions across her pleasure spot. She closed her eyes and thought of Scott, her sex slave for the moment.

Scott was Tara's latest play toy and a real gangster. He was deep in the streets, and Tara loved the thug in him. Imagining Scott was the one touching her, Tara drifted to a place of ecstasy as her hands began to provide her the needed stimulation her body craved.

The water cascaded down her full, firm breasts and splashed over her throbbing clit as she tried to contain the moans of pleasure that were stirring within her. The distant wave began to sweep across her as she reached her climax. She allowed the water to rinse away the stolen pleasure as she prepared to exit the shower, dry off, get dressed, and start another day of confinement.

The dorm began to come to life as the morning lights were turned on by the first-shift deputy. Days and time were hard to determine in jail. There were no clocks, and the windows were painted over with thick white paint. Time was measured by the turning on and off of the lights.

Deputy Lifton tapped on the door and motioned Tara to the glass.

"Hey, girl," she whispered. "I saw your name on the morning court run, so be ready. I know you want out of this hellhole," Lifton announced quietly through the door.

Tara was cool with a couple of deputies in the joint, and Deputy Lifton was one of them, as well as Deputy Harris. Tara knew Deputy Harris from her many visits in and out of the workhouse.

Harris made it a point to get to know Tara. The first night she met her back in dorm three, she knew she was someone to know. Tara had sat at the dayroom picnic table dressed in a fresh pair of designer pajamas with a matching robe. She had ruled the bid whist game the whole dorm was crowded around. Tara was in charge of the inmates, and that was clear to see. There were a few other inmates in the room that were feared, but Tara was respected. The prostitutes respected her. She was cool with the crackheads, and the drug dealers shared their secrets with her. Most of them knew Tara from one set or another.

Deputy Lifton, on the other hand, was one of Tara's best customers on the street. She bought everything Tara stole in her size.

The Moore family was connected on every set. They stacked paper from judges, lawyers, rich Jews in Upper Arlington, and bankers. If the city's elite weren't paying the family hoes, they were paying the family boosters. If a person didn't have to come see one of the Moores on one set, they'd have to see 'em on another. No hustle hit the streets of Columbus, Ohio before going through the Moore family first. Slim was even dipping in this new hustle that dealt with this thing they called crack. Tara wasn't clear on just what all the hoopla about this crack was, but unfortunately, she would soon find out.

Two

Free at Last

Tara walked into the fresh air and allowed it to wash across her face. She stood in front of her dad's ride for a moment, enjoying the sounds and smells of freedom. In court that morning, Judge Crawford was in an unusually good mood. Tara was shocked when he set her bond so low. She quickly said, "Thank you, Your Honor," and headed back to the holding cell, escorted by an overweight female deputy.

When the judge told Tara to be back in the courtroom in thirty days, she didn't even sweat it. She knew Attorney Watson would get the case continued for several months where she would never even have to show up in court, ultimately getting that sucker dismissed for some reason or another.

"Hey, hey, baby girl. Give ya daddy some sugar," Slim said, turning his cheek to Tara while adjusting the seat as she got into the car.

"Hey, Daddy," Tara said, leaning across the plush, butter leather seats of her dad's fully loaded Cadillac and kissing his cheek. She then flipped down the sun visor to check herself out in the mirror.

"You know, ya old man sorry you had to spend Christmas in the belly of the beast. I had my best attorneys trying to get that hold lifted," Slim apologized.

"I know, Daddy. It's all good."

"You know ya old man done told you about running up in Lazarus anyway." Lazarus was a department store in Columbus that Macy's eventually bought out. "Them Jews don't play about theirs. They lay in wait for you," Slim scolded his daughter as he pulled off and began to drive.

"I know. I just got greedy," she gave in.

Tara thought back to the day she was arrested at the Lazarus department store in Kingsdale Shopping Center. In all honesty, she truly had been greedy that day. She was on her third trip, all in the same day, back into the store to get the last of the Coach purses when she was caught and cuffed by security.

"All money ain't good money," Slim said, changing lanes. "Sometimes you have to know when to hold 'em and when to fold 'em."

Tara listened to the lesson her dad was teaching her about hustling and took each word to heart. She knew her father knew what he was talking about. Slim had been pimpin' hoes and boosters from coast to coast his whole life. He proudly bragged about how he had survived in the game and never did a day of time in jail; all by listening and learning from those who had played the game long before he was drafted. He was a believer in imparting knowledge to the select few who he allowed in his inner circle. There was a code of the streets, and it wasn't given to just anyone. The game was a valuable thing, and not everyone was worthy to play.

"Baby girl, you want to make some rounds with ya old man or do you want to go home?" Slim asked Tara.

"Home, Daddy. I want to take a long nap and then I got some paper to chase."

"Yeah, ya old man got some traps to check on too." Slim laughed at his daughter's eagerness to get back on the grind. A few days in jail couldn't keep a Moore down.

Tara turned up the radio and let the music soothe her. Slim looked over at his youngest daughter and smiled at her beauty. He thought to himself how true to the game she was. No father wants the streets for his children, but the streets were in Tara. She was a natural. She took to the streets like a fish to water. All his kids by M&M liked nice things, and when a man couldn't give it to Tara, she got it for herself.

Don't get it twisted, though; Tara would be the first to sit back on pulse and let a brotha hold her down. But if a motherfucka wasn't handling his, Tara would handle it herself. Hell, could anyone blame her? She had lived her entire life watching her mama and daddy get theirs, so it was only natural for Tara to want to get hers.

Slim smiled once again at the sight of his baby girl doing her thing and then focused back on the road. He leaned back in his seat and let the music soothe him as well. Like father, like child.

Three

No Place Like Home

Tara walked through the inviting doors of her split-level condo. She paused and enjoyed the smell of lilac that filled the air. She made a mental note to let the cleaning service know that they were handling their business.

Dropping her keys onto the marble countertop of the bar, she picked up the stack of mail that was laying there and glanced through it. *Nothing pressing,* she thought, dropping the mail back onto the countertop. She then headed for the upper level. As she reached the top of the stairs, she thought she heard soft music coming from behind the mahogany doors to the master bedroom. Nearing closer, the sound of Carl Thomas's "Summer Rain" could be clearly heard.

Entering and scanning the room, Tara smiled. Scott lay shirtless on her bed while the flickering candlelight danced on his caramel skin. Scott was gorgeous. He had a body that could hang in the best muscle magazines. He rocked the bald look, had piercing gray eyes and kissable lips, not to mention that his sex game was on point.

"Come over here and let me undress you," Scott ordered Tara. He planned on giving her something she could feel. He'd spent enough time on lockdown to know that once you raised up out the beast, there was always the same three things on your mind: good sex, good food, and paper. He didn't have a problem getting Karen to let him in Tara's spot with her spare key so that he could take care of one of those needs.

Tara walked across the room over to the king-size bed. Scott stood and massaged her shoulders. He then began to peel away her clothing.

"How'd you know to expect me?" Tara asked her lover.

"I ran into your girl Karen at the club and she let a nigga know you was raising today," Scott explained as he continued undressing her.

Once Tara was completely naked, Scott ran his hands across her body; taking in every perfection. He scooped her in his arms and carried her into the bathroom. There he placed her in an awaiting bubble bath.

"Ooh, this feels good," Tara moaned in pleasure as the soothing waters swallowed up her skin.

"I know exactly what you need and I'm going to give it to you," Scott bragged.

After washing Tara's body from head to toe, he helped her from the tub and began drying her off. When she was completely dry, he rubbed her favorite Victoria's Secret Dream Angel lotion over her skin. Reaching her warm spot, he began to gently spread her legs as he dropped to his knees in front of her, exploring her inner thighs with his tongue. Her moans filled the bathroom and he knew he had her just where he wanted her; the porn star was in the room. She was in control, so he allowed her to lead him from the bathroom.

Tara wanted him inside her desperately. She reached for his Timberlands belt buckle and pulled him to her. She could see the print of his rock-hard dick through his pants as he pulled them off. Tara licked her lips and pushed him onto the bed. She pulled a condom from the night-stand and joined him.

Scott was rough in bed; he knew Tara enjoyed his roughness. She was like a wild stallion as well, and he was catching feelings for this thoroughbred. He wasn't sure if he was ready to settle down with just one filly. Deep down, a part of him knew Tara was somebody to have in a brother's corner.

He lay on his back watching Tara work her hips like a pro. With each arch of her back, he dug deeper inside her while palming her juicy ass.

His body went numb and he could no longer control himself. His release filled the condom as he came.

Just like always, Scott had broken her off something proper. After the sex, money was on Tara's mind. She popped up, kissed Scott, and then headed for the shower.

Scott cleaned up at the sink while Tara showered. He exited the bathroom and got dressed. Shortly after, he returned to the bathroom where Tara was drying off.

"Hey, boo, holla at ya boy when you get a minute," Scott told her as he planted a kiss on her moist lips and smacked her on her fat ass.

Tara admired how fine he looked with his black folk rag tied tightly around his head. "For sure," Tara said as she watched him walk away and then shortly thereafter heard the sound of him peeling out on his Harley motor-cycle.

After getting dressed, she grabbed her pieces and left her condominium. She had enough fast movers to come up on a nice bank. She would take her father's advice to heart and slow her roll. A bitch wasn't trying to be stupid; she just liked making that money.

Tara backed her silver BMW 750ci from her garage and thought of Scott. *That's a thug I might just have to keep.* He was just so raw and real. When it came to Scott, Tara knew that what she saw was exactly what she was going to get.

Tara remembered the first time she ever saw him. He had walked up on her like he knew her. It was at Mr. Larry's East Nite Club, the hottest joint on the east side of the city. Every old- and new-school player made it a point to do a walk-through in that spot. One never knew what or who might come up in there. Tara's family were regulars at Larry's East. So when Scott stepped to Tara, he only knew of her, but didn't know her per se.

"Nigga, I don't know you," she had told him.

He confidently stated, "But you're going to," and walked away.

"That nigga got game," Tara turned to her girls and said before making sure that she had Jimmy, the bouncer, slip Scott her number that night. They'd been fucking ever since. The sex was good and Scott was a true hustler in every sense of the word, but he was a young G, and he had a lot of street and hoes to get out of his system. Tara enjoyed the time they shared, but she knew she had to let a gangster be a gangster.

He was deep in the streets, and the folks were his true fam. Tara knew they would always hold him down and he would be fine. So she decided at that moment as she drove down Cleveland Avenue toward her grandparents' house that she had to start letting him go. But something inside assured her that their paths would cross again.

Tara was a twenty-five-year-old on a mission. She didn't

have time to get stuck on some good dick. She missed some prime moneymaking days, lying in jail. Black folks would speed their bill money up to Christmas day, but reality always set in the day after. She planned on being out all night if it took that long to get rid of her pieces.

Four

Back to Business

Tara pulled her Beemer onto I-71 and headed up north. She parked her car in front of her grandparents' house. Mama Grace and Granddaddy had long since moved from the small, cramped house from her childhood. The family now enjoyed a large, stark white Victorian six-bedroom home. It was a Sunday tradition for the children, grandchildren, and any stray church members to stop by unannounced to enjoy whatever Southern delights Mama Grace had prepared.

As Tara made her way up the long walkway to the enclosed front porch, she could hear her grandfather, sitting in his favorite chair by the front door, giving Mr. Davis, his next-door neighbor, his daily cussing out.

The porch was decorated with a yellow metal swing and a set of patio chairs and other odds-and-ends furniture. An assortment of flowerpots were decoratively placed everywhere. There was an overstuffed recliner reserved just for Granddaddy.

"I don't give a gotdamn, Davis," Granddaddy snapped. "Get yo' black ass off my porch!"

"Granddaddy, you ain't right. You ain't right," Mr. Davis moaned.

"Walking ain't crowded, so walk yo' ass off my porch," Granddaddy ordered in a hateful tone.

Tara could hear the drunkenness in her granddaddy's voice. Mr. Davis started off of the porch as Tara was approaching.

"Hi, Mr. Davis," she chimed.

"Hey, Tara baby," Mr. Davis said. "Ya granddaddy is an old fool," he added, turning around and cutting his eyes at Ernest before heading to his humble abode next door.

"Whose baby?" Granddaddy said, greeting Tara as she entered the porch.

"Yo' baby," Tara replied, smiling at the familiar greeting of her beloved granddaddy.

"You ain't been by in a while. Where you been hiding?"

"I been busy with school, Granddaddy," Tara said, frowning about the fact that she had to lie to her granddaddy. The last thing she wanted to report to her grandfather was that she had been locked up. Tara led her grandparents to believe that she was going to school and living off government grant money. The elderly couple loved their grandbaby too much to even entertain anything different.

Her grandparents meant the world to Tara. She knew the sacrifice they made by taking her and her brothers and sisters in all those years ago, and she was grateful to them for it. She saw how prison destroyed families by separating children from their blood. Tara and her siblings were spared that pain thanks to her grandparents.

Mama Grace raised them to love family and fear God. She took them to church three times a week and twice on Sunday. They would often spend all day at the Prince of

Peace Holiness Church, which they believed was the sweetest church this side of heaven. They would often have what
Mama Grace affectionately called "dinner on the ground."

She would cook their Sunday dinner on Saturday night,
pack it neatly in a picnic basket and take it with them to
church on Sunday to listen to the great Rev. Richard Hairston preach the gospel according to King James. Mama
Grace was known for pulling all kinds of treats from her
baskets.

With all the wonderful memories of her grandparents
and all the efforts Mama Grace put into teaching her to
fear and choose God, Tara made it a point to make sure
nobody told them of her whereabouts while she was in
jail. It would have broken their hearts to know that their
baby girl was taking after her mother.

"Don't get so busy that you don't make time for your
family. Blood is all ya got; the rest is mud," her grandfather
taught while placing his bottle of Southern Comfort 100-
proof whiskey under his chair.

"I won't, Grandaddy," Tara said, kissing him on the
forehead and then heading for the front door.

Tara entered the house and immediately felt warm inside as she glanced around the room. The living room was
a large, spacious area. One would never know it, though,
because Mama Grace had three couches, two coffee tables, five oversized chairs, two china cabinets, and every
trinket and knickknack known to man crammed into the
room.

There were pictures of all six of her children in every
stage of their lives, her seventeen grandchildren, their
children, not to mention her parents, cousins, aunts, un-
cles, and nieces.

Tara walked through the living room, dining room, and
then into the kitchen. Mama Grace stood at the stove stir-

ring in her signature candied sweet potatoes. Tara could see her granddaddy's breakfast plate untouched on the back of the stove.

"It smells good in here," Tara yelled over Mama Grace's church music that was playing loudly from the small radio.

"Hi, sweetie," Mama Grace said, putting the lid on the pot and walking over and planting a wet kiss on Tara's forehead. "You just in time to sit down and eat with me," Grace told her sweet granddaughter.

Mama Grace prepared her and Tara a plate, and then the two sat down, ate, and made small talk. After Tara had feasted on her grandmother's Sunday dinner and listened to Mama Grace making her feel guilty about not coming by more often, she prepared to leave.

"Now you know I want to show you off at church on Sundays. Pearl and Sister Edna are always parading their grandkids around the church. I want folks to know I got some fine grandchildren myself," Mama Grace explained. She longed for the days when her grandchildren would attend church every Sunday with her like they had once done when they were smaller and under her care.

"I'll try and make it one of these Sundays. They just keep you so long at that church," Tara complained.

"Child, heaven last always; you can't sit through a few hours of service?" she laughed, putting her hands on her hips.

"I love you, Mama Grace," Tara said, smiling as Mama Grace walked her to the front door.

"I love you back." Mama Grace hugged her granddaughter with a tight, loving squeeze.

"Mama, Mama, did I eat? Did I eat?" Tara could hear her granddaddy saying as she stepped off the porch. Sometimes he would be so drunk out there in that chair that he couldn't even remember whether or not he had gone inside to eat and would have to ask Grace.

Walking back to her car, Tara passed her cousin, Bruce, and his girlfriend on the immaculately clean sidewalk. Mama Grace swept her outside walks as if they were her living room floor, grateful for the lovely home God had blessed her with.

"Hey, cousin," Bruce said.

"Hey, cousin," Tara replied. Just as she was about to get in her car, she saw her favorite aunt approaching the house. "Hey, Aunt Nancy," Tara shouted.

"How you doing, baby?" Aunt Nancy sang.

Aunt Nancy had a way of making everyone feel special. The sound of her voice made you think of lazy days and white, sandy beaches. Everyone who met her felt instantly comfortable in her presence.

"You leaving?" Nancy asked Tara.

"Yeah, I have to run," Tara offered.

"Call me when you get a minute. I'm trying to plan your cousin Rick's wedding and I need your input."

"You know I got you," Tara promised. She hopped in her Beemer and headed up the one-way street on Kohr Place. She waved at Mrs. Pollard and Mrs. Davis as they sat gossiping on Mrs. Davis's front porch. She then headed to her destination.

Tara impatiently rang the doorbell for the fifth time and listened for sounds of life coming from inside the house. *Where is Karen?* she thought to herself. She knocked again and then decided she would leave after there was still no reply.

Just as Tara turned to walk away, Karen snatched the door open. "What's up, Tara, girl?" Karen chimed.

Karen was Tara's best friend. They had known each other ever since Tara was in grade school. Every important moment in Tara's life had been shared with Karen.

Karen was a dime piece in her own right. Her skin was a rich mocha chocolate. She had a body that gave Tara a run for her money, and her waist was so small that her butt set out like a shelf. Wherever the two of them went, heads would turn. They would often compete to see who could get the most phone numbers when they went clubbin'.

Karen was also Tara's work partner. They would run up in them stores together and hit a lick. Tara and Karen would start their workday just like a square going to a nine-to-five. Nine o'clock sharp, they would begin preparations to make their rounds to all of the finest stores.

Boosting was an art; M&M had thought Tara that. A good booster learned their part and executed it well. Anybody could rip somebody off, but a good booster would leave a store with the salesclerk saying, "please," "thank you," and "come back again."

Tara and Karen would return home and add up their day's work. Of course, each of them would keep the slickest gear for themselves. All the other pieces would be sold.

"What took you so long to answer the door? I was just about ready to jet," Tara complained.

"Girl, I thought you was that nigga, Derek. He's turning into a bug-a-boo. I fucked up and gave him some of this come-back pussy and a nigga stuck," Karen said, walking into the house and sitting on her mustard-colored leather sofa. "Girl, I'm glad to see they turned you loose," she continued.

"Yeah, it's good to be out of that bitch. Eleven days in that hellhole felt like a lifetime," Tara said, sitting at the small bar in the corner of the living room.

"I knew Slim would move heaven and earth to raise you

up out of that motherfucka." Karen popped up off the sofa and headed into the kitchen. "He won't 'bout to let his baby rot in jail, huh?"

The rules to the game were complex, but the one rule that was simple—but often overlooked—was that a man handled his business where his woman was concerned, or else he was caught slippin'. No true hustler let a woman lay in the belly of the beast without trying to raise her. Karen knew the rules to the game well, and therefore knew that Slim wouldn't have his baby girl sit in jail not a day longer than could be helped.

"Them sorry motherfuckas took my girdle when they busted me," Tara spat. "And I had just broke that bitch in," she added, shaking her head.

"I've got a spare one," Karen offered her friend, walking over to the refrigerator and getting out two Jack Daniel's wine coolers for the two of them to sip on. "Hey, let me get dressed and grab my pieces. We need to check on a few new customers I lined up at Alan's spot," Karen explained after handing Tara her wine cooler and then popping open her own and taking a sip.

Karen disappeared out of view, and Tara waited on her to get dressed while she checked her voice messages on her cell phone. Her voice mailbox was on full. She listened to each message carefully and made a mental note to get back to everyone who had left her a message. But later for phone calls—first things first; she needed to get her ends straight after missing so much paper while she was in jail. Money was on her mind.

She was disappointed that she missed all the holiday shoppers, but Tara knew she could still make some quick, easy cash at Alan's spot. It was sweet having a spot where they could sell their pieces on a regular basis without any drama. She hated that door-to-door shit. She could spend hours at a bitch's house with her trying on all of her shit and end up not buy anything. In the club, it was open season. Everybody shopped after a few drinks and some good music. If the women weren't shopping, then the men were.

Tara placed her cell phone in her purse and a few minutes later, Karen reappeared, dressed, with her pieces in hand and ready to go.

"Where to first?" Tara asked her friend.

"Club Rumors, baby," Karen said. The two headed for Tara's car and then drove to the club.

Tara and Karen entered the smoke-filled Club Rumors, which was owned by Alan, an intelligent businessman with a slick side. Every old- and new-school player was up in the club. Tara smiled at Karen and they both winked in agreement at how many marks were up in the spot. They knew that they were going to break some motherfuckas tonight.

Tara headed straight for the bar while Karen claimed a nearby table that a young couple was getting up from.

"Hey, Reese, is Alan upstairs?" Tara asked the overworked bartender.

"Yeah, Tara, my sister," Reese sang over the pounding of the music that the DJ was spinning. Tara slipped behind the bar and made her way up the hidden staircase to Alan's office.

"What you up to?" Tara inquired after entering the office.

Alan sat at his oversized wooden oak desk, counting money. "Tara, Tara, bring your fine ass over here and give an old man some sugar," he all but begged, looking up from his desk at the lovely beauty who stood before him.

Tara walked over to Alan and then leaned down and kissed him on the lips. As she backed away, he grabbed her firm ass. Tara didn't trip; she knew she looked good tonight. She couldn't blame the old man for wanting to cop a feel.

She was rockin' a fresh hookup. Saks had just put out their new Donna Karan line. Karen and Tara had stolen everything in their sizes right before her little Lazarus incident. The chocolate brown wrap dress was doing her body justice. She was demanding attention tonight.

"What's poppin'?" Tara sang.

"Trying to finish up," Alan responded.

Alan was one of Slim's old-school partners. He ran a flea market of illegal hustles out of every club he operated in the hood. He had a thing for fast money and fast women. He'd been trying to get a piece of Tara for a minute. Few years her senior, Tara still thought Alan was doable, but she didn't have time to be tied down, and old men liked to tie a bitch down.

"Why don't you follow me home and we can spend a quiet night together? Ain't nothin' in these streets for a fine catch like you," Alan proposed, putting away the work on his moon-shaped desk.

"Thanks for the invitation, Alan, but I got some paper to chase." Tara noticed the lust in Alan's eyes so she played on it. "One of these days I'm going to give you some of this," she said, smacking her ass, "and then yo' ass gon' be stuck," she threatened, switching her ass. Alan laughed, placing his hand on his dick, watching Tara exit his spacious office.

Tara joined Karen in the back of the club where she was busy setting up a mini-boutique. "Hey girl, run out to the car and get the rest of the pieces," Karen instructed.

Tara made a trip back out to the car, retrieved the fastest moving pieces they brought with them, and placed them across the back of the circular leather booth. It was easy to get a customer to spend money if you had a selection of pieces under a hundred dollars. If you sold for a third of the original price, your customers were more than happy to drop a bill with you on some nice shit; they only featured the best.

The girls stood back and admired their top-of-the-line pieces as they began to do business. A few happy hour customers gathered and selected items in their sizes. Two hookers were fighting over a yellow spandex cat suit they both wanted.

"Hey, Sweets, chill. I got another one just like that in my garment bag," Tara said, interrupting the fight. Sweets was one of her good customers, known to spend big with the boosters. "That's a hundred and seventy-five dollars. If you want the orange short set too, I'll throw it in for an even hundred and ninety dollars. That's a third off the ticket price. You know I usually sell my short sets for half price, Sweets," Tara explained to the hooker.

"You know we look out for our regular customers," Karen explained, placing the pieces Sweets had purchased in a clear garbage bag.

"What's up, Tara, girl?" Tracey yelled, making her way to the back of the club. "Girl, where you been? Me and my girls been waiting for you to come through the projects and hook a sister up. My clothes game is slippin' bad. How am I supposed to rep when my shit is late?" Tracey teased.

Tracey was a good friend of Tara and Karen's; she was a hustler. Everyone knew Tracey sold the best rocks in town. She was a low-key dealer. A person couldn't step to her unless they had gotten a personal invitation. And if they smoked that shit, Tracey was the person to know. Her brothers pushed weight and they took care of their sister in every way. It didn't hurt that she looked like a light-skinned, young-ass Toni Braxton, either. The girl got respect in the streets.

"Tara, give me a deal on what you got left. I can sell what I don't want for myself to those thirsty bitches in Nelson Park projects," Tracey said.

"You can get everything for a fourth," Karen and Tara said in unison, closing up shop. Tracey was happy to take them up on their offer, ridding them of all the pieces they had left.

After leaving Club Rumors with not a stitch left in their garment bags, Karen and Tara pulled in front of Karen's sister Terri's split-level crib. Karen asked Tara to stop by there because she needed to leave some of the money she made with Terri or she knew she would blow it, and she had a bill she had to pay. Tara had to pee anyway, so the detour was right on time. She had been holding it damn near ever since arriving at Club Rumors; she hated going to the bathrooms in the club.

Terri's spot was jumpin' as always. There were fine-ass dudes posted up in the living room kickin' it, and three in the hallway just chillin'. Terri kept a houseful of niggas. As the two friends entered the kitchen, Tara's eyes fell upon the finest man she'd ever seen. He was about five feet nine and everything about him said, "Do me, baby."

The Don Juan himself was wearing jeans and one of those Don Johnson *Miami Vice* shirts and loafers. He was deep in a phone conversation with someone who seemed to be annoying him. He walked around the small kitchen as if he owned it. Tara studied his every move. There was a presence about him that made her weak in the knees. She felt warm all over just watching him.

Tara walked from the kitchen into the hallway where she spotted Karen's sister and said, "Terri, who is that fine motherfucka in the kitchen?" Just then, the topic of her conversation walked up behind her.

"My name is Julio," he said in a thick Dominican accent.

Tara tried to hide her embarrassment by saying something slick. "Nigga, why you all up in my grill? Back the fuck up," she shot back.

Julio smiled at the heart of this cutie. "Sorry, mami," he said in his sexy accent. "So what's yo' name?"

"I'm Tara," she answered. One word led to another and before Tara knew how it even happened, they were locked in conversation on the brown love seat in Terri's basement.

Each time Julio paused to gather his thoughts or search for the right word in English, he licked his sexy pink lips. His native tongue was Spanish, but his English wasn't as bad as he might have thought it sounded. Tara could understand him just fine. He was speaking her language, all right.

Tara looked down at her watch and realized she had been kicking it with him for almost two hours. There had been an instant connection between the two of them.

"Man, it's late. You want to go get a drink?" Julio asked, getting up from the love seat.

Tara knew that night she would follow this one to the end of the world. He had an edge about him that had her stuck. It was like, Scott who? Ridding her system of the young thug had seemed to be made easier than she thought thanks to the likes of Julio. His conversation was deep and interesting. He talked about everything—from his plans for the future to his little girl; he even produced photos of the beautiful little girl that looked like they had been taken in the typical department-store photography studio.

Julio was so fine; Tara had a hard time focusing on his conversation. Her thoughts kept drifting back to how gorgeous he was. His skin was an orange-ish bronze. He just had this glow about him. His wavy, jet-black hair was cut close to his head and he had a chiseled, handsome face. It could be detected from across the room that he was a hustler by the way everyone hung onto his every movement. Thugs and hustlers who normally didn't bow down to no one were giving this gangster respect. Niggas were making it a point to acknowledge Julio. Tara liked that in him.

She gained instant respect for him after watching him work the room. Everybody wanted to be acknowledged by Julio, but Tara was the only one he seemed to notice, and if it was up to her, she was going to keep it that way.

Five

Mi Casa Es Su Casa

Tara entered the foyer of her warm, inviting condo with Julio following close behind. She slipped off her Donna Karan pumps and turned on the Bose sound system. The smooth sounds of R. Kelly filled the room.

Julio was impressed at the classy way she was living. He knew she wasn't the average one-night stand. Julio knew the minute he saw her that he was going to hit it. Initially his plan was to break her off something proper and bounce. Now he was watching this down chick move comfortably in her environment, and he liked what he saw. She was a dime, and he knew he would have to see her again.

"Make yourself comfortable and chill. I'll get us some drinks and something to snack on," Tara offered as she made her way into the kitchen.

After leaving Terri's, Julio had suggested they check out a new spot in the north, but Tara suggested they chill at her place instead. She knew she had to get a piece of this thoroughbred, and her intentions could be much easier carried out in the comfort of her own home. Karen was cool with copping a ride home with her sister while her girl saddled up.

"Sounds good, mami," Julio yelled after her. *I really like her style,* Julio thought, making himself comfortable on the down-feather stuffed sofa.

Julio originally came to Columbus from Long Island City to lay low and stack some paper. That was two years ago. He now had the east side of the city on lock, and him and his crew were quickly taking over the north end. The city was not ready for the gangstas from up top. He felt like a kid in a candy store. It was amazing how easy it had been to just take the fuck over.

Julio and his crew set up shop low-key in a quiet spot on Oakwood Avenue. Before he knew it, they were pushing two ki's a week from the spot. He baited his traps with twenty-dollar double-ups. Double-ups were the ticket; you give your crack customers two twenty-dollar rocks for the price of one. The fiends had fallen instantly in love. He specialized in damn near pure Peruvian flake. And in no time at all, the local dope boys were trying to figure out how they could holla at Julio.

Hustling was his claim to fame, and he was confident in his role. He treated everyone in his circle straight up. He came from a family and city of hustlers, and he studied the family business well; something he and Tara had in common.

Julio's uncle, Rafael, taught him at an early age to always remember the bridge that brings you across. To truly be down meant that he took care of those who took care of him. His customers and his crew were his lifeline; they were the bridge. "Never fuck with your lifeline," his uncle pressed.

All of Julio's soldiers trusted and respected him. All he had to do was say the word and they were always ready to put in work. Life in this city was good for Julio, so he had gotten comfortable.

As he waited patiently on the couch for his drink, he could hear Tara moving around in the kitchen, humming to the music. A few minutes later, she entered the room carrying a tray filled with ham, cheese, fruit, and crackers.

"So, what are you drinking?" Tara asked him.

"Vodka with a little juice is fine, mami," Julio purred, licking his sexy lips.

Tara set the tray on the glass coffee table and rushed to make their drinks so she could join him on the couch.

"Tara, do you know who I am and what I do?" Julio questioned, looking into her eyes. "I'm a real gangsta; I don't play games. I believe in letting a person know the real and letting them make their own decisions from that," he explained.

"I know you're a gangsta," she enlightened him, "and I like that in you. I come from a family of hustlers, so I'm down with whatever your claim to fame is. I know I like you and want to get to know you better," Tara said in a soft, sexy, sincere voice.

"Man, it's getting crazy in them streets. There are way too many young bucks out there with no direction. It feels good to have somebody true to the game to kick it with and just chill. Terri told me who your family is, so I know you straight," Julio said, letting Tara know why it was he felt comfortable enough with her to holla at her about his background. "Motherfuckas always trying to read me and they think they know me, but they don't. I'm a regular nigga looking for the same things every other left-behind nigga is looking for.

"My family raised me in the hood, we've struggled side by side with black people, trying to get what's ours. People sometimes look at me weird when I call myself a nigga, but that's what I'm used to. I've just been dealt the street card and I mean to play it to the fullest.

"I was taught at an early age to be all you can be and that's how I do mine," Julio shared as he took off his shoes and got comfortable on the couch. He placed his hands gently on Tara's thighs and rubbed them as he talked.

After getting relaxed in each other's presence, the two sat and talked more about their lives, dreams, families, and even shared a few of each other's secrets.

Before they knew it, the sun was coming up. Tara took the crystal glass from Julio's hand and led him from the couch up the stairs. Entering the bedroom, she slowly danced him over to the bed.

Julio was enjoying this take charge honey. She pushed him onto the bed and positioned herself on top of him while planting soft, tender, wet kisses seductively on his face.

He gasped and sternly flipped Tara on her back. He slowly lifted her dress, exposing her peach-and-brown thong set. Julio planted kisses up her thighs until his sexy lips reached her kitty cat. He had Tara purring as she grabbed his silky hair and placed his lips in the right spot. She lifted her hips and rolled her kitty cat across his face. He pushed her thong to the side, grabbed her juicy butt cheeks with both hands and dug in.

When Tara couldn't stand the pleasure anymore, she eased from under him and completely undressed. She then removed Julio's clothing and got on top of him. Slowly licking and sucking his nipples while sliding his hard, firm dick inside her, she rode him like a champion while screaming his name.

When she saw his eyes roll back in his head, Tara knew she had him whipped. Smiling to herself, she thought, *Oh, he'll be back for more.*

Tara loved the power her pussy had over men. Julio wasn't a puppy, though; he was a dog in the bedroom and he was putting in work on Tara's pussy. Before she knew it, her inner self was throbbing.

Tara turned on her back and spread her shaking thighs, allowing Julio to enter her deeper. They both kissed and stared into each other's eyes, locking into an unspoken bond. Their orgasms could not be held back, and they both began to shake with pleasure. They fell off into deep sleep—one dreaming about the other.

Later that morning, once the sun was fully at work, Julio awoke to the smell of bacon frying. He tried to focus his eyes on his unfamiliar surroundings. As the fog began to lift from last night's drinking, the memories of the night before came into clear view. Relaxing his body on the inviting bed, he began to think about Tara. *Damn, last night was mind-blowing. This shit was crazy,* he thought.

He'd started his night riding by his boy Carlito's— Terri's man—to holla at him. Now he was lying in the bed of a *mamacita* he could spend some time with. The two of them had just vibed; she was cool in the game and the sex was on point. Tara had him thinking about turning his pager off and just chillin' with her all day.

No sooner than the idea entered his mind, the black square pager began to vibrate across her dresser.

"*Ahh, puta,*" Julio said, reaching for the pager and reading the number. It read 7777. That was the code for his partner, Santiago. As he reached for his cell phone from his pants pocket and dialed Santiago's number, he hoped that he was calling to hear some good news.

"*Hola,* Santiago. What's up?" Julio asked.

"Yo, I wanted you to know the shit is handled," Santiago shouted into the phone over the salsa music that played in the background.

"Carlito roll with you, right?" Julio questioned, speaking quietly into the disposable cell phone he just picked up from his Jamaican boys on the west side.

"Sí, and before you go asking, we did just like you asked," Santiago confirmed. "We put that sorry bitch motherfucka in the tub and cut his ass up in little pieces. Carlito put him in bags and we rode out Route Twenty-three and dropped that dead weight off."

"Good. That soft motherfucka is out of the way. We couldn't let that shit slide, my friend. You have to send the right message to your crew or they lose respect. Respect and balls is all we got, my brother," Julio explained to his good friend.

Julio and Santiago were boys; both were from the Dominican Republic. They were even from the same town in Puerto Plata. As fate would have it, they actually met here in Columbus. Santiago was a true hustler, and Julio trusted him with his life.

"I heard you hooked up with a chocolate honey last night," Santiago teased his friend.

"Ya man, I think I found a keeper, but I'll holla at you about her later." Julio could hear Tara coming up the stairs. "I'll call you later, partner," Julio said before hanging up the phone.

Tara entered the room and placed the tray she was carrying on the bed. She wanted to impress this one, so she pulled out all the stops. There were scrambled eggs with cheese, crispy fried bacon, waffles with hot syrup, fresh fruit, fried potatoes, croissants with creamy butter, and fresh-squeezed mango-orange juice.

"I thought you might be hungry," Tara whispered, positioning the tray in front of him on the bed.

"Come over here and eat with me." Julio began reaching for her.

Once Tara joined him on the bed, they gobbled up the breakfast and fell back onto the pillows like two stuffed pigs.

"So what are you doing later?" Julio asked his new honey.

"Nothing, just chillin'," Tara replied, hoping that Julio would see to it that those plans changed.

"Well, I'm trying to see you later; that is if you got some time to kick it with a gangsta on some laid-back shit," Julio said, pulling her into his arms and kissing her. After tonguing each other passionately, it was clear that before he departed, he had to make time for one more round. Tara gladly gave him what he craved.

Tara and Julio had been kicking it for about three months now. Tara was more than content. She found herself rushing home at night, hoping he'd call and ask if he could come by. Her girl, Karen, couldn't get her to hang out, go man hunting or even put in work. Tara just wanted to be with Julio.

Shortly after they started kickin' it, he got her a fancy attorney who got her probation on her theft case. She didn't even have to appear before the judge on two of the hearings. He was constantly handing her hundreds and telling her to get what she needed. Julio was about business, and she liked that in him.

This was some weird shit. She had never been this stuck on any man. In the past, they had all served a purpose. There was the sex partner, the money machine, Mr. Handyman, and the clubbin' partner. She never felt all anxious and excited to just chill with a nigga. But Julio was so different. She enjoyed kickin' it with him on every level. He was somebody who understood and accepted her for who she was—a hustler. He was every man rolled into one.

Although Julio was a hustler, he had a laid-back style that Tara enjoyed. Often he would call her and say he was coming through. Once he arrived, they would order carry-out and then spend the rest of the evening sexin' or just talking. It always made Tara feel special when he would turn his pager off and block out the world while he was with her.

He told her that she made him feel peaceful and re-laxed. Tara knew she had it bad for Julio; it got so bad that she started slippin' on stackin' her paper. She hadn't hit a lick in a while. As a matter of fact, she hadn't even really hollered at her girl in a minute. Thinking of such, Tara picked up the phone and dialed Karen's number and listened for her to answer.

"*Hola!*" Karen screamed into the phone.

"What's up, gurl?" Tara replied with a chuckle. She knew Karen was trying to be funny by speaking Spanish.

"So you finally came up for air?" Karen teased.

"I know I got it bad," Tara admitted.

"Girl, I don't blame you. Julio is quite the catch. You better do whatever it takes to reel him in, 'cause every hood rat and diva been tryin' to land him ever since he hit town. He's been with a few, but nothing long-term or any-thing. Terri told me that he was kickin' it with that fake-ass Pam that lives across the street from her." Karen offered her friend all she knew.

"That's cool. The nigga too fine to not have been see-ing anybody," Tara said. "I just have to tighten my game. I like this one.

"I'm broke," Karen threw in. "When are we going to work?"

Tara knew that it had been a minute since her and Karen's last run together. She owed her girl the company.

Tara looked down at her watch. "It's after four o'clock

and you know I like to be at the stores when they first open," Tara complained.

M&M taught her at an early age that the early bird catches the worm. She would often say, "Nothing comes to a sleeper but a dream." Most stores were understaffed and an easy mark for a seasoned booster.

"I know," Karen replied, "but I found this sweet spot that has nothing but teenagers working in the evening. We can run up in there two or three times and clean up."

"Okay, but you have to roll with me. I need some new kicks to match my Harve Benard pink suit," Tara whined.

"Pick me up in an hour. I'm going to pop in the shower and get dressed."

"I'll see you in a minute. Bye." Tara hung up the phone. She thought about calling Julio, but decided not to. She was getting too hooked.

She put him out of her mind and headed for her walk-in closet. Her clothes were divided into three sections: kickin' it clothes, partying clothes, and work clothes. Her work clothes were an assortment of A-line skirts and dresses. Each were classy, businesslike hookups. She had to dress the part if she was going to be believable. She planned to blend in with the rest of the working middle-class women who stopped by the mall after work.

After scanning her clothing, Tara chose a simple navy skirt with a matching blouse. In addition, she topped it off with her Gucci pumps. To complete her look, she brushed her hair back and added one of her pop-in ponytails. After her shower, she would pull her hair into a neat bun. When she wore her hair that way, she always looked like a schoolteacher on her way home from the classroom.

"I am going to put a hurtin' on that poor store," Tara said to herself before going to take her shower.

After showering, dressing, and fixing her hair, Tara went to pick up Karen and the two headed for work.

Karen and Tara parked three lanes back from the store entrance and headed for their mark. When they entered the store, they were pleased to see it was understaffed and overcrowded with after-work shoppers.

They quickly spotted the high-priced suits and spring dresses that were neatly arranged on the overstuffed display racks. Tara began blending in with the other shoppers while skillfully selecting the highest-priced items on the rack.

When she was done, she walked away and approached the pimple-faced college student. "Excuse me, may I try this on please?" Tara asked her, holding up some inexpensive yellow-and-brown capri pants.

The salesclerk turned to Tara with a look of annoyance. Tara looked over her shoulder and noticed the girl's homework spread across the back counter. It was obvious Tara had just interrupted her from her studies.

"Yes, right this way," the clerk said, not too anxious at all to help her. The salesclerk hurriedly led Tara to the dressing room that was located in the back of the store. She unlocked one of the doors for her and then went back to attend to her homework.

Before entering the dressing room, Tara glanced back at Karen, who was heading for the back of the store with all the items Tara lined up on the rack.

Once Karen joined Tara inside the plush fitting room, the pair moved with precision. They pulled their clawfoot screwdrivers from their purses and quickly began removing the security tags from the garments. Both women divided the stack of pricey garments into two neat piles and then pulled up their skirts to reveal their girdles. The long-legged girdles hugged their bodies tightly.

Tara placed each piece neatly on top of the other one and then rolled them into a large, tight ball. She then stuffed the pieces inside her girdle. Spreading her legs, she positioned the tight ball neatly between them while Karen did the same.

Tara lowered her navy blue skirt over the girdle and checked her reflection in the mirror. After checking both her back and front, she hurriedly moved out of the way so Karen could do the same thing. When the women were sure they passed inspection, the friends exited the fitting room.

Pretending she had tried on the capri pants, Tara returned to the counter with the pants in hand. "They didn't work for me," she said politely to the salesgirl. "But thank you for your help."

The young girl took the pants from Tara and hung them on a crowded rack behind the counter to put away later. "No problem," she said. "Please come again." She then proceeded to ring up an elderly lady who had just walked up to the cash register with an armload of clothes.

"Did you find everything you were looking for today?" the salesgirl asked with a big smile, happy to be getting the large sale. She never looked up, and Tara and Karen slipped quietly from the busy store.

They made two more trips into the store without being noticed before they headed from the shopping complex, pleased with the day's work.

"You want to go over to DSW now?" Karen questioned.

"No, the truck is loaded. We better go home," Tara suggested.

"Yeah, you right, but let's stop by Red Lobster and get something to eat." Karen rubbed her belly. "I am starving and they got a new special I want to try."

"I'm kind of hungry too," Tara added while pulling onto the highway and heading for the restaurant.

After arriving at Red Lobster and stuffing themselves on the deluxe seafood platter, Tara noticed Julio and two guys entering the restaurant. She watched as they headed for a booth in the back of the room.

"Karen, look. It's Julio and some of his partners," Tara pointed.

"Oh shit, I know you don't want him to see you looking like a square. I'll pay the check and you head for the car," Karen whispered and Tara obliged.

After paying the check, Karen slipped from the restaurant and joined her friend in the car. Tara sped from the parking lot and headed home.

Once they were at Tara's place, they separated their pieces. They were happy with the results of their two hours of work. The Limited was a quality store, and their pieces had always proved to be fast movers.

Tara walked around her bedroom while standing on her tiptoes and modeling the sexy slip dress she had copped for herself. Karen was busy setting aside the pieces she was going to keep for herself. Just then, Tara's phone rang.

"*Hola!* What's up?" Julio said after Tara answered.

"What's going on with you?" A grin crept across Tara's face.

"Nothing, trying to see you," Julio announced in a laid-back tone.

"You wanna get some drinks later at Club Spinners?" Tara asked, hoping to get the answer she was looking for.

"Sounds like a plan. Just make sure you don't wear that grandma outfit you had on earlier." Julio laughed and then hung up the phone.

"Hell no!" Tara screamed while hanging up the cordless phone.

"What's up?" Karen asked as she lay down across the bed, waiting to hear what her friend had to say.

"That was Julio."

"I figured that from your expression. Girl, do you know how your face lights up whenever you talk to that nigga?"

Tara sat down on the bed next to Karen. "Karen, I got it bad for him. He is everything I ever wanted in a man. He makes me feel safe and protected when I am with him. I can exhale with him. This is a new feeling for me. He is a complete package. It is rare that you get a nigga that can sex you real good, take care of the ends and handle his business in the street." Tara had a faraway look on her face.

"So are you going to see him tonight?" Karen questioned.

"He wants me to meet him at Spinners," Tara said. "Hey, come with me, please, so I don't have to go up in there by myself peeping him out," Tara asked in her begging voice.

Tara was used to going places alone, but being out on the scene with Julio made her so nervous. She liked him so much, but she didn't want him to know it just yet. She wasn't sure how he felt. She could easily fall hard for him; she had to keep things light. She would feel more on point if she knew Karen was there with her. Besides, she knew a couple of Julio's boys were bound to be on the scene. That's just how they got down. Julio rarely flew without at least one or two members of his crew. Tara thought that this would be a good chance for Karen to come up on some down niggas if she hooked up with one of Julio's boys.

"Girl, you ain't said nothin' but a word," Karen said without hesitating to accept Tara's invitation. "I've been dying to meet some true-to-the-game niggas. Julio is a class act, so I know his boys are 'bout it," Karen said. The girls gave each other a high five and prepared for the evening.

By the time they pulled up at the club, they were on point. The two friends entered the crowded club and as usual, all eyes were on them. It was Latino night, and all the Latin hustlers and drug dealers were in full effect. Tara and Karen made their way to the large bar in the center of the room.

There were eight waiters positioned behind the bar and all were fully occupied. Tara tried with no luck to get the blond, overly made-up waitress's attention. She never even looked Tara's way.

Just then, someone slid up behind her and whispered in her ear in a sexy voice, "What's your name, sexy?"

Tara spun around to see who was all up in her face. That's when she was greeted with a kiss from Julio. He scanned Tara's body with his eyes and he liked what he saw.

Tara was dressed in a black strapless slip dress that hugged every curve of her body. Every man in the room had an instant hard-on just looking at her.

"Damn, baby, you look good. You do a nigga proud every time I see you," Julio complimented. He then turned his attention to the bar. "Yo, Susan, bring a bottle of Möet to my table," he called out to the waitress.

"Sure thing, Julio," the waitress responded in her sexiest voice. It was the same waitress who had ignored Tara earlier.

Julio looked to see Karen standing next to Tara. "Yo, what's up, Karen?" he greeted her.

"You, for sure," Karen responded.

"Hey, my boys are back in the VIP section; let's head

back there and get comfortable," Julio said, leading Tara by the hand to the back of the club.

Tara was aware that all eyes were on her. Every diva, gold digger, hood rat and wannabe was trying to figure out who this was all up in Julio's face. Spinners was Julio's spot. Pussy was always being thrown at him. Women were always trying to figure out how to get next to him. It was a known fact that he was a catch, so they were always fishing.

Tara wasn't the least bit intimidated, though. She used this opportunity to send a message. She stopped to let a couple pass them by, and took the moment to plant a soft kiss on Julio's lips. He then pulled her to him and tongue-kissed her like they were in the bedroom.

Unbeknownst to Julio, in a booth in the corner of the club sat Candy, Julio's baby momma, along with four of her friends. Candy was a ghetto fabulous roughneck. She lived for a fight. Club owners hated to see her coming, because they knew it was just a matter of time before a fight broke out. She was a high yellow, thick girl with red hair. She always wore athletic hookups with crispy white gym shoes.

"Shit, did you see that?" Candy's girl, Trina, screamed.

"See what, bitch? Why you yelling?" Candy said, annoyed by her friend's outburst.

"See Julio just kiss that girl," Trina offered with a smirk on her face, hoping to get some shit started.

Candy looked in the direction Trina was pointing and her eyes became frozen on her baby daddy tonguing down some chick.

Candy met Julio when he first came to Columbus. He didn't know a lot of people then, and she used that to her advantage. She would pick him up every day in her leased Honda Accord and take him wherever he had to go. He told her he didn't like driving his car until he was able to get rid of the New York plates and exchange them for Ohio tags.

Julio's money was long, and he made sure Candy was always straight. She knew from the gate he was a good catch, and she did everything she could to land him hook, line and sinker.

Candy would put on her sexiest outfits whenever he was around. She practically threw the pussy at him, but he would never bite. They ended up becoming nothing more than friends, and he would often get drunk and crash at her place. On one of those nights, Candy put her master plan in motion.

She made each drink for Julio doubles and triples. When she saw he was no longer in control of himself, she began to undress him. He was drunk, but not too drunk to turn down pussy. Candy pulled out all the stops that night. She sucked, fucked, licked, and swallowed until daybreak.

The next morning, she just knew that she was in there, but Julio let her know in no uncertain terms that he did not want a relationship with her. They were friends and he wanted to keep it like that; however, nine months later, she gave him a beautiful daughter named Francisca. This bitch was desperate to latch on to him.

Julio was excited to have extended his bloodline when his baby girl was born. He absolutely adored her. He made sure that her and her mother had everything they needed at all times. This gave Candy certain pull in the streets. Everyone knew she was Julio's baby momma, and she used that every chance she got.

Julio had never been one to have a steady woman. None of his children were planned; just bitches trying to trap him, so it was even more shocking for Candy to see him all hugged up with a broad.

"Who the fuck is that ho?" Candy asked her girls who were seated at the crowded table with her.

They all took a good look, and then Trina spoke up and said, "That's Tara Moore. Her family is connected in the streets. They're legendary with every set. Her dad is Slim the pimp, and if you know anything about boosters, then you know her moms, M and M," Trina shared.

Candy watched as Tara and Karen joined Julio's boys in the VIP section. Tara was still all hugged up on Julio. Candy made a mental note to get the complete 411 on that bitch.

Tara could feel the haters' stares piercing her back. It didn't faze her one bit; she loved a challenge. She wanted everyone to know that she was in Julio's life and she didn't plan on going anywhere soon. She was never one to back down, so she was ready for any drama that came.

Once they reached the VIP section, Julio introduced Tara to all his boys she hadn't met. She loved the way he kept his arm firmly around her waist the entire time. It made her feel special. He then introduced Karen to his boys. Tara could tell by the look on Karen's face that she was pleased with all the fine men at the table. Karen immediately began flirting with a tall, handsome Cuban name Roberto.

"Man, Julio. Where you been hiding these beauties?" Roberto asked.

"Believe me, man, I lucked up when I found this one," Julio said, kissing Tara. "So, are you ready to hang out in my world?" Julio asked her.

"I'm ready for you if you're ready for me," Tara answered.

"This couple thing is new to me. I have been solo ever since I hit town; that is, until I met you." Julio looked into Tara's eyes. "I feel like you are someone I can have a future with. Someone that makes a nigga want to come home at night. I don't know how this couple thing works; I need you to teach me. Can you do that?" Julio said very sincerely, whispering in Tara's ear while they sat in the VIP booth.

"Yes, I can teach you. All you need to know is always make me feel safe, protected, and loved, and everything else will take care of itself," Tara explained, whispering back. "I just want to love you and feel your love. I don't need anything from you but that. I know how to take care of myself and I got my own already."

"Listen, I know how you get down; running up in them stores. That's cool. I don't knock the hustle, but I need you to let me be the man. As long as you are with me, I got you, not the other way around. I know that you are a strong woman that's used to taking the lead, but I got this." Tara could see the sincerity in Julio's eyes. "I want you to let me know how much it costs for you to maintain your lifestyle, and I got you. I want you to just chill and enjoy the ride with me. Fast money don't last. I want us to enjoy it. I have fallen hard for you, and I want you to know I love you. Just don't hurt me," Julio explained. He never took his eyes off her.

Tara almost fainted. He had said the words she wanted to say to him so many times before, but she was afraid to let her guard down. She knew she was going to fall in love with him their very first night together. She was used to being in control of everything around her. Letting her guard down was new to her. This felt so right. It had to be right. For the first time in her life, Tara felt she could exhale, just relax and be the woman to *her* man. She had always been in charge and in control. Every man in her life served a purpose. There was no purpose or plan with Julio; there was just a deep wanting and this new thing called love.

"Oh, and promise me I never have to see you in that old-lady hookup again." Julio began laughing.

Tara playfully punched him on the shoulder and then led him to the dance floor. He resisted at first, but then gave in to her because she looked so cute pouting in front of him as she swayed to the music.

Dancing wasn't something he did often, so once on the dance floor, he just moved to the music and enjoyed being with the woman he'd fallen for so quickly.

He couldn't get over just how different Tara was from any woman he had ever known. She was tough when she needed to be. She knew how to take care of business if necessary, and she knew how to make a man feel like a man in the bedroom. To top it off, she could cook. He wanted to spend some serious time with her. He planned on making all of her dreams come true.

She told him about all the no-good niggas in her life before him. They were all imitators. He was a real man, and he couldn't wait to prove that to Tara.

The two of them danced in each other's arms until the slow song ended. Julio led Tara from the dance floor and back to their table. He held on to her as if he would lose her forever if he let her go.

"Karen, go with me to the restroom," Tara asked, wanting alone time with her friend to talk about everything Julio had just said to her. Besides that, she wanted to make sure her appearance was still on point.

Karen and Tara headed for the ladies' room in the back of the club. The club was packed; there were people everywhere. They had to force their way through the crowd just to get to the bathroom, only to find a line of hoochies waiting to get in.

"Damn, girl, I think I saw that nigga Derek over by the dance floor," Karen announced.

"I hope he ain't on no shit tonight. He will get his feelings hurt fucking with them Spanish motherfuckas. They play for keeps," Tara said.

"I saw you and Julio talking. It looked serious," Karen said as they stood in line.

"Karen, I think he might be the one. He asked me to make a commitment to him," Tara shared.

"Hell no, I know you told him what he wanted to hear, right?"

"And you know this!" Tara shouted.

"I knew my girl would land the biggest catch in town." Karen high-fived Tara. "So what does this mean? Are you going to move in together or what?"

"We haven't talked about all that yet. He wants me to chill on boosting and just hang with him on some wifey shit," Tara explained, hoping her friend would understand.

"I'm happy for you, girl. I am trying to find me a man that will put my ass on some just chill shit. You know I am down with whatever makes my girl happy. I can tell you really like him. This could be it."

Tara was relieved that her best friend understood. She was worried that her girl would look at it as some form of desertion; putting a man before their work together. Good work partners were hard to find, and Tara valued Karen. Although they wouldn't be putting in any more work together, Tara told herself that she would make sure her girl was all right.

By the time Karen and Tara made their way into the bathroom, it was packed with women trying to freshen up. After using the toilet, Tara washed her hands and checked her hair and makeup. She was pleased with the way she looked. Everything was in place.

As she patted down her hair, she noticed a high yellow,

thick sister staring at her from the other side of the bath-room. *Damn, what she staring at?*

Just then, Karen exited the bathroom stall and walked over to the sink next to her. "Hey, girl, do you know that hood rat over by the door?" Tara questioned Karen indis-creetly while nodding her head toward the girl.

"No, but I think I noticed her checking you out earlier in the club while you and Julio were dancing." Karen squinted. "You know I be scoping out shit."

Candy had planned to confront Tara in the bathroom, but after getting up close, she realized that this ho wasn't some wannabe gold digger. Something about her said to proceed with caution. She would have to come up with a well-thought-out plan for this one.

She had been successful in running off all the other hangers-on in Julio's life, but somehow she knew this one would be a challenge. Candy exited the bathroom know-ing that she would have to regroup, but she wouldn't give up. She was going to run this bitch out of Julio's life if it was the last thing she did.

Six

Take Away the Pain

Julio lay across Tara's bed in his silk boxer shorts and reached for the glass tray that was overflowing with white powder. He put the tiny straw to his nose and inhaled the white crystal powder into each nostril. He loved the rush the drug gave him. He had been fucking with drugs his whole life. He tried everything at least once. He'd now narrowed his choices down to just speedballing on occasion and cocaine.

The heroin in the speedball kept him calm, but he didn't like the side effects. There was too much money to make; he couldn't spend all day nodding from the heroin, so he mostly stuck to the cocaine.

Every player in the game had some kind of vice. Drugs were a way of life for niggas in the street. They needed something to take the edge off. Every day they took their life into their own hands in the streets. They played either Russian roulette or threw bricks at the penitentiary. So when Tara first learned of Julio's drug use, she didn't trip, nor was she surprised. His woman understood a hustler. He could just be himself with his girl and he loved that.

Julio watched as Tara entered the bedroom from the shower. Little beads of water danced across her skin and fell to the floor. She began drying herself in front of the bedroom mirror while she swayed side to side in rhythm to the music that flowed from the bedroom speakers. He watched as she rubbed the towel across her juicy booty. He loved the shape of her body. He could feel his dick coming alive in his silk shorts.

Tara knew her man was watching her, so she moved in front of the bed so that he could get a better look. She loved the way he looked at her. He always made her feel like he could eat her alive whenever she was in his presence.

Tara and Julio had been living together in her condo now for over a month, and even though she had never lived with a man before, she had not gotten tired of sharing her life with him.

Julio only kept a small spot on the east side for mail and his clothes. He never was one for the wifey and home shit until Tara. He ate, slept, and breathed the streets. He would still hang with his crew until daybreak, but with Tara was where he laid his head on a regular. She was so happy in their new life together.

They were like teenagers; every chance they got they made love. He called it making a baby. He would call her and say he was on his way home to make a baby. This always put a smile on her face.

Tara was a very sexual person, and she had never found anyone that could match her in bed until Julio. They spent most of their time making love and enjoying each other. Some days they wouldn't even leave the house. This was a new experience for both of them. Whenever Julio did leave the house to take care of business, he would often take her with him. He wanted to be with her every waking moment. She had become his world and he hers. Julio and Tara were so comfortable with each other that they knew what the other one was thinking without speaking a word.

As Tara finished drying off, she knew by the look in Julio's eyes that he wanted a piece of her pie, so she began gently massaging her breasts while she positioned herself between his legs. She then took his hand and placed it between her legs. She moved his hand in a circular motion across her clit, watching as his manhood danced within its confinement.

Tara took her man's rock-hard weapon in her hands and stroked it up and down while staring into his eyes. He licked his lips and then placed his fingers in his mouth. He then placed them between her legs, searching for her moist spot. When he found what he was looking for, he entered.

Arching her back with pleasure, Tara closed her eyes and began her journey. Her body moved with the rhythm of Julio's fingers. Just when she was about to reach her peak, he flipped her onto the bed and studied her body as if he was deciding where to begin.

"*Mami,* I want all of you. I want to feel you, taste you and touch you. I just can't get enough of you," Julio whispered softly.

"I want all of you too, baby. I want you inside of me. Please give it to me. I can't stand it. I need my dick now. Give it to me," Tara moaned as she stretched across the bed studying his movement.

Julio began kissing her soft chocolate thighs. He inched

his way between her legs, all while planting kisses wherever his lips touched. He stood over her, and for a moment, all he could do was smile.

Damn, he thought, *can a man be this totally satisfied?* He began stroking his manhood as he watched Tara moaning and begging him to enter her. He slid his rock-hard dick inside her with one hard stroke. Their eyes met and locked in place as they both melted into each other and began their ride together.

Tara arched her back and hung on for dear life. She was in the zone. This was her man, and their lovemaking had reached a completely different level. They both began to moan as they reached their orgasms together. Julio slid his hands under Tara's soft ass and drifted off to sleep.

"Whew ooohh," Tara moaned, waking from her sleep and pushing Julio off her. She quietly moved from the bed and headed to the bathroom for a quick shower.

After her shower, she began brushing her teeth. Her tooth had been killing her lately. She had been putting off a dreaded trip to the dentist for months now. The pain in her tooth was getting measurably worse each day. Tara didn't know why she hated going to the dentist so much. Perhaps it was the horrible sound the drills and dental equipment made that only added to her fears.

As she turned the water off from the shower, she could hear Julio speaking loudly on the telephone in a mixture of both Spanish and English. She could tell by his tone that this wasn't a pleasant conversation. She continued listening.

"Yo, that motherfucka messed with my ends and we gon' have to step to him sooner than later. I told you not to give that *wa puta* that much rope. I knew he would hang himself," Julio spat into the phone. "I'm gon' have to make an example out of that *primo*. His ass gon' have to be the poster boy for the other *wa putas* that are even thinking about crossing me."

Tara entered the bedroom and smiled at her man as he blew her a kiss. She prayed that the conversation did not mean that there was trouble in their future. Their life together was so good, and she didn't want her happiness interrupted by anything or anyone. But right now, with all the pain she was in, it seemed something as small as a little ol' tooth was trying to interrupt her happiness.

"Baby?" Tara said as she watched Julio hang up the telephone and reach for the tray of white powder. "Can you run and get me some Anbesol for my tooth? It is killing me, baby. I'm in too much pain to go myself," she said, holding the side of her face.

"*Mami,* I am fucked-up. I can't drive anywhere right now." He looked down at the tray. "Here, put a little of this 'caine on your tooth and it will numb the pain," Julio said, scooping up some of the white powder onto his index finger and holding it up.

Tara stared at it with her nose turned up. "I don't know, baby. I ain't never tried that shit," she cautioned.

"Here, we gon' just put a little bit on it. It won't hurt." Julio began rubbing the powder across Tara's gums.

The drug tasted bitter but sweet at the same time. Tara could feel it draining down her throat. She felt instantly alert. Everything seemed brighter. After a few minutes, there was a warm stirring feeling inside her and the pain was gone. She kissed her man and reached for his crotch all at the same time, while pulling him to the bed.

Julio was truly her everything. She would do anything to please him and he would do anything to please her. Who knew he could even find a way to take her pain away?

Seven

Addicted

Tara licked the remaining fine white crystal powder from the silver tray and looked around the room nervously. She was alone, but the drug heightened her hearing and the sound of the house settling scared her. The drug always gave her an instant rush. She felt like she could build a new world and hear everything from just a quick "one and one" of her newfound friend.

She lay back down in the bed and thought back to that first night she tried the 'caine. That night, the sex with Julio had been crazy off the chain. They fucked all night long. Each time she came, her orgasm reached a different level. After that, she began using it to heighten their sex. Julio loved the fact that she would kick it with him all night long. He was a night owl, and she was becoming one fast.

Everything came into perspective once Tara snorted the crystal powder into both nostrils. Drugs had never been of interest to her until now. She would smoke an occasional blunt with her girl, Karen, when they planned on hangin' in the clubs all night just to kick it, but she never

tried the hard stuff. Tara wasn't worried, though. There wasn't a person, place or thing that could ever control her or get her off her game; surely not something that resembled baby powder. Life was good and she was with the man of her dreams; she deserved to be able to enjoy her life however she wanted.

Julio questioned her the first time she asked for a "one and one." They were preparing for a night out on the town and she wanted to have a good time with her man and their friends. When he pulled out his silver tray and snorted the 'caine, she asked for some.

Julio was surprised and a little worried. He did not want his girl to become a fiend. He'd seen way too many fiends that would do anything for drugs.

Shit, the crackhead fiends were selling their babies for the shit. He trusted the fact that Tara came from the streets and she knew just as much as he knew about drugs. He was confident she could handle it. So, he told her, he didn't want her using the drug in public, and it was only for their personal use.

He asked her if she was sure she wanted to fuck with the shit or she was feeling pressure because he used the powder himself. Tara assured him that she enjoyed the high and she liked chillin' with him in this newfound way.

Tara was a sex fiend without the drug, but she became a porn star with it. Once she got the drug in her system, all she wanted to do was chill and fuck. She began trying things in bed that she never thought she would do, and she liked it. Julio loved the way the drug relaxed her, and he was glad they were able to share their high together.

Opening her eyes, the morning sun beamed through the bedroom window like a spotlight and warmed Tara's face. She rose leisurely from her bed and went to the living room. Turning on the TV, Tara turned it to the church station.

The Sunday morning church music blasted from the television. She hummed along to the music of her youthful days in Mama Grace's house. Tara moved across the living room floor with a bounce in her step.

She wanted to call Julio, but she did not want to be a bug-a-boo, so she decided to give her mom a call instead just to get an update on her family. She hadn't spoken to M&M since she had taken a trip to Canada on a mink coat run. Tara felt like talking, and she knew her mom would get her caught up on all the latest gossip.

"What's up, baby girl?" M&M sang into the phone as she laid across her king-size bed with imported mattresses.

"Nothing much, just chillin'," Tara answered, making herself comfortable on the new chaise lounge she picked up from City Center Mall last week.

She'd been eyeing the powder blue chair for months. Thanks to her man, she was able to splurge all the time now. Her condo was beginning to look overcrowded with all her new purchases. She reminded herself to mention to Julio that they would have to start looking for a bigger place soon.

"I'm waiting on that slow-ass Eddie to come pick up these pieces. His ass is so slow, if his money wasn't so good, I would kick his ass straight to the curb," M&M complained.

"What's been going on with you and Daddy?" Tara asked.

"Oh, now you want to come up for air? You over there all in love and ain't nobody heard from yo' ass. Karen told me that you don't even go to work with her anymore.

"She asked if she could ride with me and Tina on our next trip. You know I don't like riding three deep, but I will make an exception for Karen; she family.

"Slim got me pissed off. He took my best two minks out of here last week to show to Mrs. Abrahams, his good customer, and he ain't brought me my money yet. I know she bought them, 'cause she been worrying me to deaf about a black diamond mink in a plus size. I could have rolled up three minks and carried them in my girdle for the space that fat fucker took up.

"Damn, I'm burning up my cornbread. Hold on, baby, please," M&M said, all in one breath.

Tara smiled to herself, listening to her mom. Talking to her was not talking at all. It was listening. A person couldn't get a word in edgewise if they wanted to.

"Ma, what you cooking?" Tara asked when M&M returned to the phone.

"I'm finishing up my bread now. I got fried pork chops, cabbage, fresh fried corn, and hot water cornbread and sliced tomatoes and onions," M&M announced.

"I'm on my way." Tara laughed into the phone.

"Bring me a 'one and one' when you come. I know Julio got that pure shit."

Tara's mind drifted to when she was younger, all the times her mom would sit on the side of her bed in the middle of the night after all her company was gone, high on cocaine. M&M would often dance into her young daughters' room and share life lessons with her girls.

M&M was a beautiful woman. She bragged that her cheekbones were high and graceful because of her Indian ancestry. She was a lovely pecan color. She always dressed as if she were ready for her close-up. M&M told her girls that they only had one time to make a first impression. Everything she did, she did with style, and she demanded the same from her children.

"I can't come right now, Ma, but put me a plate up. I will take care of you when I come by."

"Slim told me that he stopped by your place and kicked it with Julio. He said that boy got the best powder in the city. You know your nephew wants to do some business with Julio and he wants you to introduce them," M&M explained.

"Ma, you know Tee don't play by the old-school rules, and I don't want to be in the middle of no shit with my man and my family. I would rather leave that alone."

Tee was Tara's gangsta nephew. He, like Tara, was born into the game. He was the youngest son of Tara's oldest sister, Karen. Mama Grace raised Karen from the time she was born. M&M raised Tee from the time he was eighteen months old. Tee was a raw gangsta. He had his own rules, and the only thing he respected was his family. He was born and raised a straight hustler. Tee barely remembered going to his great-grandparents' and going to church with Mama Grace.

"He just needs a break. Everybody in the streets knows you with the biggest dope man in the city. What it look like if yo' blood still grindin'?" M&M asked, putting a guilt trip on Tara.

"Ma, let me think about it and get back to you," Tara contemplated.

"Tee said he saw Julio at Papa Jack's last week and he was thinking about stepping to him."

"Ma, tell Tee not to do that. I will talk to Julio and see if he wants to meet Tee. I'll call you and let you know. I gotta go, Ma."

"Okay, baby, talk to you later. Bye," M&M yelled into the phone with a mouthful of the food she had just tasted.

After hanging up the phone with her mother, Tara poured herself a drink and dialed Julio's number. She tried her best not to call him, but she wanted to hear his voice. They'd been spending so much time together that now she felt lonely whenever she wasn't with him. She tried to play it cool, but she knew as well as everyone else that she was addicted—she was addicted to her man. She wanted to be with him all the time.

The drugs made her think and worry a lot. She thought about how Julio used to ask her to ride with him when he went out, but lately he had been rollin' solo. This worried Tara. From the conversations she overheard him having with Carlito and Roberto the past few weeks, there was something going on with their crew that wasn't cool. Julio hadn't shared any of his business with her, but she could put two and two together; even from a one-sided conversation.

After Tara dialed Julio's cell phone, it rang four times and then went to his voice mail. "Baby, call me when you get this message," Tara spoke into the phone. She hung up and tried not to worry, but it was hard. He had always answered the phone when he saw that it was her on the caller ID.

She decided to take a nice long, hot shower to calm her nerves. She headed up the stairs just as the phone started ringing. She almost broke her neck trying to get to the cordless phone on the kitchen counter.

"Hello, hello," Tara said into the phone.

"Hey, *mami*, what's up? I got your message. You sounded worried," Julio said.

"Hey, baby. Where are you?" Tara questioned.

"I'm headed home to you. Put on something sexy. I'm taking my baby out to dinner. Roberto and Karen are gonna meet us there. You didn't tell me that Karen and my boy was kickin' it," Julio yelled into the phone over the music bumping from the sound system in his Range Rover.

"I thought Roberto would have told you. He's been

creepin' with Karen since that night they met at the club. I told her not to get in too deep because he's living with some chick. She said that she could handle it, so I'm gon' let her handle it," Tara explained.

"You know that's my boy, but he's a dog. I just want to warn you. I know how close you and Karen are, and I don't want this to come between us if it backfires on her," Julio warned.

"I know, baby. I'll probably try to have another talk with Karen. Anyway, how long before you get here?" Tara asked.

"I'll be there in an hour. Be ready. There's something I want to show you before we go to the restaurant. I love you," Julio added with excitement. He'd been gone all day, getting things right for his baby. He hoped she liked his surprise. "Bye."

"Bye," Tara said, hanging up the phone.

Tara searched her walk-in closet for just the right outfit. She could tell by the tone of Julio's voice that he had big plans for them, so she wanted to look breathtaking. She always enjoyed the way he looked at her when she looked nice. Whenever they went out, he always made a point to take time and truly look at her from head to toe. She was a representation of her man, and Tara made a point of reppin' for her man to the fullest.

She decided on a burnt orange silk dress with matching Fendi shoes and bag. She showered and slipped into the body-hugging dress and applied just the right amount of M•A•C makeup to her face and a dab of Chanel No 5 behind each ear. She decided to keep her jewelry simple: diamond studs and a teardrop diamond necklace.

Tara stood in front of the full-length mirror and admired what she had created.

"Damn, ma, you look good," Julio sang as he entered

the room and hugged his girl. "I've been making my way back to you all day. It's getting crazy out in these streets. Real gangstas are getting harder and harder to find. Keep a nigga making moves. But fuck that, come over here and give me what I need," he demanded of Tara.

Tara glided across the room into the arms of her baby. She planted a wet kiss on his soft, full lips, lingering for a few minutes before moving to his neck and then his chest. Tara gently pushed her man against the front door, massaging his dick with her right hand as she worked at his zipper. She could hear Julio moan in surrender as she got down on her knees and placed his throbbing penis deep inside her mouth. As Julio's body began to shake with pleasure, he grabbed Tara by her shoulders and pulled her up to him.

Staring into her eyes, he whispered, "I love you, *mami*, and I want to spend the rest of my life with you like this. Marry me," Julio pleaded. "I been playin' games with females my whole life, and nothing really mattered until you rolled up on a nigga. I ain't never thought about havin' no future or getting out this game, but I can see that shit with you. Damn, *mami*, you done showed a gangsta something different, and I like it."

Tara looked into Julio's eyes and she knew that she was safe. She could finally put her guard down forever. "I love you," she cried, burying her face in his chest. "Yes, I'll marry you."

Tara and Julio made mad, crazy love and then prepared themselves for their night out with their friends.

The two of them sped up I-71 north, headed toward the restaurant. "Baby, you just passed our exit," Tara warned, looking out of the tinted window of the Range Rover.

"I got this, girl. Sit back and chill. I want to show you

something before we head to the restaurant. You always tryin' to run something," Julio said, playfully mugging her face.

"Okay, Daddy, I'm gonna let you have it then," Tara said, mugging him back.

After exiting I-71 north, Julio pulled slowly onto a tree-lined suburban street. He stopped the car in front of a ranch-style, split-level brick home with blue shutters. Before Tara could ask a question, he hopped out of the car and opened the passenger-side door for his woman.

"Baby, welcome home," Julio said, handing her a key ring with a single key on it. "If we gonna start this family shit, we need a place that is ours." Julio smiled and led a speechless Tara up the walkway and to the front door.

With moist eyes, Tara nervously unlocked the door and gasped when she saw that the inside was completely decorated. The front door opened to a marble foyer. The marble was beige with streaks of cobalt blue. A full-length mirror hung on the wall, with a matching marble table filled with fresh flowers.

The sunken living area sat to the right of the door. Tara smiled at the imported white silk couch; it reminded her of her mother. M&M rocked a white couch in her living room for as long as Tara could remember.

The living-room decor was beautiful shades of blue, white, and cherrywood. Flowers were planted tastefully throughout the room. Custom-made drapes flowed from the picture windows and matched the accent pillows on the sofa.

The kitchen was all stainless steel with black appliances; the floor a black-and-white marble pattern.

Their master bedroom was breathtaking. A king-size bed sat on a raised pedestal, and there had to be at least twenty pillows of all sizes arranged on top of the tan, burgundy, and green comforter set with the matching drapes.

There were African art pieces on all the cherrywood sur-
faces.

"I don't want nothing in the house you had when you
was with them other niggas. I kept your spot because it's
yours and you can decide what we do with it. It's a cool
low-key spot, so I kept it. I got us all new shit because I
want us to start this thing fresh. You my woman, and I
want you to have everything. I will kill any motherfucker
that tries to fuck this up. I want you happy and safe always," Julio said with the most sincere look in his eyes. He
then led Tara back downstairs with both his hands around
her waist.

Tara stood in the center of her sunken living room and
watched as her designer leather sling-back sandals disappeared into the plush white carpet. A balcony that led to
the master bedroom could be seen from the front door.

Tara ran through her new home like a kid in a toy store
for the very first time. She finally slowed down in her bedroom. She did a belly-smack dive onto her king-size bed.
Damn, if I'm dreaming, don't wake me, Tara thought, burying
her face in the pillows.

Julio entered the room and joined his girl on the bed.
"You like, *mami?*" he questioned.

"I love it, baby. Thank you. Nobody has ever done no
shit like this for me before. You make me so happy. You're
always thinking of me. I don't ever want this to end. I want
you to promise me that once we move in here, you'll start
backing up out of them streets. I want us to slow this shit
down and for us to really get a shot at the American
dream. I don't want to lose you. Promise me," Tara said,
looking him in his eyes as tears ran down her face.

Julio wiped her tears and held her close before turning
her face to him and saying, "I want the same thing you
want. I always thought I would die out there alone. I never

thought I would find someone like you, besides my kids, that matters more than my homies and paper. Damn, girl, you all I think about.

"I been trying to tie up some shit out there and turn some things over to Santiago. Will you give me a little time? I need to do things the right way.

"I want you to come with me to New York to meet my family soon. I want them to know my wife." Julio had a look of seriousness on his face that Tara had never seen before.

"I will give you anything you ask me for, baby, and that includes time," Tara replied to Julio and then kissed him tenderly, ready to begin their new life together.

Eight

Mo' Money, Mo' Problems

Tara inspected every inch of her new home before returning to the car with Julio and heading for the restaurant. The Reflectory was packed with well-off suburban families and couples enjoying an evening out. Tara felt intimidated by all the people of power in the room. She was used to dining out, but her family always stayed on their side of town.

Julio believed he had every right to rub elbows with the rich and famous. He told Tara they were no different from him; hell, they were the ones that dealt the cards people like him were forced to play. He saw himself as a businessman just like them; therefore, belonging at the table with them.

Julio confidently stepped to the hostess and said, "Table for Julio, please."

The petite blond hostess studied her clipboard and then replied, "Right this way, sir." She led them to a private, secluded table along a drapery-covered wall in the center of the room, where the other guests had been waiting for their arrival.

"What's up, G?" Roberto greeted Julio, getting up from the table and hugging his friend. Karen smiled and waved at her girl from the booth.

"Hey, girl, you look nice," Tara complimented her friend as they greeted each other.

"Bring us a couple bottles of champagne and some of your best appetizers," Julio instructed the hostess.

"I will give your waitress your request, sir," the polite hostess announced as she turned and walked away to do just that.

"What's poppin', Karen?" Julio offered, noticing something about Karen was a little off. She was dressed nice, but there was a glassy look in her eyes and she seemed nervous. He'd seen that look before, just never on Karen. It could be seen on every street corner in the hood, though.

"Yo, man, Roberto, roll with me out to the car. I think I left my phone out there." Julio covered for a chance to speak privately with his boy.

Once they reached the parking lot, Julio turned to Roberto and said, "Tell me you ain't turn that girl out."

Roberto grinned and nervously looked at his caramel-colored snakeskin shoes. "Man, you know I like my freaks wild. That filly is teaching a nigga some things in between the sheets. When she smoking that shit, it's on," he bragged.

"Man, that girl's like family to my girl. How you gon' turn her out on that shit? Damn, man, do you ever think about anything but yo' dick? That shit is foul," Julio screamed.

"I didn't turn her out on the shit; she was playing around with it when we met. She just greedy with it and she's a freak. It's cool, *primo*. I got it under control. I ain't gon' let nothing happen to Karen. Hell, I kind of like her and plan on keeping her around," Roberto told his partner as he nervously paced back and forth in front of the restaurant's entrance.

"This shit better not come back to haunt us. I got a bad feeling about this whole thing. How the fuck you talking 'bout keeping her around and you already got a wife?"

Roberto treated his wife so bad people sometimes forgot he had one. The poor girl was so glad to be in the land of opportunity that she let him get away with murder on the regular. Fuck, sometimes he'd bring his latest pussy home with him and they'd all fuck. He had no respect for any woman.

Julio knew it would be just a matter of time before some shit went down with him and Karen. The shit was too close to home. He was happy with his life right now. He didn't want some petty bullshit to fuck up his happiness.

"Motherfucka, you always wanna play with fire. We got enough shit in the game without you bringing more drama. Damn," Julio complained as he watched a group of noisy teenagers dressed in prom attire exit the restaurant and enter waiting limos.

Roberto did his best to calm his friend down before they joined the girls back inside the restaurant. Tara was happy to spend some time with her friend, so she didn't notice that Julio had returned to the table upset.

"Baby, you ready to order?" Julio asked Tara as he sat down and picked at one of the appetizers, not sure exactly what it was.

"Boo, I was starving, and these appetizers weren't hittin' it, so I ordered for us," Tara said. "I figured you'd want to try the lobster. The menu says they fly it in fresh daily. I ordered the same thing for me. I can't wait. My guts are growling," Tara whined, picking at the calamari appetizers the waitress had brought to their table.

Julio's cell phone began to ring. "*Hola*, where you at?"

Julio questioned. "Sí, stay there. We coming through." He hung up the phone and looked at Roberto. "That was Carlito. They're at Spinners and the spot is jumping, he said."

"Aw shit, I'm ready to get my party on. I ain't been out in a minute," Karen began to complain as she danced in her seat.

"Girl, it stay packed in there. You can barely get on the dance floor. The DJ keep it pumpin'. I swear the walls be sweatin' in that spot," Tara explained as she watched two skilled male waiters arrive at the table in unison, place their meals in front of them, refill their drinks, and clear their appetizer plates.

The two couples ate the delicious food and shared conversation. They ordered cheesecake for dessert and sipped on glasses of wine and talked.

"Karen, come with me to the restroom. I want to fix my makeup. I know I ate my lipstick off along with my food," Tara teased, licking her lips playfully.

"Don't take all day. My peeps are waiting for us at Spinners," Julio reminded her.

"Baby, if I do take all day, I know you gon' wait for your boo." Tara leaned down and kissed her man.

The two friends then made their way to the pristine bathrooms located in the front of the restaurant.

"I didn't know white boys be sweating a sister all like that. Did you see the one at the table with the two old ladies? He stared me down," Tara questioned Karen when they entered the bathroom.

"I thought you knew; white boys love them some sisters, and they can fuck. Shit, I got me a white boy in the south end I keeps on standby." Karen laughed.

"I ain't never tried me no white boy. But that one was fine," Tara said as she entered the bathroom stall.

Karen nervously entered the stall next to her friend. She tried to get the door to lock but was having difficulties, so she gave up. She removed her glass crack pipe from her navy blue Dooney & Bourke purse, gently placing the last of her crack rock on her pipe and quickly lighting the drug. Anxious for the rush, Karen hurriedly sucked at the pipe and dropped her purse on the marble bathroom floor. All its contents rolled onto the marble floor and spilled into the adjoining stall.

"You getting clumsy. Here, let me help you," Tara politely offered after flushing the toilet. She picked up the contents at her feet and then exited her stall and pulled open the rose-colored stall door that Karen stood behind. The two friends froze as their eyes locked. Karen sat on the toilet with a glass crack pipe in her mouth. There was fresh smoke billowing from the open end.

"Hell no, Karen, you ain't fuckin' with that shit. Damn, Karen, you know that shit crazy," Tara said, staring at her best friend with a look of fear on her face.

"Karen, you know what crack has done to a lot of people. I'm scared as hell of that shit. I know you trying to get next to Roberto, but you got to be careful how far you're willing to go with him. You know he got a wife and family at home. He's been with a bunch of sisters and all the relationships have ended bad.

"I want you to be careful with your emotions; I don't want you getting into no deep shit with him that's going to hurt my girl," Tara warned her friend, wanting to spare her the pain of falling for the wrong nigga. The thought of her friend getting addicted to crack worried her.

"Girl, I'm cool. You know ain't nothing I can't handle," Karen announced, nervously putting the pipe away. "You know I been fuckin' with something my whole life. I like how this high feels. It make me wanna relax, and I be putting a hurtin' on Roberto when I'm high on the shit. That nigga been shooting through my spot every night. He even stayed all night on Tuesday. I think I just about got him hooked. I got this, friend.

"I'm trying to work my plan where the boy stuck and I'm sitting pretty on some laid back shit like you and Julio. I'm tired of being solo. I want a man that's all mine. I'm trying to make Roberto forget those other hoes. A girl got to put in extra work when you dealing with a brother with paper," Karen explained as she washed and dried her hands at the sink.

"Well, I guess this is a good time to tell you that I been messing around with some powder with Julio," Tara confided.

"I knew you were losing weight. Yo' ass been holdin' out on your girl. How long you been snortin'?" Karen questioned.

"Not long. Julio doesn't want me using it in public. I don't think he wants me off guard in the streets. I like it, though. I've been pinching from his private stash. When he's out in them streets and I'm alone, I like snorting it to keep my mind occupied. I am so afraid of losing what we have that I constantly worry about him getting caught up in them streets.

"Damn, I ain't never cared if a nigga even called before; now I'm worried all the time. This love shit is hard." Tara sighed.

"Shit, all we go through for it, I hope it's worth it." Karen shook her head as they exited the restroom after she had put all of her contents back into her purse.

"Yo, let's bounce. Julio's pulling the car around now," Roberto ordered as the girls returned to the table. He popped Karen on the ass and they headed for the exit.

Tara got in the car and kissed her man as Roberto and

Karen went to their car. Tara really was happy to have him in her life. For the first time, she knew she was loved. There were always so many games in all her other relationships. She never trusted anyone with her heart, so she constantly played games.

Karen and Tara were masters at playing games. They were pros at getting men to do whatever they wanted. They could get a man to do anything once they had them under their spell and hooked.

Her gut told her that their Latin lovers were not to be fucked with, though. She especially had an uneasy feeling about Roberto. Something in his eyes was cold and dark. She felt as if she were looking into a black hole whenever she looked at him. The man was ruthless; she just knew it. Tara would have to have another talk with Karen about her new conquest.

Pulling down the sun visor, Tara checked her lipstick and turned up the radio. The bass thumped through the Bose speakers, flooding the car with the upbeat salsa music. Julio began moving to the beat. Tara reached for his hand and relaxed in her seat. He leaned over, kissed her on the forehead, rolled back the sunroof, and headed for Spinners with Roberto and Karen following close behind.

It was standing room only as usual for Latino night at the club. There was an impromptu car show in the parking lot, along with someone selling knockoff NBA leather jackets inside the entrance to the club.

The two ballers made their way through the club like royalty, stopping to greet their admirers as they passed. Tara held onto Julio's hand for dear life. It was as if they were walking the red carpet for a major movie premiere. She recognized some real heavyweights in the game paying their respects to her man. She knew he held weight in the streets, but this was the first time she saw how much pull he truly had.

People were everywhere. You couldn't find an empty table if your life depended on it. The beauty of Spinners was the melting pot of culture. Brothers, sisters, Jamaicans, white folks, and Latinos blended effortlessly. There were so many different languages being spoken in the spot that it sounded like a day at the United Nations.

Julio led them to the VIP section located at the left of the revolving dance floor, where Carlito and a girl were sitting.

Carlito rose to greet their leader. "*Hola,* dog. What it look like? I want you to meet my new friend, Angel," he said, pointing at the Playboy bunny–looking girl who sat in the booth with her legs folded beneath her butt and her shoes off.

"What's up, baby?" the girl purred as she licked her lips and sat up straight in her seat.

"It's all good," Julio replied. "Meet my girl, Tara, and this is Roberto and Karen," he informed the centerfold as they all got comfortable at the table.

"I already ordered Moët and Heinekens all around. If you want anything else, let me know. Rocco, the owner, has a tab with me. The motherfucka snorts more 'caine than Scarface and we gon' drink the fucker dry until he pay up. If y'all want to get some food, just let me know. The kitchen stays open until three and the food is good in this bitch too," Carlito offered, almost all in one breath.

"Oh, girl, your hair is bumping," Angel said, running her fingers through Karen's silky hair. "Where you get it done?"

"I go to Natural Motions over on Livingston," Karen replied. "Trey does my hair and Tara's. He's bad, but be prepared to stay all day. Those gay boys over there don't get in a hurry for nobody. They worth it, though. Your hair be bouncing and behaving for weeks." Karen laughed and shook her fresh 'do.

"Hey, y'all want to dance? They gon' be talking business all night and I want to have some fun. I just got this outfit and I want to get some mileage out of it before I take it back to the store," Angel said as the trio headed to the dance floor.

Angel was a tall, light-skinned girl with honey blond hair. She wore a skintight cat suit with six-inch heels. She appeared to be mixed with black and Asian. Her blond hair hung in wavy curls down her back. Her eyes were black as coal, and she had full brown lips. She sported a set of breast implants that were the best Tara had ever seen.

Tara didn't get close to strangers often; there were way too many perpetrators in the game. She was taught to keep a close circle, but there was something about Angel that made Tara like her from the gate.

"Hey, hold up. I need to run to the bathroom first," Tara announced to the girls.

"I need to check my hair too," Karen said.

The girls pushed their way to the restrooms and entered. Tara almost ran over a thick, light-skinned woman on her way out. It was Candy.

Candy and Tara locked eyes, and then Candy moved out of the way, allowing the girls to enter. Candy was dressed in a two-piece denim hookup with a pair of clean white Air Force Ones. Her hair was pulled back in a tight ponytail. Her road dog, a skinny and shapely sister, was dressed in a matching outfit and stood behind her.

Ain't this a bitch. Every fuckin' time I turn around it's this bitch. This bitch is really trying my patience. I thought this ho would be history by now, and she still all up in my mix and shit. This hooker ain't trying to back the fuck up. I'm going to be forced to show her I ain't no joke, Candy thought angrily.

The girls entered the restroom and Candy and her girl followed behind them. Tara watched their every move from the bathroom mirror.

"So you think yo' ass all that, parading around here like you really Julio's woman. I been down with him for a minute, and I done seen bitches like you come and go," Candy spat while Karen and Angel circled around Tara.

"Is there something you want to say to me?" Tara questioned calmly as she checked her hair in the bathroom mirror.

"Hell yeah, there's something I want to say to you. You think he belongs to you? Well, I want you to know he's still fuckin' me every chance he gets. He ain't ever gon' be through with me and our baby. I hope you know that shit," Candy hissed, stepping to Tara. Karen and Angel stepped up at the same time.

"Listen, bitch, he fuckin' me real good too, and taking care of me real good. So we both should be real happy. What's the problem, huh?" Tara said calmly, giving Karen some dap while never backing down.

Candy noticed the huge diamond on Tara's wedding finger, and she could not believe her eyes. He was really serious about this girl. That explained to Candy why Tara was so damn cocky; she was rocking a rock. Julio was planning to marry this girl.

The thought of him getting married had never crossed Candy's mind. He didn't seem like the settling-down type. She'd seen hookers come and go, and never did she think he would marry any of them. The only attachment he showed was for his children.

The three girls stared Candy and her friend down and they turned and left the bathroom. Tara used the restroom, washed her hands, and checked her makeup.

"Fuck that stuck-up bitch. Them ghetto fabulous hoes is off the chain," Tara spat. "I ain't even gon' let them ruin my night with my baby and my friends. Let's get this party jumping," Tara ordered, dancing from the bathroom.

There wasn't a bitch young or old that she was afraid of. This was the happiest day of her life, and she wasn't going to let Julio's baby momma spoil her mood.

"How long you and Carlito been kickin' it?" Tara questioned Angel as they walked over to the dance floor, wanting to know more about this chick. She liked the way Angel had been ready to put in work for her back in the bathroom. Tara felt like Angel had some balls, and she respected that. Even though the girl was a sex freak, she was a down, true-to-the-game sex freak and man hustler. Tara had been around enough hoes, sex freaks, and hustlers in her lifetime to recognize her game from the gate.

"Hell, if you count the time he spent trying to get me to leave my husband, I guess you could say a year. I love the partying he does. He keep a girl on some excitement shit. I don't give a damn he got other women. I take what I can get with that nigga," Angel yelled over the loud salsa music as she danced closer to Tara.

"Julio is so fine. He looks at you like you the only one in the room. I've seen him around, and I never seen him give a bitch the kind of time of day. I need to get some tips from you, girlfriend," Angel teased.

"We just vibed from day one. I guess you can call it fate. The shit was meant to be," Tara explained.

"Y'all look good together too. I bet you and Julio would make some pretty babies together," Angel complimented.

"It's hot as hell in here. My shirt is soaked. Let's take a break," Karen suggested after they all had danced to a couple of songs. The three left the dance floor.

"Yo, sweetie, what a nigga got to do to get a dance?" a buster in a lime green leisure suit asked Tara as he grabbed her by the arm.

"Clown, you are way out of your league. I suggest you back the fuck up before you bite off more than you could ever chew," Tara warned.

Before she could get her next thought out, Julio was standing beside them with Carlito and Roberto positioned behind him on either side. Tara could see Roberto's gun was drawn. Just then, two bouncers appeared and escorted the man to the door.

"*Mami*, let's raise up out of this spot. It's too thick in here. Let's take this party back to the house. I'm sick of looking at motherfuckas," Julio said to Tara before turning to Carlito.

"Carlito, take the girls to the car. Roberto, come with me and I'll meet y'all in a few minutes out front."

Tara could tell by the look in Julio's eyes that he was in business mode. She knew to just follow orders when he was like this. She followed Carlito to the car without any questions.

The group sat in Carlito's jeep and waited patiently for Julio and Roberto.

"*Papi*, roll the window down. I want to see if that's my girl, Trina, over there by that Cadillac," Angel whined.

"Girl, shut up and sit back. You always thinking you know somebody," Carlito said as he admired himself in the rearview mirror. Carlito was gorgeous. He had jet-

black hair and a chiseled face like a movie star. He reminded Tara of Manny from the movie *Scarface*. He was always flirting with the ladies, and they were always flirting
with him.

Angel sat back against the dark green leather seats and
relaxed. She pulled a folded-up dollar bill from her purse
and began unfolding it. The crystal powder overflowed inside the confines. She skillfully snorted two blows in each
nostril and then passed the folded dollar bill to Carlito,
who did the same. He turned to Karen, who was sitting behind him, and offered the dollar bill to her. Karen reached
for it like a baby reaching for a bottle.

"Good looking out, Carlito; I need a wake-me-up,"
Karen chimed as she hurriedly snorted the powder and
passed the dollar bill to Tara.

"Thanks, guys, but I'm cool," Tara covered, remembering what Julio told her about blowing in public.

Just then, Julio pulled the car up next to Carlito's ride
and got out. Roberto was bumper to bumper behind him
with his music blasting as usual. He got out as well. Julio
looked a little nervous as he glanced anxiously around the
parking lot.

"Tara, let's go, baby. We gonna have to pick this party
up another night real soon. We didn't get the chance to
celebrate our engagement like I wanted to," he explained.

"Aw, hell no! You engaged, *primo*?" Carlito and Roberto
said in unison as they high-fived their partner.

The girls screamed and hugged each other. Karen
grabbed Tara's hand and inspected the large solitaire diamond ring with twenty-one baguettes that sat on her friend's
finger. Karen had not noticed the ring before because her
mind was in the clouds from smoking.

"Aw shit, we got a wedding to plan," Karen said excitedly. "I know just where I'm going to get your wedding dress. I saw it last week out at Tuttle Crossing Mall. They just opened up a new bridal store out there.

"I need to act fast before the spot gets hot. It's just a matter of time before it's a done deal. It's like taking candy from a baby in the whole shopping complex. They got every young kid in town out there working. I been going out there every day for two weeks.

"You have to go with me, though, Tara. I don't want to take a chance on rolling that fat bitch up and you don't like it," Karen explained to her friend.

"All right, call me tomorrow and I'll come by and pick you up and we can go see what they have. I'm not sure I even want to wear a traditional wedding dress, but it will be fun to check them out," Tara said as she got in the car.

Julio smiled at his boo, but his thoughts were in another place. He'd just gotten a call that someone had kicked in the door at his spot on Main Street and two of his best workers were shot. The word was that the boys who did it were teenagers and his soldiers had to take them out. What a waste.

The bigger their operation got, the more problems they faced. The young bucks in the game were getting harder and harder to control. They had little respect for the game. They were like wild animals. It was every man for themselves and fuck everybody else.

Julio now had to constantly let cats know just who he was, that he was ride or die for his. His crew would have to send a message soon. He knew they were always ready to put in work, but nobody wanted war. It was bad for business.

Can't we all just get along? He wished the timing was better. The young bangers were fucking with his plans. They had begun knocking over spots just for GP (general purpose). The young boys weren't even waiting to be introduced to the game; they were just jumpin' the fuck in. The body count in the streets was reaching an all-time high.

Julio promised Tara he was going to start backing out of the game, but now shit was out of control. He'd have to put his promise on hold . . . indefinitely

Nine

M&M's House

Tara knocked at the gold-frame glass security door to her mom's house. She smiled up at the peephole in the burgundy steel front door. The smell of lilac blossoms from the manicured flower beds on either side of the spacious porch tickled her nose. She prepared to knock again when Rabbit opened the door swiftly.

"Hey, baby girl, get your fine ass in here; lookin' just like your mama," Rabbit sang as he lowered his shotgun and secured the deadbolt lock on the door.

Rabbit was M&M's bodyguard. He was a stocky older man who looked like he could give Mike Tyson a run for his money. He was dressed in his signature wife beater, T-shirt, and jeans. He was employed by Slim to protect the house and everything in it.

At any given time, M&M might be sitting on tens of thousands of dollars' worth of pieces. She might have a couple ki's she was flippin' for a friend or she might be sitting on hot ice for some B and E boys. You name the hustle and M&M fucked with it. If there were some dollars to be made, she made them.

There were too many people depending on her. Her kids were grown and she was now taking care of three of her grandchildren. Her children could always count on her for whatever help they needed. If someone in her family was in need, she was gonna move a mountain to help. Her friends could count on her as well.

Her home was a gathering place if you were lucky enough to get in. Once in, you didn't want to leave. You were guaranteed something good to eat, good to smoke, and some good conversation. Tara's parents were teachers, and you were given some life lessons in their presence. People came from miles away to soak up game from them.

"Rabbit, where Ma at?" Tara questioned.

"She back in the kitchen cutting up some chickens," Rabbit answered.

Tara moved through her mother's elegant living room with ease. The living room looked like the cover of *Better Homes and Gardens*. The color scheme was rose, burgundy, and white. M&M didn't play about her white silk couch and the matching rose- and burgundy-flowered Queen Ann chairs; all were imported from Italy. There was a large assortment of crystal knickknacks placed throughout the room.

"M, it's Tara. Get over here and give me some sugar," Toby said, reaching her arms out invitingly as she rose from the mahogany two-leaf dinner table.

Tara hugged her mother's best friend and then kissed her mom, who was busy seasoning chicken in the large kitchen sink. There was a bowl of cabbage crisping in ice water on the counter and six large sweet potatoes waiting to be sliced in the double stainless-steel sink.

"Mom, what time is dinner gon' be ready?" Tara asked.

"You know it don't take me long to get my dinner ready. We gon' be ready to eat by the time my peach cobbler come out the oven," M&M promised her baby girl.

"Tara, go in my bedroom and get them pieces off the door. I need you to take the dye packs off for me before Eddie comes to get them. You know I don't like taking them things off.

"It's getting harder and harder to find stores in town that ain't putting them things on their good pieces," M&M complained. "I remember when you didn't have to work on your pieces after you got them home. Those snatch-and-grab thieves messing shit up for us pros."

"All right, Ma," Tara said, getting up and heading for the bedroom. Tara happily jumped at the chance to assist her mother. She snuck a chicken wing as the familiar smells of home comforted her.

"Baby girl, can you do my two suits too?" Toby asked.

"I got you," Tara yelled as she stopped to look at the latest school pictures of her nieces and nephews that crowded the tables in the dining room.

M&M's room was decorated in the same colors as the living room. The bed was centered in the middle of the room on a raised platform. There were beautiful Lladró figurines on every surface.

Tara learned when she was a small child that she couldn't mess with her mom's antiques. M&M knew good stuff, be it clothes, furniture, jewelry or food. She only dealt in the best and she only stole the best. No matter what, she always kept the best things for herself.

Hustlers would often come to her to learn the value of their day's work. She knew knowledge was king, and she loved crowning her subjects. M&M would let someone know if they were sleeping in any area of the game. She kept it real, and she didn't tolerate perpetrators.

The family was taught to study the game well, because that was the only way to beat the odds, stay free, and survive the streets.

Tara removed the pieces with dye packs from the door and placed them on the bed. To remove the dye packs, she had to burn the plastic until it melted and the inside metal springs and screws were exposed. This released the back from the front without causing the dye to explode.

Tara opened the bedroom window to allow the smoke from the burning of the dye packs to escape. She was a pro at removing the ineffective security devices.

The dye packs did not set off any alarms when a person exited the store, and every good booster knew how to remove them. They served very little purpose in preventing shoplifting.

"Hey! Hey! Baby girl," Slim sang as he entered the room and hugged his daughter. The scent of his Cool Water aftershave tickled her nose.

"What's up, Daddy? You just in time for dinner. Mom's making peach cobbler. I flew over here to get some. I'm going to have to take Julio some; he's never had it," Tara explained as the pair returned to the kitchen.

"I ain't know you were here, Calvin," Tara shouted as she greeted her father's lifelong friend with a long, warm hug.

Tara had a crush on Calvin ever since she was a little girl. He would tell M&M when Tara was young that she was going to be a heartbreaker when she grew up.

Calvin was a pimp through and through. When he spoke, the words came out smooth as silk. He would look at a woman like she was the only one on the planet, his eyes penetrating her soul. Every mannerism was as if he were performing live onstage. His looks were distinguished and regal all the way down to his manicured fingernails.

"Girl, you look good enough to eat. What's been going on with you?" Calvin asked. "I done heard you all in love and shit. How you gon' break an old man's heart like that? I was planning on retiring with you," he teased as they all sat down to dinner.

The table was spread with all of M&M's heavenly creations. There was fried chicken stacked high on a silver serving platter. Delicious, hot candied sweet potatoes loaded with pure vanilla and butter sat to the left of the chicken. Fresh, steaming hot cabbage was stationed to the right. There was a napkin-covered straw basket filled with homemade rolls positioned at the head of the table next to Tara's father.

Homemade rolls were Slim's weakness, and M&M made a point to make them for him often.

"Rabbit, pass that iced tea, partner," Slim said with his mouth full of food and a hot dinner roll in his hand.

"You interruptin' my flow," Rabbit joked, passing the ice-cold drink to his boss. "I heard them north punks ran up in Fast Black's spot and robbed them for everything. They even pistol-whipped his bottom bitch, Goldie, and raped her daughter. What the fuck is wrong with these young gangsters, man?" Rabbit asked, shaking his head in disgust. "Shit getting crazy."

"Man, the game is changing. You got kids with no grooming out there now. They making up shit as they go along. There's long paper to be made with this crack thing, but we sleeping. We need to be prepared for the game to change forever. Hell, hoein' ain't even the same; crackheads out there giving the goods away. We gon' have to come correct and adjust our game or stay home," Slim taught.

"Young boys getting thirsty; they tired of being left behind. They getting theirs by any means necessary. You can't hardly blame them, either; most of them out their raising themselves," Tara offered.

"Everybody want dessert? I got hot peach cobbler with vanilla ice cream," M&M announced as she got up from the table and removed a gallon of Häagen Dazs ice cream from the side-by-side refrigerator.

"It's simple. Either we start giving them some respect on the streets, or we all better be prepared to take some losses. We need to start taking them under our wings or the game is going to suffer forever." Calvin sighed with a faraway look in his eyes.

The old Gs sat at the table and thought of better days. Each man viewed their hustle as a dying art. It was getting harder and harder to find thoroughbreds like them. Each had survived and flourished off the streets; it was hard to watch how fast things were changing. There were lives being taken over by a little bit of money. Families were being torn apart over the rock. Things were out of control, and they all knew it would get worse before it got better. Babies were raising babies and boys were teaching boys how to be men. Niggas were just jumping in the game and the penitentiaries were filling up fast. Something had to change or the old Gs would be right . . . the game would never be the same.

Ten

Ain't No Love in the Heart of the City

Tara backed her BMW out of the gravel-paved driveway of her mother's home. She really wanted to stay and continue the conversation with her family, but she had promised Karen a trip to the mall. It was hard for her to concentrate on planning a wedding when there was so much shit going on in the game.

Tara turned up the volume and allowed the sounds of her favorite Jodeci CD to fill the car. She sang along with the words of "Get On Up" as she headed to Karen's house.

Spring was arriving early in the city, and the hood was jumping. Tara cruised slowly down Livingston Avenue to see who was posted up. Hoochies were in full effect with their $10-or-less outfits on. The dope boys hugged the corners and took orders. The smell of BBQ grills working overtime filled the air.

Tara pulled into the Brothers beer and wine drive-through and got in line with the other customers waiting to be served. Slowly inching to the entrance, she noticed a tall, thin man quickly approaching her passenger side. A wave of fear swept across her body as she reached for the locks.

"Hey, sis, you want to buy some CDs?" the crackhead asked, smoothing out his wrinkled, too-small Cleveland Browns jersey. He nervously held a stack of used disks inside of the window; none of them were in cases.

"I'm straight, my brother. Maybe next time," Tara said as she rolled up the window.

"Thanks anyway, and have a nice day," the crackhead yelled over his shoulder in a polite businessman's voice as he moved swiftly to the next car.

The shelves of the drive-through were practically empty. The primary business was cigarettes, alcohol, and drug transactions. Brothers was owned by one of Julio's boys, Dre, who was also one of Tara's old customers.

A pimple-faced young buck approached Tara's car on the passenger side and said, "What's up," as he pulled his cell phone from his pocket and checked his numbers.

"Let me get ten large bags of Grippo's BBQ chips and hurry up, partner," Tara ordered, casing her car toward the checkout booth. She always stocked up on her favorite chips when she was in the hood. The young boy continued at the same pace, ignoring the line of cars behind Tara.

As Tara pulled her car to the small office, she could see Dre crowded inside with two easy-on-the-eye gangstas who were busy rolling blunts.

"What's poppin', Dre?" she shouted over the hard-core rap music pouring from the booth.

"Hey, what's shakin', Tara, with yo' sexy ass? Where you been hidin'? You know I need to holla at you. You got a nigga rockin' late gear and shit. I'm tryin' to be fresh this summer," Dre complained jokingly.

"I been on some wifey shit. I'll send my girl Karen by to holla at you. She knows what you like," Tara assured him.

"Do that, do that, and tell ya man I need to holla at him. He can't be forgetting about us little fish. We need to eat too." He looked her up and down with wanting eyes. "And let me know if he ain't takin' care of business right. Can't nobody give it to you like a brother can," Dre said, sucking his teeth with a look of disgust on his face. It was almost as if he was wondering why a dime piece like Tara from the hood was fucking with a Spanish motherfucka. And it only added salt to the wound that the Spanish cats were taking over in his hood.

"I hear you, Dre," Tara yelled over her shoulder as she exited the drive-through and pulled onto Livingston Avenue, heading toward Oakwood. *Damn, all that for some chips,* Tara thought, placing the bag on the passenger seat.

The block was on blast. People were everywhere. There was a line of cars inching their way down the street. Teens crossed back and forth between the cars and music blared from every direction.

The driver in front of Tara stopped his car abruptly and got out. He ran to the corner, purchased a dime bag of 'dro from a young thug on a ten-speed, and got back in his car. The young thug yelled, "I got two-for-ones all day," to the cars behind Tara as the traffic finally began to move again.

Tara reached Karen's house and parked out front. She bounced from the car and headed for the door, avoiding a four-year-old racing down the sidewalk on a tattered Big Wheel that had seen better days.

Tara approached the door and noticed that it was open. This was strange because Karen never left her door open.

Tara entered the living room; it was in disarray. The coffee table was turned over and the couch lay on its side. She could hear what sounded like people shouting in the back room. Tara rushed to the kitchen to find the doorway blocked by a set of twin gorillas dressed in matching jogging suits.

Karen's brother, Jay, was being held in the corner by a Mike Tyson wannabe. "Come on, Dagga Man, man. Come on, you ain't gotta do this," Jay nervously pleaded with his young friend as sweat ran down his face and landed on his soaked shirt.

"Yo, man, ya sister think I'm a punk," Dagga Man said, standing over Karen, who was balled up on the floor and sobbing. "She done gone and fucked up my shit and now she tryin' to play me like I'm dumb. And to put the icing on the cake, the bitch fuckin' around on a nigga," Dagga Man explained, kicking Karen in the stomach as she cried out in pain.

"Dagga Man, you ain't got to handle this shit like this," Tara shouted as she tried to enter the kitchen, but was pushed back by one of the gorillas blocking the doorway. "This ain't yo' fight, Tara, so stay out of this," Dagga Man warned.

Tara used the opportunity to give Karen the signal. Jay broke free from his confinement and continued reasoning with Reggie as Tara slowly backed away from the kitchen and raced to her car. She quickly pulled the car to the back of the house and anxiously parked, keeping her eyes glued to the back door.

Suddenly, Karen bolted from the back door and raced to the car. "Pull off, Tara! Pull off!" she ordered.

Tara put the car in reverse and began backing from the backyard. When she turned to look at the front door, Dagga Man was rushing to the car with his gun drawn and staring Tara dead in the eyes.

Tara quickly closed her eyes and yelled "Jesus!" as a million thoughts raced through her head. She wished she had stayed at her mother's house and enjoyed her family. Or she wished she was just chilling with Julio laying in bed. She ached to be at home with her boo right about now. What the fuck was happening? Time stood still.

Tara opened her eyes to see Dagga Man laughing wildly. She put the car in drive, backed from the yard and sped up the alley. The sick bastard took pleasure in seeing the fear in their eyes.

"Friend, I am so sorry. I been playin' niggas all my life and I ain't never think a motherfucka would trip like that over some product," Karen apologized. "Shit, takin' losses is a cost of doing business. I gave the young boy some pussy a few times and now he think he owns this. Don't no motherfucka own this pussy," Karen shouted as if speaking to Dagga Man.

"It's all good, friend. You all right?" Tara asked, looking at the knot forming on Karen's forehead.

"You can't keep a good bitch down," Karen teased, closing her eyes and leaning back in the seat to ease the pain in her stomach.

Tara sped up Livingston Avenue and fled from the grips of the hood. Shit was crazy. What the fuck was she thinking, getting in the middle of that shit? She wasn't using her head when she ran up in there like Captain Save-a-Ho. But Karen was her girl; loyalty to a friend was what drove her to make such a foolish choice. Tara had lived her whole life watching her back and avoiding the traps of the system. She had become a master at that. Now she had to guard against a new enemy on her own turf.

Tara longed for a simpler time. She turned on the radio and searched the stations. She stopped on a local gospel station and allowed the familiar music to flood her mind.

The mood felt like a Sunday morning service at the Prince of Peace Holiness Church. She hummed quietly to the soothing music, finding comfort in it.

Tara watched the cars pass at the intersection of Livingston and College Avenue. Her mind drifted to another time and place as she longed for the safety of her family:

"Mama Grace, tell Rick to move over; he's smashing me," Tara complained to her grandmother.

"We all smashed," Mama Grace shot back and moved closer to the door of the late-model Cadillac.

Grace and six of her grandchildren were crammed in the backseat of Deacon Clark's prized status-symbol Cadillac. Deacon Clark, who was a 400-pound country bumpkin who loved to eat, would haul the world in the back of his Caddy if he thought there was a plate of food in it for him.

Mama Grace was known for her Sunday dinner, and he had no problem picking her up for church like clockwork for every service. He would pull up in front of Grace's house each Sunday at 11:00 a.m. sharp. He never blew the horn or got out because he knew Grace would always be ready to roll when he pulled up.

Grace didn't drive, and she appreciated the rides she was able to get. She reached inside of her black snakeskin purse, pulled out a roll of LifeSavers candy, and lovingly handed each of her grandchildren a piece.

"Oh, let's see how long you can make yours last. You have to suck it and you can't bite it," Rick explained to his cousins.

"Benny already bit his," Tara blabbed, scooting back on her brother's lap.

"Don't y'all start that playing and mess up your clothes," Grace warned.

Deacon Clark pulled his Caddy onto the church's unpaved parking lot. The children jumped from the confines of the car and began to straighten their clothes before he could put the car in park.

They all knew Mama Grace didn't play about how they represented her at Sunday morning service. Church was Grace's life, and she made sure that her grandchildren respected the House of the Lord.

The children each had three Sunday best outfits that they cherished. Grace had an eye for quality things and only bought the best for the children. Although the clothes were handed down, they rarely wore out. This was during the time M&M was locked up; otherwise, best believe the children would have had far more than just three Sunday best outfits.

The sound of loud organ music and drums filled the sanctuary as they entered. The choir was up on their feet singing, and two missionaries were shouting around the building, waving tambourines. The walls seemed to be sweating and vibrating as church members randomly jumped from their seats and began shouting also.

Elder Richard Hairston leaped from his King Solomon chair, grabbed the microphone and screamed, "If God's been good to you, stand up on your feet and say 'Thank You.' " He then dropped the microphone and ran around the pulpit. The entire choir broke out in a shout.

This was a typical Sunday morning service at the Prince of Peace Holiness Church. All who attended left knowing that God was good and He answered prayers if they called on Him.

"Whew, service sho' was good," Grace sang once the service was over, returning to the confines of the cramped Cadillac.

To the dismay of everyone, Deacon Clark had offered a ride home to Sister Tatum, and she sat smashed between his sweaty, fat body and Sister Bosley, who hadn't missed a meal in a lifetime herself.

"Grace, ya grandkids getting so big. What grade you in now, baby?" Sister Tatum questioned Tara. "I remember when you were in diapers, with your cute little self."

*"I'm in the fourth grade and my teacher's name is Mrs. Fields.
I go to Eleventh Avenue School. You like my dress?" Tara responded, peeping over the seat at the funny-looking lady in the
silly big hat.*

*"And what grade are you in, little boy?" she asked Benny while
handing each of the kids a peppermint.*

*"I'm in the fourth grade and I'm going to be a pimp when I
grow up," Benny proudly announced to the church saints as they
headed home from service.*

Tara was jolted out of her daydream by the sound of the
horn of the car behind her. She sped through the light.
She had watched her grandmother pray for her children
and her children's children many times. Tara knew that
Mama Grace's prayers had protected her that day.

It had been a beautiful day in the hood and the block
was winding down. Young and old folks sat on their
porches and reflected on another day in the hood. Children chased each other through their yards. The sound of
police sirens could be heard in the background.

Julio cruised down Berkley Avenue. He decided to stop
by Happy's house before heading home to Tara. Happy
ran one of Julio's biggest money-making spots on the east
side. He was an old-school hustler who Julio could count
on to keep his paper straight.

Julio's day had been full of drama, so he was glad to
swing by the drama-free spot on the way home. Every spot
he stopped by to collect, he was hemmed up with one
problem or another. His crew was acting like they forgot
how shit go. He had to check motherfuckas left and right
all day.

Even when he tried to stop by and see his baby girl, that
shit was crazy too. Candy was in rare form. Somehow she'd

found out about him and Tara, and the bitch was trippin'. The shit pissed him off so bad that he had slapped her.

He couldn't understand why she was so upset. He never gave her any reason to think that they ever had a future to- gether, but the bitch was still trippin'. Shit was crazy, and he just wanted to raise up out the drama.

He confidently parked his car and hopped out. A group of jailbait girls passed the Latin lover and stared him down.

"What's up, *papi?*" one of the young girls said, giving him a seductive smile and a wink.

"Little *mamis*, y'all out ya league. Stay in ya lane," he schooled the girls as he watched them continue down the sidewalk, giggling.

Julio sighed to himself and leaped up the stairs two at a time to Happy's old Victorian-style house. He knocked at the door and patiently waited. Happy's son, Man-Man, snatched the door open.

"Come in, Julio, man," the young buck said and returned to his spot on the worn-out couch in the living room. Man-Man stared into the screen of the TV as the sound of bombs dropping could be heard coming from his video game.

"Where your pops?" Julio questioned, closing the front door behind him.

"They all downstairs," Man-Man said, looking up and pointing toward the basement door.

Julio went to the door, opened it, and paused. The smell of ass, dick, and pussy smacked him in the face. His eyes slowly adjusted to the dim, smoky light of the base- ment as he made his way down the creaky wooden stairs.

A young G was lying on the dingy blue sectional couch getting his dick sucked by a blond-haired white girl, who, at the same time, was being fucked from behind by a Rick James–looking motherfucka. Happy sat in a recliner in the corner, rubbing his dick and enjoying the live porn show.

"What the fuck is going on, *primo?*" Julio shouted over the hard-core rap music that was blaring out of the stereo system.

Happy was a loyal employee. He was given the name Happy in elementary school. His teeth were so big that they barely fit in his mouth; he always appeared to be smiling, so he was nicknamed Happy by his friends.

Black, who was gripping the blond girl's hips, paused and looked at Julio with disgust. "Motherfucka, you fuckin' up my groove; now kick bricks," he spat in Julio's direction.

"Slow ya roll, young buck," Happy said. "You know who you talkin' to, Black? This here is our boss, Julio." Happy smiled nervously at Julio, hoping not to get caught up in no shit. He knew he should have just stayed upstairs.

Julio and Black stared each other down for what seemed like forever. Julio then remembered that he wasn't strapped. He'd left his heater in the car. *Damn, I'm slipping.* With or without it, though, he damn sure wasn't backing out of the staring match.

"My bad, G," Black apologized and continued laying the pipe to the young freak.

"Let's take this upstairs where we can talk privately," Happy said, standing.

"Let's do that, *primo,*" Julio ordered, backing out of the room as he studied Black's face. Happy led his boss back up the stairs.

As they left the basement, Black rammed his dick deep

into the ass of the white girl and took pleasure in her screams of pain. His thoughts were in other places.

"Fuck that rice-eating motherfucka," he mumbled under his breath once Julio and Happy were no longer in sight. *We sleepin'; lettin' them wetbacks come over here and get rich on our block. He ain't my boss. Shit, I'll show these chumps what a real boss look like,* Black thought, pulling the white girl's hair and slapping her on her ass.

As soon as Julio and Happy reached the first floor, Julio began shouting at Happy. "What the fuck you call yo'self doin', *primo?* You fuckin' got my spot wide open with nobody on the door while you getting ya funky on. You know you don't mix business with pleasure. And where the hell is Roberto? I told him to post his ass up at the door until Rick gets back from handling business with Carlito."

"He brought that young buck, Black, by here and dropped him off with that other nigga down there. He told me they was cool and he'd stop through later. He left here with that freak, Angel. I swear I think they fuckin'. She's the one that left that strawberry here. That girl been suckin' dicks and smoking all day. I wish they would come back and get her ass," Happy said, rubbing his dick as he reached for the shoebox full of Julio's paper. It had been a busy day and he was proud to show off the day's take.

"Get this house under control and find out everything there is to know about that young boy Black," Julio commanded. "I want a full report first thing tomorrow. When Roberto gets here, you tell him he needs to get at me."

Happy nodded as Julio headed out the front door.

Julio cautiously returned to his car and hopped in. He started the engine and headed home. Black's face danced in his head. There was a primal look behind his cold stare. He knew the kid had seen way too much at an early age and didn't give a fuck. Those same eyes were showing up more and more on the set.

It used to be that the young bucks kept a look of admiration and respect for the old Gs. Now he was beginning to see more and more looks of "fuck 'em." It was this mentality that threatened Julio's work.

Eleven

Someone to Watch Over Me

Julio turned the key in the lock to his home. An instant feeling of peace flooded his soul. If he had his way, he would never leave the lap of luxury that his home provided. The familiar floral smell from the fresh-cut flowers filled his nostrils.

Tara rushed to the front door to greet her man. They collapsed in each other's arms and simply held onto each other as if each one was returning home from some unknown war. The bond they shared was so close that they both knew that the other had experienced some disturbing drama that day. And each put the day out of their mind at the sight of the other.

"Baby, come with me," Julio pleaded, leading Tara by the hand to their bedroom. Tara obediently followed her man. She would follow him to the ends of the earth if he asked her to. Once in the room, Julio slowly peeled away Tara's clothes until she stood naked before him.

He gently planted wet kisses on her forehead and down

the side of her face. He swiftly spun her around and began passionately kissing her entire back.

"Let me hold you. I want to feel you in my arms," he whispered, leading Tara to their king-sized bed.

The two lovers lay in each other's arms and blocked out the world. Julio laid his head on Tara's chest and ran his hand down her thighs and across her womanhood. He couldn't decide which one he wanted more; just to hold her or to feel himself safe inside of her familiar walls.

Tara made the decision for him. She eased from under him and passionately kissed him, sucking on his tongue like it was her lifeline. She then moved her skilled lips to his chest, sucking on each nipple equally. Then she quickly moved her lips to what she truly craved: his dick.

She massaged the weapon with both hands and gently licked the head before she practically swallowed it whole. Julio moaned with pleasure and grabbed her head as it moved up and down on his manhood.

When Tara felt the throbbing of his dick inside her mouth, she knew he was reaching his orgasm. She quickly climbed on top of him and placed his rock-hard tool deep inside her wet pussy.

Tara slowed the pace to steady up-and-down pumps. With each upward stroke, she arched her back, tightened her pussy muscles, and called her man's name. "Julio, I love you. Oh, Julio, I love you. Julio, Julio, Julio!" she cried as the eruption of his warm cum caused her body to shake with pleasure.

She laid her head on his chest and drifted into a safe and secure sleep with his dick still inside of her. Julio nestled his head against hers and fell asleep as well.

Later on, Julio woke to the sound of his phone vibrating in the pocket of his pants that lay in a heap at the foot of the bed. He hesitantly rose from the bed and kissed Tara tenderly on the forehead. She looked so peaceful lying there; it pained him to leave her side.

He tiptoed to the spacious bathroom and closed the wooden door behind him. "Yo, what's up, *primo?*" Julio whispered into the phone as he slid the glass door to the shower open and turned on the water.

"My bad, boss. I made a run and it took longer than I thought it would. You know how it is out here," Roberto explained anxiously.

"What I know is you better get yo' ass over here. We need to talk, and don't keep me waiting," Julio yelled into the phone and then hung up. *Damn*, he thought, hoping his shouting didn't wake Tara.

He stared into the wide-width mirror that hung over the double sinks. He liked the man he saw staring back at him: a man in love. He'd found happiness and he wasn't even looking for it. Julio didn't know this part of life existed. All this time he thought happiness was stacking paper and having respect on the street. Now he knew that happiness was the love of a good woman. Tara's love was more valuable than any treasure the streets held.

He would protect what they had with his life. There were a lot of things he needed answers to, and he planned to get those answers that night. He stepped into the steamy shower and began washing the dirt of the day from his body. The shower refreshed him as he exited the glass stall.

Julio pulled on his Nike drawstring wind pants and slipped the matching wife beater over his firm chest. He ran a brush across his silky, jet-black hair and then applied Paul Sebastian aftershave to his face. Peeking into the bedroom, he assured himself Tara was still fast asleep. He quietly left the bathroom and headed downstairs.

Karen had stayed at their place that night. She was asleep in the guest room when Julio arrived home earlier. Now she sat at the island in the center of her girl's kitchen. She felt relaxed in one of Tara's bathrobes as she sipped at the rum and Coke she had poured for herself.

Her head ached and she wanted to smoke. *Where the fuck is Roberto?* She had been calling and paging him all day. Every time she thought she had him just where she wanted him, he'd flip the script on her.

She was constantly starting over with him. Roberto was work, and Karen stayed on the job. She did whatever he wanted. Last week he brought Carlito's woman, Angel, to her house and the three of them fucked all night long. Karen was so high that she didn't even know how they all had ended up in bed. *Damn,* she thought, *I need to blaze.*

"What's up, Karen?" Julio sang as he entered the kitchen. He opened the refrigerator, removed a gallon of orange juice and turned up the jug, drinking the ice-cold liquid down in big gulps.

He positioned himself on the chair across from Karen and then looked at her face. On Karen's forehead sat a large black-and-blue, egg-shaped knot. Her cheek had a purple-and-black rug burn on it. She smiled at Julio and lowered her head.

"What the fuck happened to you?" he questioned, standing up and moving closer to her.

"I made the mistake of fuckin' around with one of them young dope boys over on the east side and now he done got all possessive of a bitch," Karen explained with a nervous grin, while she lit a Newport cigarette and blew the smoke over her shoulder.

"Was Tara with you when this happened?" he asked.

"No. She just picked me up. She wasn't in no danger. That nigga don't really want no beef. He just be tryin' to flex in front of his boys. It's all cool; this shit ain't nothin'. My stepdad used to hit me harder than this," Karen offered, taking another sip of her drink.

"Let me make something real clear to you, Karen. I respect the fact that you are Tara's girl and all. I know she'd walk through hell with gasoline drawers on for you. I understand that shit and I respect it. What I ain't gon' ever understand, or accept, is if something happens to her and you got something to do with it. You feel me?" Julio warned, staring Karen in the face and then returning to his seat. Karen tried to play it cool, but she was visibly shaken by the ice-cold look Julio gave her as he sat across the table from her.

After what seemed like an eternity, he spoke again. "I want the name of this east side dope boy and I want to know where he lives. I need to pay him a house call.

"Roberto's on the way. I'm gonna have him take you to your place to get your things and you gonna chill at Tara's old spot. I know you fuckin' with that shit, Karen. You need to let that shit go. You too good of a woman to let that monster take you out. You need to get your head right," Julio scolded. The sound of the doorbell ringing interrupted him.

Karen was so glad for the interruption. She quickly headed upstairs to the guest bedroom to try to fix her face. She wanted to look her best before she saw Roberto. She knew he would have some rocks with him, and she planned to use her charm to get her smoke on. If she played her cards right, she would put it on him real good and he would stay with her all night. She would have to borrow something to wear from her girl. *Damn, Julio love some Tara,* she thought.

Karen knocked lightly on the door of the master bedroom; she hoped her friend was awake.

"Come in," Tara whispered from behind the door.

Karen slowly pushed the large door open and peeked her head in. "Girl, you up yet?" she questioned, entering the room.

"Yeah, I'm up. I didn't plan to sleep this long, but my baby rocked a sister to sleep real proper," Tara teased, getting up from the bed and slipping into her robe. "Was my boo out there?" Tara asked, walking into the bathroom and turning on the shower. Karen followed behind her closely.

"Yeah, and Roberto just came in too. You got to give me something to put on. I look like shit," Karen complained to her friend.

"Come over here and let me look at your face." Tara examined where Karen had tried to touch up her face with what looked like powder. It only ended up making her look ashy. "I just got some new M•A•C concealer. It'll get you right together," Tara promised, placing her makeup bag on the marble counter.

"I hope so, girl. I think I'm losing ground with him. I need something sexy to wear too," Karen ordered anxiously, standing in the doorway of the bathroom.

"Just work your magic and you'll land him."

A few minutes later, the girls joined the men in the cozy living room and sat silently on the silk sofa. The atmosphere was thick with tension when they entered the room.

"Hey, Roberto, how you doing?" Tara questioned, breaking the silence.

"It's all good, little *mami*," Roberto said in that sexy Latin accent of his. He then got up, roughly reached for Karen, and kissed her wildly.

"Aw yeah, baby, I been missin' this all day," Karen purred, rubbing up against his dick. Roberto's dick sprung to life and he didn't even notice the faint bruises on Karen's face that peeked through the heavy makeup.

"You good, baby? How you sleep? Come here," Julio questioned Tara all at once, wrapping his arms around her. He kissed her tenderly and smoothed out her hair. He looked her up and down again and again until he was sure she was physically okay and then he let her go. "We need to talk," he whispered into her ear as he released her from the safety of his arms.

"Come on, Karen, let's bounce. I need some private time with you, and I know the lovebirds want to be alone," Roberto said, nervously getting up to leave.

"I'll call you tomorrow, Tara," Karen yelled over her shoulder as the couple moved with Julio to the door.

"Make sure the both of you remember our conversation," Julio warned the departing couple and then closed the door behind them. "Tara, let me holla at you."

He walked over to the crystal-stem lamp on a table near the sofa and turned on the light. The soft light flooded the room and lit up Tara's face. She looked so beautiful and innocent with her legs folded under her as she sat on the couch. All he wanted was to protect her from the cold world. He didn't have a problem laying a nigga down over her. He didn't give a damn who they were.

"I know you know what I'm gonna say before I even say it," Julio told her. "You know I ain't on that shit you did with Karen. How you just gon' put us in jeopardy like that? Look at me and listen," he said, sitting up straight on the sofa and staring into her eyes.

"The game is changing by the minute. Gangstas are dying out here for nothing. These young Gs ain't playin' by the rules we're used to. We at war, baby, and we got to act accordingly. The streets got me questioning niggas I used to think I could trust with my life. Crack done fucked the game up forever. You got thirsty motherfuckas out there thinking they gangstas. Loyalty is getting harder and harder to come by. Everything you thought you knew about the streets don't even apply no more," Julio schooled Tara.

The look on his face was so serious that it scared her. She grabbed him and held him close. Hot tears filled her eyes and spilled down her face. The thought of never seeing Julio again swept across her soul.

Tara broke their embrace, looked into her man's eyes, and said, "Baby, you have taught me the meaning of true love. I am complete when I'm with you. All I want is to spend the rest of my life making you happy. The thought of never being in this moment with you again scares the hell out of me. I feel you when you say shit is changing out there. I will never put us in danger like that again," she promised.

Julio kissed her gently and wiped the tears from her eyes. For the next hour, they simply held each other, clearing their minds of all the past drama—drama that had only really just begun.

Twelve

Here is Where I Want to Be

The happy couple lay on pillows on the floor in their relaxing bedroom. Tara and Julio had just finished making love for the third time that night. The sheets and comforter hung half on and half off the mattress. Julio retrieved the glass tray full of powder from under the foot of the bed and placed the metal straw up his nose. He inhaled deeply and repeated the ritual on the other nostril. He then passed the tray to Tara.

"I ain't fuckin' with you, baby. I want to go to sleep," Tara said, getting up from the floor. Julio pulled her back to the floor and kissed her.

"Just lay here with me for a few more minutes, please," he begged in his sexy voice.

"For you, baby, I'd lay here forever," Tara said, smiling. She removed the straw from the tray, snorted the magical drug up her nose, and waited for the rush. The room instantly got brighter and Tara believed she could fly.

The two of them shut out the outside world. They had been holed up in their home for days. Neither one wanted to let the streets break through their happiness. They couldn't care less if they ever went out again. Tara lay back in her boo's arms and enjoyed the warmth from his body. He molded himself to her and relaxed.

A few hours later, after the couple had moved from the floor to the bed and drifted off to sleep in each other's arms, Julio rolled over and reached for Tara. He jumped up and looked around the room nervously when he didn't feel her next to him.

He began to leap from the bed as Tara burst through the bedroom door carrying a tray full of breakfast treats.

"Where you running to, boo?" Tara questioned, placing the tray on the bed and sitting beside him.

"What you got for your *papi?*" Julio asked as he relaxed his shoulders on the soft cushions on the bed.

They devoured the enticing feast together and then lay back and relaxed.

"I just finished talking to my mom and she's really buggin' me about you putting my nephew on, baby. I know you ain't trying to get involved with no new shit. He a young G, but he family. Can't you just jump-start him with something small and see what he do with it? If he fucks it up, then it's on him," Tara asked.

"Tara, I ain't got time for no shit. I'll send Carlito to get him straight. If he put in some decent work, I'll holla at him," Julio responded.

"Thanks, baby. My mom's gon' make sure he keep it real," Tara added.

Julio got up from the bed and opened the door to their walk-in closet. He studied his side of the closet for his hookup of the day. Appearance was very important to him, and that was one of the things he loved about Tara. The girl looked good in anything. She had a way of bringing style to everything she touched.

He settled on a pair of black slacks with a black linen shirt, then he moved to his belt drawer and selected a dark brown leather belt. He skillfully chose a pair of Italian leather loafers to complete the look.

"Baby, get ready. I want you to roll with me to a few spots and then we can go by your mom's house," Julio announced to Tara as he exited the closet.

"Okay, but I'm getting in the shower before you. You always use up all the hot water," Tara said, racing to the bathroom door. Julio leapt over the bed and beat her to the entrance. They playfully wrestled at the door until Julio tickled her away.

"Come on and get in with me and we can use up the hot water together. If you're lucky, I'll let you play with my friend," Julio said, swinging his dick in the air. Tara chased him into the bathroom and got undressed.

Julio's phone rang loudly, disrupting the lovers' playful moment. Instantly, Julio put on his business face and answered the phone. "Yo, holla at ya boy," he spat into the phone.

"Yo, Julio, ya baby need some new shoes. You be trippin' and shit all laid up with that bitch and you just done forgot about us over here. I never thought you'd let some pussy come between you and your flesh and blood. What the fuck you thinkin', huh?" Candy yelled into the phone.

"Don't call me with that bullshit, Candy," Julio shot back. "You know I ain't the one. If my baby girl needs anything, you know she got it. You better check the tone of your voice too. You ain't talkin' to them soft-ass niggas you be fuckin' with. I know you don't want me to come over there and split your wig," he threatened.

"All right, all right, baby. You know I get emotional about our daughter, Julio. When you comin' through? I need some groceries too," Candy added.

"I'll shoot through there later today. Now get off my jock," he said and hung up the phone.

Tara was already in the shower, so he joined her there. He slid in behind her and removed her pink sponge from its holder, carefully massaging shower gel onto her skin. She took his sponge and returned the favor. His dick stood at attention at the touch of her hand on his skin. They cleaned each other and prepared to exit the shower. They would pick things up where they left off once they returned home.

Black stretched across Candy's small bed and watched her fat ass shake like jelly as she paced around the room naked. Candy's apartment was small, but it was clean. There were fuzzy stuffed animals everywhere; a brother felt like he was at the zoo. Black sat up on the bed and pretended to be watching the porn flick on the TV. The star of the film reminded him of a crackhead he gangbanged with three of his boys last week in a geeker's spot. He played with his dick and listened to Candy.

He lucked out when he met the ghetto freak at the club three weeks ago. The bitch was a true gold digger. He gave her a few big faces for the mall and she was hooked. She ran her mouth like a federal informant about everything and everybody. She knew the streets well; she bragged that she had connections, promising Black that she could hook him up with some real gangstas, and she delivered. Before he knew it, he wasn't nickel-and-dimin' it anymore. He was stacking some serious paper.

He couldn't believe what he was hearing. She was screaming into the phone at that soft-ass nigga, Julio. *I don't believe this shit,* Black thought. His new freak had a baby with the motherfucker that he hated most. He couldn't stand that greasy bastard. He hated the way he paraded through the hood like he owned it. Black spent his whole life trying to get a piece of the pie and some respect on the streets. Here this wetback motherfucka comes and just takes over. Fuck that shit. As far as Black was concerned, Julio wasn't gon' take shit in his hood. His little freak Candy had a baby by the chump. That was calculated to know. He might need to use that information to his advantage later, when the time was right.

He watched Candy hang up the phone and then sprang into action.

"Get over here and take care of this dick, baby. You know I want some more of that good pussy," Black said, rubbing his chest with one hand and massaging his dick with the other.

Candy got on the bed and slowly crawled toward him. "You know I loves that Black dick, don't you, baby?" Candy replied and allowed his dick to disappear into her mouth.

Black was a hunter on the streets. He studied his prey to perfection and had learned his skill the hard way. His mother was a seasoned crackhead and his father a bank robber who had been locked up in Lucasville State Penitentiary ever since Black was in kindergarten. He raised himself, barely remembering his father. But he did remember that when his dad was there, life was easier.

He hadn't seen his mother since he was sixteen, when he left home to join the Crips. He'd been putting in work ever since. A prostitute on Main Street named him Heartless Black because of his ashy black skin and evil stare. He lived up to the name daily. He'd rob the Pope if he had something that he wanted. The bright-eyed, happy baby boy, De'andre Martin, was long gone. He was Heartless Black.

Things were looking up for an orphan from the wrong

side of the tracks. Black had taken everything that he owned. Nobody had given him anything.

He had to ride daily for his, and he was tired of the grind. He had plans of taking the fuck over, and for some reason, he was sure that the light-skinned freak between his legs would play a very valuable part in his plan.

Thirteen
There's No Place Like Home

Tara entered the kitchen to find Carlito sitting at the kitchen island enjoying a cold beer. Julio was sitting at their glass breakfast table and talking on his cell phone. She poured herself a glass of pink grapefruit juice and sat down at the table with Julio.

"Let's go," she mouthed and then got up and went to the half bathroom near the kitchen to check her hair. She loved to wear dresses, so she was glad the weather was getting nice and she could rock her summer wardrobe. She wore a body-hugging burnt orange sundress. The fabric was scarf-like and flowed over her skin effortlessly. She wore her hair straight, and it hung freely and framed her face. She looked good, so she returned to the kitchen.

Julio and Carlito were standing by the door when Tara walked back into the kitchen. They both jokingly looked at their watches and said, "Let's go."

"Fuck the both of y'all," Tara teased back, leading the way out the front door. Tara knew without asking that Carlito was riding strapped and ready to put in work if the call came.

Julio parked his car in the back of Alan's club. The lot was full with deliverymen and construction workers. Alan was having a patio added to the back of the club, and during the day, the sound of saws and power tools could be heard for blocks. They maneuvered through the cars and trucks and entered the club through the back door.

A cute, dark-skinned waitress was behind the main bar stocking the beer coolers. "Yo, where Al at?" Julio questioned the waitress.

"He's back in the VIP section auditioning some strippers for his new club," the waitress replied and returned to her work.

Alan was sitting in an oversized booth watching a middle-aged, big-tit stripper in a G-string bend over and make her ass clap. It was obvious from the look on Alan's face the audition was becoming more about pleasure than business for him.

"What's poppin', Al, man? I see you gettin' your freak on. You know damn well you ain't gon' open no strip club. You'll be your best customer," Julio teased as they all slid into the booth with him and sat down.

"I ain't know you was with them, Tara, baby. Give an old man some sugar," Alan greeted Tara fondly.

Julio pulled a folded ten-dollar bill from his shirt pocket and took a one and one. He passed the dollar to Alan, who lit up like a Christmas tree when he snorted the pure powder. He then pulled a hundred-dollar bill from his pocket and tossed it at the stripper. The girl quickly picked it up and hurried to the back room to change.

"Julio, I keep telling you there's money to be made if you line up with those Detroit boys. Either we get in bed with them, or we keep taking losses at all our spots," Alan warned, handing the bill over to Carlito.

"Alan, I ain't tryin' to meet them. You handle the sells, and Carlito will make sure your supply keeps flowin'. You need anything, you see him," Julio instructed.

"It's all good. Now let's make this paper," Alan toasted, raising his shot glass.

The businessmen gave each other dap and said their good-byes. Julio felt refreshed to conduct business with a real gangsta as he watched Tara kiss Alan good-bye.

"Let's get it pushin'. If you want to spend some time at yo' mom's house, we need to get moving," Julio warned Tara as they left the club and headed for the parking lots. Although Tara promised they were just going to drop off some product and look at a few pieces, Julio knew any visit to Tara's people's house was not going to be quick.

His plan was to slowly start turning things over to Carlito and Santiago. He felt good about his plan now that Santiago was returning from Puerto Plata. His old friend had been gone for too long, and he was anxious for him to return. But in order for everything to go as planned, he would have to bring him up to speed on how things were changing.

Julio parked his car two houses down from M&M's spot. The joint was jumping. Cadillacs were everywhere. He wasn't in the mood for socializing, but knew it was important to Tara that he really get to know her family. Her father dropped by their house a lot, and Julio felt they had gotten to know each other well; the two men trusted and respected each other.

He'd been to her mom's on several occasions, but never stayed for long. He could tell by the way M&M rolled out the red carpet for him when he came around that she liked him for her daughter. It was only right that he get to know his soon-to-be wife's family

"I'll stay for a while, but I'm not trying to be here all day, Tara," Julio warned. He knew if Tara had her way, she would stay with her family all day.

"Don't even act like that. I don't be tryin' to be up in all your spots all day, either, but I do," Tara shot back and rolled her eyes as the three of them got out of the car.

"All I want to know is can a brother get a plate," Carlito said, rubbing his stomach.

"And you know this. Half the people here right now are here to get they belly right," Tara explained as they reached the front porch.

Tara knocked on the door and prepared for the wait. To her surprise, Rabbit opened the door immediately. "What it look like?" Rabbit greeted.

"Hey, Rabbit, this is Julio and his partner, Carlito," Tara announced while Rabbit gave her a bear hug and a wet kiss on her cheek.

Both Rabbit and Julio sized the other up and then gave a nod of approval to Tara. Rabbit had heard a lot about the new man in Tara's life, and he was glad for the chance to finally size him up. The old-school player looked at Tara like one of his own children. He knew without even asking that she was happy. It showed all over her face.

Word had it that Tara's young G came correct. Rabbit knew that he had been schooled by some real contenders because Slim had already signed off on him, but Rabbit wanted to see for himself if he was worthy of their precious Tara. He liked what he saw so far. Tara was their baby girl, and he would take a motherfucker out about her.

The house was alive with people and business deals. Her

mother was known for having last-minute get-togethers, and this one caught Tara off guard. When she spoke to her mom earlier, there were only a few people at the house.

She promised to bring her some product and look at some pieces. Now they were in the middle of a social event. She hoped there wasn't any shit in the game while they were at the house. *God*, Tara thought, *please don't let the young boys come through.*

Two pimps Tara recognized from New York were sitting on M&M's precious couch with two strawberries between them. One was wearing what appeared to be a pink-lace jumpsuit with a matching bra and panty set underneath. The other one looked like she'd just gotten off of the bus from Mississippi. Both sat silently as the two pimps discussed their business.

"Hey! Hey! Tara, what's going on?" one of the pimps said as they passed.

"What's up, y'all?" Tara responded quickly, hoping they wouldn't realize that she didn't remember their names. She led the way to the backyard where the action was in full effect.

There were two grills blazing and loaded from end to end with barbecue. The picnic table along the fence was covered with food. Four ice coolers were lined up at the bottom of the steps with cold drinks of every kind.

The smell of killer 'dro smacked them in the face as soon as they stepped off of the porch. There was an instant feeling of belonging that overtook the trio once inside the yard.

Carlito was quickly snatched up by two young girls and they started fixing him a plate. He was in his element: pretty women and good food. He planned on staying awhile.

Tara finally spotted her mother at one of the bid whist tables slapping cards. M&M loved a good card game. She would stay up all night playing if there was a good game going down.

"Baby, you want me to fix you a plate now or you want to wait?" Tara asked Julio while her eyes scanned the food.

"It smells good. What's all over there?" Julio asked.

"There's barbecue chicken, barbecue ribs, greens, baked beans, macaroni and cheese, roasted corn on the cob, potato salad, macaroni salad, and all kinds of cake," Tara answered.

"Are you eating now? I don't want to eat by myself," Julio responded.

"Aw, baby, I'll eat with you. Everything looks so good. I'm ready to get busy. I'll fix our plates and we can eat inside. I don't want no flies getting on my food out here. Let me run over and speak to Ma and then we can go eat inside," Tara explained.

"What's up, young man?" Slim greeted, walking up behind Julio.

The two men gave each other dap. Tara greeted and kissed her father and walked away to greet her mother. Julio was in good hands, and she was glad that her dad arrived when he did.

"Hi, Tara. When did you get here? Did you get something to eat?" M&M questioned her daughter. She got up from her card game and joined her baby daughter in the yard. She hadn't seen Tara in weeks and instantly she could tell something was going on with her. Anyone else would think Tara looked fine as hell, but M&M knew her child, and she didn't even have to ask the question. Her baby was using drugs . . . and heavy. She knew it.

"Come on, let's go look at the pieces I told you about. I got some Harve Benard suits I know you gon' want," M&M announced as the pair made their way inside. "Rabbit, put some more drinks in the coolers; they're out in the garage. And change that music. That blues shit you playing is depressing. This is a party, not a funeral," she instructed, closing the screen door behind her.

"Mom, you ain't tell me you was having a cookout. Julio really don't like meeting new people. I'm so glad Daddy is here to keep him calm. Who are all those people out there under the tent?" Tara questioned.

"They're with Tee. He ran to the store to pick up some shit. He'll be back in a minute. They cool. Janice Sadiq's boy, Rocmon, hit a huge lick down South and they been partying all week. He brought twenty slabs of ribs for me to cook. You know those kids love my cookin'," M&M explained, studying her daughter. The two women moved through the familiar space of the house and breathed in the smell of Southern BBQ that filled the air, each woman studying the other.

Tara knew her mother well, so she knew her mother wanted her to do more than just look at some pieces when she invited her into the house. Her mother made her living at reading people. There was no way she could ever hide anything from M&M. She prepared herself for the questions she knew were coming.

"How long you been snorting?" M&M asked as she sat down on her inviting bed.

"Not long," Tara was quick to respond. There was no need in even trying to lie to her mother. "I've been spending a lot of time at home and it relaxes me," she offered, joining her mother on the bed.

"What you need relaxing for? You with a man I know you love, and he's taking care of you real good. What you worried about, huh?" M&M asked, looking Tara in the face.

Tara was her baby girl and the toughest of all her children. She was attracted to the street life like bees to honey. Hustling came natural to her, and she could hold her own with the best of them. M&M saw so much of herself in Tara. She lived life to the fullest. She'd learned that from watching her parents. M&M chose the street life, but Tara was born into it. She knew Tara felt she could control everything, but M&M's gut told her that her daughter was headed for self-destruction, and she had to try and stop her.

"Ma, I love Julio so much, and I want to just kick back and enjoy the life we have, but for some reason, I keep feeling like he ain't gonna be with me for long. I always feel like I'm dreaming and I'm going to wake up and he's going to be gone. I keep having that feeling, Ma. How do you deal with Daddy being out in the streets taking chances all the time?" Tara inquired with a serious look on her face.

"I've always used drugs for recreation, not for a crutch. When you find yourself needing something, it's time to step away. You need to ask yourself that question: Am I just having fun or do I need this shit? Have you asked yourself that? I've watch some of the best of them be taken out because they didn't realize they had a problem. I ain't going to let that happen to my daughter. You still my baby, and I'll hurt whoever I have to if something happens to you." M&M stroked her daughter's face and then continued.

"Down South, I learned at an early age that you can't control life. You just got to live it. Enjoy every moment and forgive yourself every day for the mistakes you make. You can't worry about everything. You'll go crazy," M&M warned as she hugged her daughter tightly while tears rolled down her face.

Tara felt the tears hit her shoulder as she began to cry also. Mother and daughter held on to each other for dear life. Neither wanted to let the other one go.

"Hey! Hey! What's going on in here? The party's outside. Baby, I'm starving. Come on and fix my plate," Slim whined, lightening the mood in the room. He knew M&M was having a serious conversation with their daughter and he knew they'd felt each other, so it was time to move on. His baby girl was just like him. She was smarter than most of his sons that were out there chasing paper. She could hold her own.

"I'm starving too," Julio said, sticking his head through the bedroom door and rubbing his belly. Tara hugged her father. The mood had changed, and they all joined the party in the backyard. The yard had filled up with young thugs and gangstas.

Tee, Rocmon, and their crew returned from the corner store with the blunt wraps and Black & Milds they needed to continue the party.

The young dope boys had been getting high for seven days straight. They'd closed down every strip club in the north end. Now they were hungry and enjoying the lazy spring day with their peeps.

"Tee, roll one, nigga," Rocmon shouted from the tent, pulling his latest gold digger onto his lap.

"You roll one, partner. I'm 'bout to get with this grub. That shit can wait," Tee shot back, stacking his plate full of honey-glazed BBQ chicken.

"I'm right behind you," Rocmon yelled, getting up and knocking the gold digger to the ground.

The crew jumped up to join them as the tent fell down around them. The scene looked like something from a comedy routine, watching them all scramble from under the tent, trying to get to the grub.

Julio jumped out of the way of the falling tent and stepped over a body crawling from underneath it. He balanced the drink he'd just poured from the bar.

The two men froze in their tracks as they instantly recognized each other. *What the fuck is this nigga doing here?* Julio thought as Tara walked up beside him.

"Tee, I done told you about acting all wild when I got company. Take that shit in the basement," M&M scolded, coming out the back door.

"What's up, boss?" Black offered sarcastically with a smirk on his face as he got up from off of the ground. Carlito witnessed the exchange and joined Julio.

"What the fuck is up?" Tee said, coming between them.

"My bad, Tee. I didn't recognize our boss at first," Black explained, falling back. He had been surrounded by the entire clan before he even had a chance to think. He had to fall back; he needed to do his homework on this family. He wasn't messing with no easy marks and he knew it.

"It's all good, Tee. You and the young folks take your party to the basement. Us old folks want the yard to ourselves," Slim instructed, breaking the tension in the yard.

Black took his place in the food line with the rest of the crew. He never took his eyes off Julio and Carlito. His blood boiled watching the two wetback motherfuckas walk around the yard like they owned it. He wanted to step to them right then and there, but he had respect for the old Gs on the set. He wasn't gon' bring the drama to Tee's grandma's house, but best believe he was working on a plan to holla at the Latin lover real soon.

Fourteen

A Whole New Life

Tara sat at the oak dressing table and combed her hair. The sound of Julio singing some upbeat song in Spanish could be heard over the running water of the shower. She checked the time on the alarm clock on the table beside the king-size bed. The honeymoon suite at the Radisson hotel had been their home for the last two weeks.

So much shit was going on in the streets that Julio had come home one night and ordered Tara to pack a bag because they needed to lay low for a while. She had tried questioning him, but she knew by the look on his face it wasn't a good time for questions.

They had driven to several hotels before he finally parked in front of the Radisson at the airport and told her to get out.

Once inside the dark hotel room, he began to kiss her deeply, stating, "Baby, I know you wanted to have a big wedding and I wanted to give that to you too, but I don't want to wait for all that," Julio panted as he kissed her in between words. "I want to get married now, tonight." He held her close.

"Julio, we can't get married tonight," Tara responded with a puzzled look on her face.

"Why not? We got them blood test papers, right? You said that's all we needed to get married," Julio questioned, sitting down on the oversized chair near the door.

"Yeah, we have the blood test papers, but we have to get a license and we have to have a minister to marry us. Where you think we gonna get a minister and the license this time of night?" Tara laughed, looking at how cute and innocent her baby looked sitting in the huge chair.

Tara joined him on the oversized chair and kissed him passionately. "Baby, I can't wait to start a life with you. I can exhale with you. I know I'm safe in your arms. Promise me it will always be like this. Promise me you will do everything you can to make sure we're together. I'm so afraid that what we have ain't gonna last," Tara demanded, staring in her lover's eyes.

"Baby, I got the same demons haunting me. I get scared sometimes that I'm going to lose you too. I promise you that I will do everything in my power to protect what we have. I'm in this forever. I want to get old with you, make some babies, and live the good life. I'm doing everything I can to get things in order so I can raise out the game the right way. I just want to be with you and experience some happiness," Julio whispered in Tara's ear as he lifted her face and planted tender kisses on her lips.

It had taken Tara a few days to contact Mama Grace's pastor, Reverend Hairston, at the Prince of Peace Holiness Church. It took her even longer to convince him to agree to marry them. Now, lying across the king-size poster bed, Tara thought about how she'd gotten to this moment. All her life she'd run from love and commitment; now she craved it. It dictated her every move. All she wanted was to start her life with her man.

In less than an hour, Tara would be married to the man she loved with all her heart. Her mind told her the timing was awful with all the street drama going on, but she eventually put that negative thought out of her mind. She loved Julio and he loved her. Together they could conquer the world.

Julio still hadn't told Tara why they had been holed up at the hotel, and she didn't want to know. Not right now. She just wanted to enjoy the happiness she felt at this moment.

The sound of the loud knock on the door caused her to jump. She quietly left the master suite and answered the door.

"What's up, girl?" Karen greeted, hugging her friend.

Karen was dressed in a pale blue two-piece suit. The miniskirt hugged her hips in all the right places. Tara was happy to see her girl looking so nice. Karen looked like her old self. Her swagger was back.

"Where you want me to put all these bottles of Moët?" Roberto asked, rushing through the door behind Karen with bags in both hands.

"Put them over there on the bar by those food trays," Tara instructed, pointing toward the kitchenette to the left of the hotel door.

"Girl, why aren't you dressed? The minister will be here any minute," Karen scolded her best friend, joining her in the doorway to the bedroom.

Just then, there was another knock at the door. "Get the door for me, Roberto, and can you get some ice from the hallway?" Tara shouted over her shoulder as she rushed from the room, heading to the bedroom to get dressed.

"What's shaking, partner?" Julio sang, entering the room. He tapped Tara on her ass as she rushed by. Julio was dressed to kill in a charcoal gray Armani suit. He wore a crisp white Armani dress shirt with a cream-and-gray tie that matched Tara's dress perfectly. He completed the look with a pair of diamond-and-gold square cufflinks.

Karen helped her friend slip into her wedding dress. The dress was beautiful. It was a pearl-colored, hand-beaded dress that fell gracefully to the floor. The back was completely out, down to the small of Tara's waist. She looked like a princess from a childhood fairy tale standing before her friend.

Karen had driven all the way to New York to roll up the designer gown for her friend. Karen loved her girl, Tara. The thought of her girl getting out the game for sure and permanently settling down pleased her. It was hard for a sister in the streets; most didn't survive.

"You did it, girl. You found the man of your dreams. I am so happy for you. Julio loves you so much. You are truly blessed," Karen told her friend as she began to cry.

"Don't you start crying, you're going to make me cry. Thank you for being here. Everything is happening so fast, but I know this is right. My family is going to kill me when they find out we got married without telling them," Tara whined, smoothing out her dress.

Mama Grace was one of Reverend Hairston's best members, and he wasn't quick to keep her secret. Tara promised him she would tell her family the news as soon as possible.

Karen kissed her friend on the cheek and said, "Let's do this." She opened the doors to the master suite and Tara moved through the entrance. Carlito, Angel, Roberto,

Santiago, Reverend Hairston, and Julio rose to welcome her.

The only person Tara saw, though, was her beloved Julio. She joined him by the fireplace as their friends gathered around them. The ceremony was all a blur for Tara. She just held onto Julio's hand as they stared into each other's eyes the entire time.

Julio took the words the minister spoke to heart. He planned to give Tara the world and protect her at all costs. He took his vows seriously, vowing before God and all their witnesses to make Tara happy, and he would not let anything stand in the way of their happily-ever-after.

After the ceremony, Reverend Hairston pulled Tara aside and spoke softly to her. "Tara, I am happy for you. I can tell your husband really loves you. I've known you since you were a little girl and I want you to be happy.

"You know only what you do for Christ will last. The two of you need to get closer to God. You know the devil comes to rob, steal, and destroy. If you want this marriage to last, the two of you need to be in church," Reverend Hairston told Tara as he prepared to leave.

Tara walked the reverend to the door and thanked him. "I know you're right, Reverend. Will you pray for me?" Tara asked seriously.

"I have always prayed for you, Tara, and I always will," Reverend Hairston explained, closing the door behind him.

"I thought the reverend wasn't ever gonna leave," Santiago teased, turning on the sound system and pouring champagne for all of them. "To the best damn friend a motherfucka could ever ask for, and to his beautiful bride," Santiago toasted the newlyweds.

Roberto pulled a silver tray full of powder from under the couch and took a one and one. He then passed the tray to Angel, who did the same. Angel then passed the tray to Julio.

Julio snorted the crystal powder and then he kissed his bride. He handed her the tray, giving her permission to also snort the powder. Tara took two heaping snorts of cocaine and passed the tray to Karen.

The wedding reception lasted two days. The friends hung out at the hotel suite drinking, listening to music, and snorting cocaine until they passed out.

Santiago shook Julio from his sleep on the floor next to Tara and asked him to join him on the patio. The two of them looked so peaceful that he hated to disturb his friend. Tara was good for his old friend. She calmed him. As long as he'd known Julio, he had never talked about getting out of the game, but now things were different. Tara allowed him to think of a life other than hustling. His friend deserved that life, and he planned on giving it to him. He wished he didn't have to have the conversation they needed to have.

Julio wiped the sleep from his eyes and joined Santiago on the patio. "Tell me something good, *primo*," Julio said, taking a sip from the bottle of Heineken he'd brought with him as he sat down in one of the two patio chairs.

"We've kicked in the doors of every known spot on the east side, and that chump Black is nowhere to be found. I got our best soldiers ready to put in work at a moment's notice; we just can't find the motherfucka," Santiago explained, pacing back and forth on the small patio.

"Somebody knows something. I want him found and brought to me, *primo*. That bastard is a wannabe gangsta. You mean to tell me we can't find a wannabe?" Julio questioned, getting up and staring out into the still night.

"We'll find him. You have my word, friend.

"I wanted to talk to you about Roberto also. He's been making some shady decisions lately, and I'm starting to question his judgment," Santiago explained, joining Julio at the railing.

"I don't want him on this Black thing. Give him his usual work and keep an eye on him. Let me know if things get worse. You know that nigga thinks with his dick. He'll be all right, though. He needs to stop trying to juggle all them women at the same time. His dick should be worn out by now." Julio laughed and sat down.

"You know he's fuckin' Carlito's girl, Angel. Shit gonna hit the fan when Carlito finally gets wind of that shit," Santiago warned just as Tara joined them on the patio.

"How you gon' run off and leave your boo all alone?" Tara purred, squeezing between Julio's legs.

"I could never leave you, baby," Julio said as he stroked her hair.

"Tara, take good care of my friend. I know you're going to make him happy. I hope I can find a good woman and settle down one of these days," Santiago sighed as he left the patio.

Tara and Julio lay there in each other's arms for a while before they went back inside. Karen and Roberto were the only ones still left in the suite when they returned. They were both passed out on opposite ends of the couch.

Tara woke her friend and told her that they were going to bed and they needed to do the same. "Your back is going to be killing you if you stay here," Tara warned.

"Good lookin' out," Karen whispered as she drifted back to sleep. The newlyweds headed to their suite, closing the doors behind them.

Tara got completely naked and joined Julio on the king-size bed. She kissed him gently. Julio returned the kiss and then rolled on top of her.

"Baby, I really felt the words the preacher was saying during the ceremony. Especially the part about the two of us becoming one," Julio shared with his bride.

He kissed her long and hard, and then he moved his lips to her breasts. He sucked at her nipples until they both stood at attention, while he searched between her legs. His dick was rock-hard in his pants, so he quickly removed them and tossed them on the floor beside the bed. He buried his head between her legs and went to work.

Julio enjoyed the sounds Tara was making as a result of the pleasure of his tongue. He knew his baby's body well, and just as he licked at her clit, she arched her back and screamed his name. He watched as her body shook from her orgasm.

Julio slid his dick inside her warm, wet pussy and he was home. Tara's hips rose and fell with his as she stroked his hair. "I love you," she whispered in his ear as his orgasm exploded inside her.

"I love you too."

Fifteen

The Beginning of the End

Tara listened to the fifteenth message on the answering machine and then pushed the stop button. The last message was from her precious grandmother. Mama Grace was shouting through the phone that she was very upset that Tara had gotten married and she wasn't there. She warned that Tara had better call her so she could plan a proper wedding reception. Tara could hear her Aunt Bootsie in the background fussing as well. She would have to call her grandmother back later.

There were twenty-two more unheard messages and she was tired of listening. She was happy to be home, and she just wanted to kick back and relax. She enjoyed being spoiled at the hotel, but nothing compared to the comfort of their home. There was a peace that she could not find anywhere else when she was safe at home with her husband. Everything around her told her she was loved. She couldn't care less about going outside into that mean, cold world.

Julio was out making runs, and she could not wait for

him to return. She hated when he was out in the streets. She worried every minute until he returned safely to her.

Tara sat down on her floral chaise lounge chair, next to the glass-front fireplace, and stared out the window, as her mind reminisced back to another time.

"Tara go outside and tell them boys to get in here and wash they hands for dinner," Mama Minnie ordered, pulling the cornbread from the oven and placing it on the warmer in the center of the kitchen table.

"Mama Minnie, I went last time. It's Karen's turn," Tara whined, getting up from the yellow plastic chair with the metal legs and stomping toward the door.

"Don't worry about what Karen's doing. She gonna set the table," Mama Minnie explained, shooing Tara out the back door.

Tara bolted through the screen door and out onto the weathered wooden porch. The backyard was small and full of an assortment of used, mixed-matched lawn items. There were even two plastic pink flamingos in the yard. Tara's brothers, Michael and Reggie, and her cousin, Rick, sat on the lime green porch swing and stared at their Marvel comic books.

"Mama Minnie said get y'all's nappy heads in here and eat, stinky boys," Tara teased, sticking out her tongue and putting her hands on her hips. The boys ignored her and continued examining the comic books.

"Where is Benny? Do y'all hear me? Mama Minnie!" Tara screamed, heading back inside.

"Here we come, you old bighead girl," Reggie teased, pushing Tara's forehead backward as they chased each other into the kitchen.

"Quit that playing in my kitchen and go wash your hands for dinner," Mama Minnie scolded as she poured the fresh-squeezed lemonade into the small kiddie-size cups that were placed around the table.

She then placed the meat loaf on the table next to the mashed potatoes and sat down to dinner.

"Karen, go tell ya grandma and granddaddy dinner is ready," Mama Minnie instructed, straightening the silver knife and spoon that lay before her.

"Yes, ma'am," Karen sang, skipping from the kitchen, happy to get her grandparents because they were having her favorite, mashed potatoes, and she was more than ready to eat.

When the family had all gathered around the table and sat down to dinner, Mama Grace bowed her head and said the blessing over the meal. "Dear Heavenly Father, make us truly thankful for this meal we are about to receive. Make it nourishment for our bodies."

"Amen," Grace and the family said in unison.

"Mama, where's the hot peppers Mickey brought me from Tennessee?" Granddaddy questioned, piling his plate full of string beans.

"They in the bowl over the stove. You know you gonna be up all night with heartburn if you eat them peppers this late in the evening," Grace warned, sipping her lemonade.

"Why you picking at yo' food, Rick? You ain't eat nothing," Mama Minnie questioned, glancing down the table at her tiny great-grandson.

"I'm full, Mama Minnie. My stomach hurt," Rick whined, rubbing his belly.

"How you full? You ain't eat nothing. You ain't done nothing but drink your lemonade."

"My stomach hurts 'cause I ate too much candy," Rick explained, frowning.

"Where you get some candy, boy?" Mama Grace questioned, looking up from her plate.

"Benny got a big bag of candy he brought from the store and he

said I could eat all I wanted and I ate too many Tootsie Rolls," Rick sang in a sweet voice, falling across the table and putting his hand on his forehead.

"Where did you get money for candy, Benjamin?" Mama Grace questioned sternly, staring at Benny from across the packed table. Benny held his head down and stared into his plate.

"He got the money from Mama Minnie's purse," Tara chimed in, wanting to please her favorite person in the house. She knew Mama Grace well enough to know she was mad, and Tara did not want her mad at her.

"The three of you finish eating and then I want to see you in the living room," Mama Grace ordered as she got up from the table.

"Lawd have mercy; help us raise these children right," Mama Minnie cried, looking up at an invisible God. The children looked up with her, hoping to see who she was always talking to.

"Aw, old lady, them kids just being kids. They be all right. You worry too much," Granddaddy chimed in, getting up from the table and getting his favorite shot glass from the kitchen cabinet. After the children finished eating, Grace led them to the living room.

She sat on the worn-out green, square-shaped sofa and worried about her grandchildren. She could not fail these children, Lord help her. She'd watched her smartest oldest daughter be lured away by the temptations of the world, and now she was paying a horrible price for her choices. She did not want the same thing to happen to her grandchildren. She raised them in the church and she prayed on her knees every night that their lives would be different from the one she and her daughter had known. She wanted more for them.

Tara walked slowly into the living room and joined Mama Grace on the couch. She scooted in close to her grandmother and smiled up at her brightly, hoping to put a smile on her grand-

mother's face. Her grandmother was a beautiful, kind woman and Tara loved her dearly. She hated disappointing her.

"Mama Grace, I didn't take no money. I just ate the candy. Benny said he wasn't gonna give me none if I told," Tara immediately started talking.

"No, I didn't either," Benny lied, bucking out his eyes and looking at the floor.

"You three listen to me and listen to me good," Mama Grace started. "Nothing good happens to liars and thieves. God smiles on those that are good. I am raising good boys and girls, and good boys and girls do good things, not bad. To lie and steal is bad. When you take things that do not belong to you, God is sad. Your bad choices always catch up to you. And for you, Miss Tara, when you cover up the truth, that makes you just as bad," Grace taught her grandchildren sternly.

"We sorry, Mama Grace," the children said in unison, hugging their precious grandmother.

The sound of the phone ringing shook Tara from her dream. She sprang from the lounge chair and leaped for the phone. "Hello, hello," she yelled, knocking her cocaine straw from her lap.

"Hola, mami," Julio sang into the phone as he puffed on his Cuban cigar and blew smoke rings into the air. Every sister in the room wished they were that Cuban cigar, stuck between his sexy lips.

"Hey, baby, where you at?" Tara questioned, wanting him there with her. She lay back on the cozy chair and retrieved her straw from the floor.

"I'm at Spinners and I want to come home, but I ain't on that driving shit right now. Fuck that shit. It's fuckin' hot as hell out there; motherfuckin' feds everywhere. I'm trying to lay low and chill with you, plus I'm drunk as fuck too. Come get me, baby?" Julio asked his wifey.

"Baby, I'm high as fuck. I told you to come home earlier, and you just had to bounce with your boys. Have yo' boys bring you home," Tara ordered, getting up from the chair and checking her hair in the mirror over the dresser.

"Tara, stop acting like a hard-ass gangsta all the time and come get your nigga, girl," Julio demanded, looking around the club angrily.

They argued back and forth for what seemed like an hour, and Tara finally gave in and agreed to go pick him up. She didn't want to argue with him anymore, so she slipped on a pair of jeans and a crisp white shirt and went to get her man.

Tara sped up State Route 161 to Club Spinners. She pushed her Beamer to the limit. She hated being high out in public. She spent so much time getting blowed alone with her boo that she always felt uncomfortable in public. Her awareness was always heightened when she was under the influence, so she noticed everything. She got so tired of staring down chickenheads that were always giving her man the eye that she preferred staying home when he went out. He was usually home at a decent hour, and she was cool with his clubbin' it. He loved the sound of the Latin music on Latino night, and he seldom missed Thursday nights at Spinners.

She pulled her Beamer into the packed parking lot and finally found a space way in the back. Crossing the busy lot, she headed for the front entrance. The doorway was filled with people waiting impatiently to get in.

Fortunately, one of the bouncers who knew her was working the door. He quickly waved her to the front and let her in the noisy club. She waited a few minutes for her eyes to adjust to the darkness of the room as she checked her appearance in the mirrored hallway. She looked good as hell and her hair was poppin'. She was rockin' the hell out of her new caramel snakeskin boots and the matching cowhide Coach purse she picked up at the City Center Mall.

As her vision cleared, she located Julio at the bar with an overly friendly waitress all up in his face. The bitch whispered something in his ear and then pulled away and stuck out her breasts implants and smiled.

Tara hurriedly pushed her way through the crowd and stepped to her man. "What the fuck is going on with you and this bitch?" she demanded to know as she turned and stared at the scared-shitless white girl. The waitress swiftly moved to the opposite end of the bar and began taking the drink orders of two horny white grandmothers. The grandmothers were trying to get their groove on up in the club with some Latin lovers who were undressing them with their eyes.

"How you gonna disrespect me and let that bitch be all up in your face?" Tara demanded to know. The couple seated next to them suddenly got up and left. Tara sat in the seat next to him and asked again, "What the fuck is up, Julio?"

He raised his head from his drink. "Why you trippin', baby? Chill out. You all salty and shit. Chill the fuck out. Ain't nobody thinking about that *puta*," he spat as he nodded his head to the familiar music.

"You must have been thinking something about her; she all up in your grill," Tara shot back angrily.

"Come on, boo, you trippin' and shit," he begged, pulling her to him.

She snatched away and got up to leave. Julio pulled her back down into her seat.

"You gonna let a bitch be all up in your face and shit when I ain't around, disrespecting our relationship and shit? I ain't on that, not ever, Julio. Fuck you," Tara yelled, pulling off her wedding rings and placing them on the bar next to him. "Don't bother coming home, either. You can stay here with that bitch," she instructed as she got up and headed to the door.

Tara ran from the club and got in her car to leave. She backed her car from the parking space and headed for the exit at the front of the lot. She passed the entrance just as Julio burst from the gold glass double doors. He rushed to the car and motioned for her to pull over. Tara stopped the car and rolled the passenger-side window halfway down.

"What the fuck is wrong with you, Tara? Yo' ass is trippin'. How the fuck you gonna take off your fuckin' wedding rings and leave them on the bar like that shit ain't nothing?" Julio demanded to know.

"How the fuck you gonna let a bitch be all up in your face like that shit ain't nothing?" Tara shouted as she started pulling off.

Julio was so angry that he could not get his point across to her. He pulled the glass from the window and broke it with his bare hands. He held onto the car door as Tara sped away.

She was so angry that she cried all the way home. Julio kept calling her on her cell phone, but she refused to answer. After the fifth unanswered call, he left her a message.

"Stop acting so crazy all the time. I love you. You know I ain't thinking 'bout no other bitch," Julio spoke to the answering machine.

She tried to ignore the beeping of the phone, so she turned up the radio and stuffed the phone deep down into her purse.

By the time she got home, he'd called her six more times. Tara placed her keys on the wooden, round antique table by the front door and rushed upstairs. She climbed the spiral staircase and crossed the hall to the bedroom. She could hear Julio enter the living room as she closed the bedroom door and locked it.

Julio climbed the stairs two at a time and leaped for the door as Tara closed it in his face. "Tara, you better open the fuckin' door before I break the fucker down. I ain't playing with yo' ass either," he said, banging on the door.

Tara got undressed and got in the bed as he continued banging on the door. She tuned him out while she reached for the glass tray piled high with cocaine on the dresser. After taking a long, hard snort of 'caine in both nostrils, she lay back on the fluffy, down feather–filled pillows on her bed. The rush of the drug spread through her brain and swept across her body. Tara forgot for a moment that the two of them were having a heated argument as she placed her hand between her legs and thought about Julio inside her.

Bang! Bang! She heard the door pop as Julio broke through the lock.

"I told yo' ass to open the door," he said, examining the broken door hinges that lay on the floor. He then walked over to the bed.

Tara lay there looking sexy as hell, and he wanted to just jump in bed and fuck the hell out of his baby, but he had to get his point across. He needed to let her know that she couldn't just put his manhood on Front Street like that in public. He had a reputation to uphold and he needed her to know that.

"Don't you ever do no shit like that again," he spat, staring her down. Tara closed her eyes and ignored him. "Do you hear me?" he yelled, grabbing her as she jumped with fear.

"Get yo' fuckin' hands off me," Tara shouted, sitting up on the bed. She pushed him away roughly and sprang from their bed. He chased after her and blocked her as she tried to leave the room.

"Yo' little tough ass gonna listen to what the fuck I got to say, girl," he ordered. She tried leaving the room again, and he held her in his arms tightly and said, "I love yo' stubborn ass, girl, and you always testing me like you a nigga. Ain't a bitch out there I want. I want you. When you gon' get that through yo' hard-ass head?" He pushed her back onto the bed.

Tara jumped up and smacked him. He went to smack her back when his phone rang. The two of them froze in their tracks and stared into each other's eyes as they both instantly realized they'd taken the argument too far. Julio snapped from the dark place he'd allowed his anger to take him and answered the phone.

"Yo, what's up, Carlito?" Julio spoke into the phone. Tara could hear Carlito shouting on the other end. "Swing through and pick me up. I need to get out of the house. Tara trippin' and I need some air," Julio instructed his soldier.

"I don't give a fuck what you got to do; I said come and get me now," he screamed in the phone. Julio wondered why everybody was challenging him tonight. He ended the call, left the room, and went downstairs.

Tara ran to the bathroom and closed the door. She glanced at herself in the mirror and shook her head. She couldn't figure out why she was letting her temper get the best of her. She wanted everything her way and she always had to be right. She knew deep inside that Julio loved her with all his heart, but the constant drug use had her thinking crazy thoughts lately. When she was thinking sanely, she knew beyond a doubt how much Julio was in love with her.

She washed her face, brushed her hair, and then reached

in her makeup dish on the rose-colored marble counter and retrieved her M•A•C lip gloss. Tara applied the shiny lip gloss to her lips and checked her hair before heading downstairs.

When she reached the living room, Julio was already headed out the door. "Where you going?" she questioned, standing barefoot before him, staring up into his eyes. She knew he was leaving to clear his head. She didn't want him to go, so she stalled by asking a question. She hoped he would just let the shit slide and come back upstairs with her. She was sorry.

He wanted to give in to her cute plea for forgiveness, but he had to teach her a lesson the hard way. *Her cute ass was getting out of hand,* he thought as he closed the front door behind him.

Tara fell to the floor and burst into tears. She lay there wishing she knew when to put the breaks on with her temper. She was always backing herself in a corner because she never wanted to back down, learning that shit from parents and running in the streets. She had to win by any means necessary. "Keep fighting" was the rule she'd been taught. Why couldn't she just trust his love?

Tara lifted herself from the floor and dragged herself up the stairs after laying there for over an hour. She cried all the way up to her bedroom. She looked around the room for her purse, grabbed it from the dresser, and fished for her phone. She hoped he'd called her to say he was coming home.

There were no missed calls. The house phone hadn't rung either, so Tara crawled in bed and tried going to sleep. She wasn't so lucky. She reached for the remote control and began searching the channels. Thinking of Julio, she fought back her tears.

It was as if she could hear the cocaine on the table calling her, and she automatically reached for the tray. She snorted the drug into her body and lay back in the bed. Before she knew it, she'd drifted off to sleep.

When she woke from her sleep, hours had passed, and she quickly checked her phones. There were no calls from Julio still, and she began to worry and pace the room. Her gut told her something was terribly wrong. She called his phone back-to-back for over an hour and he never answered.

By dawn, Tara was in a panic and high as hell. She'd snorted so much cocaine that the rims of her eyes were swollen and red. She'd been dialing his number back-to-back all night when she finally got an answer.

"Hello," a strange voice spoke through the phone. Tara could tell by the sound of the voice that the man was white.

"Who is this?" Tara questioned nervously.

"If you're waiting up for Julio to come home, you're going to be waiting a long time," the strange voice said and then hung up. A crippling sense of loss swept across her as she stared into the phone and cried uncontrollably.

The phone rang, startling Tara as she quickly answered. "Hello," she yelled, praying it was her baby.

"*Mami*, it's me," Julio said in a controlled voice. He didn't want to upset her any more than he knew he was going to have to with what he was about to tell her. He cleared his throat and spoke in a calm, even tone. "I love you, baby, and I'm sorry I lost my temper with you," he apologized tenderly.

"I love you too, baby. Where are you?" she questioned, afraid of the answer, then lowered herself to the bed and held herself tightly.

"The feds arrested me and Carlito. They trying to say

we had some weight in the car. There was a large amount, and they trying to book a nigga with that shit. I need you to be strong and call my attorney and get him down here tonight.

"Keep yo' head up. I'm gon' be posted up in this bitch for a minute, and I need you to be strong and handle our business, baby. The shit is strange. I need to get some answers. Roberto ain't roll like that. Shit real strange. Can I count on you to be down with me? Tara, can I count on you?" Julio questioned her then paused to hear her answer.

Tara wanted to fall apart. She could not live without her husband. How could she go on without him? He was her world.

She had to be strong. She'd watched her mother and her father be strong for each other when the streets separated them. She'd learned from the best. She could do this. She had to; he needed her.

Tara fought back her tears and spoke in her strongest voice. "I'm down with you forever, baby. Whatever you need me to do, I'm going to do it," she sang into the phone, trying to sound strong for her husband's sake.

"They waving me off the phone, baby. I got to go; I'll call you tomorrow. Check and see if there's a block on the phone. If there is one, get it off as soon as possible. I need to talk to you every day.

"Tara, the only way I'm gon' get through this is to know you're okay. Take care of yourself. I need you. Lighten up on the one thing. Be careful. I'm going to send somebody to watch you as soon as I figure this thing out.

"I love you for life," he said and hung up the phone.

Sixteen

Don't Hate the Playa, Hate the Game

Black continued to follow the Cadillac Escalade. He had been behind that chump, Carlito, ever since he left the bitch Angel's house. He knew the soft-ass nigga was headed to his boss Julio's house when he got on I-71 north.

Black had been following the duo for two weeks now. Neither was the wiser. Both of the marks were so pussy-whipped that they had let their guard down, so he knew eventually he'd have them right where he wanted them and he could make his move.

As Black kept up with the Escalade, he thought about how much pull he had in the streets. He made a name for himself and had to keep his shit under control. Heartless Black looked at himself in the rearview mirror, grinned, and felt like a soldier holdin' his ground.

The north end belonged to brothas. What the fuck would it look like letting Spanish niggas make more money off the streets than them? It was Crip territory, and he wasn't just gonna fall back and watch that shit go down. He'd let them know he wasn't no soft motherfucka. Black put in work on the regular. He was a gangsta.

Carlito dipped through traffic, gripping the steering wheel with one clenched fist and smoking a blunt with the other, until he jerked the wheel, cut in front of a minivan without looking, and leaped onto the exit ramp at Dublin-Granville Road. At the second light, his cellular phone went off. He set the fatty in the car ashtray, took his phone out of his jacket pocket, and answered.

"Si, que passé?" Carlito held the phone to his ear with his shoulder, grabbed his joint, and sparked it. "No problem," Carlito said to Julio on the other line, holding in a thick hit. Exhaling, "I'll be up there in a second." Carlito hung up the phone and cut across three lanes to turn at Cleveland Avenue.

Black watched Carlito turn onto Cleveland and started to get over, but was cut off by a dark blue Nissan Altima. The eagerness of the car caught his attention. Then it hit Black and he nodded at the familiarity of the scene. He wasn't the only one following the pair. The drug-dealing kingpin had himself a tail, and from the amount of weight he pushed in the streets, the boys in the Altima most definitely were feds.

Black lucked up when he followed Carlito's silver Escalade and it pulled straight into Julio's driveway. *Two birds wit' one stone*, he thought. He killed his headlights and waited at the curb a block away. The feds waited at the next corner.

Julio rushed from the house, and Black could tell by his body language, even from a distance, that shit wasn't right. Julio got in the car and it sped off quickly. Black waited for the feds to follow suit, then he joined the chain.

Carlito held the blunt up to Julio. He took it without looking and hit it hard.

"You forget an anniversary or something?" Carlito

laughed, trying to lighten the mood. He could tell things were heated with Tara and Julio the moment Julio entered the car.

Julio passed back to Carlito. "She's trippin'. I had to get the fuck outta there," he said, and then he reached into his pocket, removed his pager, and quickly checked it.

As Carlito relit the fading flame of the joint, his cellular phone rang. *"Hola?"* Carlito answered.

Roberto spoke smoothly into the line. *"Hola, Carlito, como estas?"*

"You know how it is. Same shit, different day."

"Sí, sí. Where you at?"

"On my way. I had to roll up to the suburbs and pick up Julio." Julio looked up at Carlito again.

"Julio? Man, why you got Julio wit' you?" Roberto asked with a little nervousness in his tone.

"Julio and Tara goin' through some shit. He had me get him up out of there."

"So, you droppin' him off somewhere or he rollin' with you?" Roberto questioned.

Passing back to Julio, who was now rechecking his pager, Carlito said, "Nah, man, we headed that way now. See you in a few. Peace." He hung up the cell phone.

"What was that shit about?" Julio said, sitting up in his seat.

"Roberto just got back with my shit. Told me earlier he wants some product. Got his money straight, so he payin' up front this time."

Black followed a little closer as Carlito's car pulled into the far end of the Swifty Mart. The headlights shut off but the engine kept running. Watching the Escalade, Black lowered his sun visor and killed his headlights.

A few seconds later, he watched Julio go into the convenience store. As Julio pushed through the store's front door, Roberto pulled into the parking lot and parked next to the Escalade. Roberto got out of his car, walked to the passenger's side of Carlito's ride, and jumped in.

Inside of the Swifty Mart, Julio stalked the freezer aisle looking for his girl's favorite drink. Even though Tara could get under his skin, she was the Bonnie to his Clyde. He knew she had a temper when he met her. It would take more than some bullshit arguing to change his feelings.

He walked over to the coolers section, but the doors were blocked by a pair of chickenheads. One was wearing cutoff Daisy Dukes, a brightly colored halter top, and a gold chain. The other reeked of hairspray and her tits were spilling out of her shirt, exposing a rose tattoo. When Julio approached, the girls looked him up and down and smiled.

"What's up, *papi?*" the first purred, showing that she was missing one of her front teeth. Julio ignored them and went straight for the door handle.

The taller of the two girls stepped out of the way and continued to watch his every move. "A sista would love to get wit' a playa like you. I can give a brother something he can feel."

The other girl giggled flirtatiously. Julio reached into the freezer, pulled out two cases of Jack Daniel's coolers, and shut the door. He turned to the girls, said, "I'm straight on that. I got a wife," and started toward the checkout counter. The girls watched him pass then went on with their conversation.

Out in the Escalade, Carlito and Roberto made small talk while Roberto put an envelope of Benjamins into the glove compartment. Carlito reached under his seat, retrieved a small duffel bag, and tossed it onto Roberto's lap.

"We're straight now?"

"Yeah," Carlito said, nodding. "Hit me up if you need to

holla at me later." Looking over at Roberto, Carlito noticed his expression change, even in the dark. Just as Carlito sensed uneasiness in Roberto's look, a swarm of officers surrounded the car, including the DEA, FBI, Immigration, and Columbus police. Roberto jumped out of the car.

"Motherfucker!" Carlito shouted and hit the steering wheel.

At the cash register of the Swifty Mart, Julio dropped a twenty onto the counter. He looked over the impulse items, grabbed a pack of gum, and laid it by the coolers. "Shit," he heard someone behind him say. He turned around and saw that the man standing behind him was looking outside toward the parking lot.

Julio followed his gaze and saw a posse of cops covering Carlito's car. Four suits were running toward the front doors of the store. Julio took a deep breath, stood his ground, and waited for the apprehension. He slowly turned around as the undercover agent pointed a weapon in his face.

Black watched the excitement like he was at the movies. Cops were everywhere. They had punk-ass Julio's face so far down in the pavement Black couldn't even see his nose. A pimple-faced rookie cop placed yellow safety tape around the telephone poles to block off the crime scene as a crowd began gathering.

Two detectives placed Carlito in an unmarked police car and locked the doors. A manly-looking female cop in plainclothes who wore her cop badge proudly on her suit jacket questioned him through the window.

Crowds of teenagers and a few elderly people gathered round to watch the excitement as the traffic on the busy street slowed to a complete stop. Black decided to pull off, and he got stuck between a Sun TV furniture delivery truck and a COTA public transportation bus.

Black was forced to creep by the scene just as a cocky detective was roughly placing Julio in the back of his police car.

He could hear the officer say, "We finally got your ass, Julio. You belong to us now."

Julio's eyes locked with Black's, meeting face-to-face through the car windows. Black pointed his fingers at Julio in the sign of a gun as he passed. Julio returned the gesture and smiled a sinister smile at the young punk.

For a brief moment, a wave of fear spread through Black's body, but he didn't let his enemy see his fear. He sped away and thought about his plan B—getting to that fine-ass Tara.

Seventeen

The Great Escape

Tara woke from her drug-induced sleep and adjusted her eyes. Her eyelids stuck together from the day-old mascara and dried tears as she sat up on the bed. The room was a mess and she couldn't find the phone. She began to panic, ripping through the covers, and then she heard it hit the floor. She picked up the phone and dialed Karen's number and prayed she'd answer.

"Speak, and it better be good. It's eight in the morning and I need my beauty sleep," Karen warned into the phone after she had snatched it from the nightstand and placed it close to her ear.

Tears ran down Tara's face at the sound of her friend's voice. "Karen, I need you. I need you, friend, to come over now. Julio's been arrested and I'm scared," she cried in the phone as she fell back on the bed.

"Don't move, and don't answer the door for nobody; I'm on my way," Karen instructed Tara while she slipped into her jeans and searched for her purse and keys.

"Hurry, friend, I need you," Tara begged.

"I'm on my way."

Tara got up to take a shower and then she began straightening up the bedroom. The room was cluttered with balled-
up tissues and pillows from her bed. The smell of stale
Newport cigarette smoke lingered in the air. The thick, floral
drapes were closed tightly and the room was dark.

Tara opened the heavy drapes and turned on the clock
radio on her dresser to the local gospel station. Kirk
Franklin's "Stomp" blared through the small speakers.

She returned the pillows to the head of the bed, gathered the crumpled-up tissues, and tossed them into the
trash. The tissues fell from the top of the pile of other
trash already filling up the trash can.

Damn, this room is dirty, Tara thought as she headed downstairs to get a garbage bag. Picking up the turned-over
chair in the hallway, she returned it to its place. Tara's
eyes beamed in on the antique claw-foot ivory table, and
there shining up at her sat her wedding ring. Next to the
ring was a note from Julio that simply read, *I love you,
mami.* He'd written the note while she was playing tough
bitch with her man.

Tara gasped and cried as hot, salty tears spilled onto her
pink camisole. All of a sudden, she heard a loud thud and
bang that sounded as if the front door had just been
kicked in.

Peeking over the banister, she saw Tee's friend, Black,
coming through the front door. He was dressed all in
black, with a Mac 10 drawn. Tara thought about running
to the room and retrieving the gun Julio kept in the dresser
drawer next to the bed. But tears still burned her eyes
from reading Julio's note. She also thought about what
would happen if she fired shots at Black but missed.

Don't get it twisted; she wasn't no punk. She could go
toe-to-toe with the best of them, but she never had to

shoot anybody. She wasn't sure she could; the shit was too final. Life was too important.

So she decided to just hide. Her legs shook as she tiptoed to her walk-in closet and squeezed behind the neatly-hung pants and skirts that lined up, one after the other, on the double-hung pole in the spacious closet.

Tara placed the oversized shopping bags from her favorite stores at City Center Mall over her feet and held her breath.

Through the speakers, Kirk Franklin sang of the joy of the Lord as Black entered the bedroom. Glancing around the room, looking for Tara, Black tiptoed across the plush carpet.

"I know yo' fine ass in here somewhere," Black taunted, peeping in the master bathroom. "I'm going to find yo' ass. My dick is getting hard just thinking about all the things I'm going to do to you," he threatened, moving toward the closet door.

All of a sudden, Tara heard another sound; the sound of her best friend calling her name. "Tara! Tara! You upstairs?" Karen screamed, running up the stairs once she saw that the door had been kicked in.

Black ducked into the bathroom and exited through the door that led to the spacious hallway. Simultaneously, Karen entered the bedroom with her .45 in her shaking right hand.

Black escaped down the stairs and out the front door. He wasn't sure if the bitch Karen was alone or not. He couldn't take that chance, so he bounced.

His plan was to have a little fun with the dime piece; he didn't have time for no petty drama. He had bigger fish to fry. There were some crackhouses he needed to pay a visit before word reached the street that the almighty Julio got popped.

The phone rang loudly, causing the two friends to jump. Tara crawled from the closet and answered the phone. The automated recording from the correctional facility came on as soon as she picked up the phone. "Hello! Hello!" she screamed, hoping it was Julio.

After the prompts were finished, Julio's voice came over the phone. "Hi, baby, how are you?" he questioned, pacing back and forth in front of the concrete wall that housed the inmate phones. He only had a few minutes to tell Tara so many things; he barely knew where to start.

"Baby, the house was just broken into by that nigga Black while I was in here," Tara cried into the phone as she got up from the floor and sat on the bed for just a second, before hopping up to get her suitcases from the hall closet.

"Fuck no," Julio yelled at the top of his lungs, punching the wall.

"Baby, I'm okay, but I'm getting the hell out of here. I'm not staying another minute in this house," Tara shouted into the phone as she stuffed clothes, pictures, and personal items into the suitcases.

"Tara, listen to me. I don't have long to talk. That bitch Black was there when we got arrested. I need you to get somewhere safe and keep your cell phone on. I'm going to call you through a three-way from now on. My visiting days are Sunday and Thursday. We'll talk when you get here on Sunday.

"I love you, baby. I'm handling things from in here; all I need you to do is take care of yourself. I want you to go to your mother's and stay there until things calm down," Julio instructed anxiously.

"I'm not going to my mom's. Her house is like Grand Central Station, and if I go to my grandparents', I will go crazy with them treating me like I'm two years old. I'm going to check into a hotel and try and get my head right.

"I'm okay, baby; don't worry about me. I'll be there on Sunday. When do you go to court?" Tara questioned while Karen helped her move the suitcases to the hallway.

"I don't know yet. I talked to Attorney Watson, and he's on his way down here to try and see if he can get me a bond. He said for me not to get my hopes up, but it's worth a shot.

"I love you, Tara. I'll call you later tonight. Somebody wants to use the phone," Julio explained, leaning against the wall.

"I love you too, Julio. I will be waiting for your call," Tara whispered, trying her best to be strong for her husband.

Before she could say anything else, the phone went dead. There was so much more she wanted to say, but she trusted Julio would handle things, even from inside.

She wanted to curl up in a ball and cry, but there was no time for that. She needed to get far away from this place, the place that had been her home.

The two friends loaded some of Tara's belongings along with Julio's stash of cash and product into her car. She wasn't leaving her shit behind; they'd have someone pick up Karen's car later. Tara did a final walk-through of the house before they prepared to leave.

"This shit is crazy, Karen. I mean, how do you go from feeling completely safe to not knowing what tomorrow is going to bring? What am I going to do without my baby?" Tara questioned as she stood in her beautiful living room staring at all their expensive things.

"Girl, we are going to make it. We are survivors; we always have been. You know I'm here for you, and together

we gon' get through this," Karen told her friend, hoping
to lift her spirits as she hugged her tightly.

"Let's get the hell out of here. I need to get somewhere
safe and get my head right. I'll be able to think more
clearly once I calm my nerves," Tara explained.

"You have some product?" Karen asked eagerly as Tara
locked the front door to her home after they exited.

"We got enough product to last us for months," Tara announced, getting into the car and starting the engine.

Tara slowly backed the car from the driveway. She
stared at her home for a long while before pulling off. She
knew deep inside she would probably never live in peace
in the home she shared with her Julio again. From the
moment they moved into the beautiful suburban dwelling,
Tara felt she was living someone else's life, and now the
fantasy was over and only God knew what the future held
for the two of them.

Eighteen

How Can I Ease the Pain?

Tara checked the deadbolt on the steel hotel room door for the third time. Confident the room was secure, she took off her shoes and began to relax a bit. She could hear the sound of cars rushing by on the nearby highway as she closed and locked the patio door.

She pulled the thick burgundy curtains back and stared into the night. She could see the shiny cars speeding by, heading to their destinations. Tara closed her eyes and wished one of the cars coming toward the hotel had Julio inside.

This had to be a dream. She would wake up from this, and Julio would be calling her, asking if she needed anything before he raised up out the streets and jetted home to her.

She missed him so much, her body ached for him. She did not know how she would survive this. For the past year and a half they'd spent most of their time together. Just the two of them against the world. Julio was her life. She couldn't breathe without him. How would she go on?

Tara slid down to the floor and cried uncontrollably. Her whole body shook. She wanted to fix this, to do something to change it. There had to be something she could do, somebody she could call.

She'd call her dad. He'd know what to do, Tara thought, getting up from the floor as she wiped the salty tears from her puffy eyes. She pulled her cell phone out of her purse, sat on the couch, and dialed Slim's number. As the phone rang, Tara tried to hold back her tears, but she couldn't swallow the knot in her throat.

The phone stopped ringing and she heard someone lifting the phone to their ear. "Hello," Slim answered. He was sitting back in his favorite chair in his family room. The sound of his voice on the line made Tara feel even more alone.

"Daddy," Tara cried into the cell phone as tears spilled from her sore eyes.

"Baby girl," he said warmly and switched the phone to his other ear.

"I need your help," she said in almost a whisper, trying to control her weeping.

"I'm already working on it for you," he said. "I got the word an hour ago and I been all over it. I done had people at both your spots looking for you. I've been worried sick. Are you all right?" Slim questioned his child.

"Yeah," Tara replied, exhaling deeply to calm herself. "I need to call Julio's attorney and—"

"Don't worry about that, Tara. Just take care of yourself," Slim said. "Everything's gonna be all right. You doing all right, baby? I don't like hearing you like this."

"I'll be all right," Tara said, more to reassure herself than Slim. "I just got spooked earlier. That young boy Black kicked my door in."

"Black, huh?" Slim said contemplatively. "Yeah, don't

worry about that, either. Karen called and filled us all in on his shit. I got something for him. I'm gonna send Tee and the boys to take care of him."

Tara felt better already. She felt like her old self, sitting on the side of the plush designer comforter. Slim's calm, even tone let her know he was calling the shots and giving orders on the street.

"Baby girl, you know your mother is worried about you. I want you to call her. I know you want to handle your own business and shit, but there's some shit you have to seek wise counsel on. That's what experience is for: to keep the next one from slippin'. You young folks need to learn that lesson," Slim taught over the phone.

"I hear you, Daddy," Tara said with a small laugh. She wiped a tear from her eye.

"Don't hear me, feel me," Slim stated. "That shit is hard as hell; to watch somebody you love lay it down and you want to save them. The game ain't fair like that, Tara. Keep ya chin up and let ya old man handle this shit.

"I'll call you tomorrow. Be ready to spread about five grand around town to see what we can get dropped on the state side. The feds is another story.

"Get some rest. Your old man got everything under control," Slim concluded with his daughter and hung up the phone.

Tara hit the off button on her cell. She set it on the nightstand and at the same time reached for a tray with fine lines of coke. Just then, the hotel room door opened and Karen entered wearing a red dress and matching heels.

"This hotel is poppin' tonight," Karen said as she sat on the couch next to Tara and started to fix a strap on her shoe.

"Where you going with your catching dress on?" Tara questioned Karen, handing her the tray of white powder.

"I know you need some alone time to get your cry on and your emotions straight. I'm going to go downstairs and see what's up," Karen said.

"I need to check out the surroundings. You should take a bath and chill, girl. Shit, that Jacuzzi tub ain't no joke. I could have stayed in that bitch all night. There's some bath salts in there that make your skin feel like silk." Karen set the tray on her lap, leaned forward and snorted a line of powder into both of her nostrils. Instantly, she collapsed into the couch cushions and closed her eyes, forgetting her clubbin' plans.

Tara smiled and headed for the bathroom. As she waited for the tub to fill with warm water, she looked at herself in the full-length mirror that hung on the bathroom door. Standing on the cold tile of the bathroom floor, she wrapped her arms around herself for a moment and wished that they were Julio's arm.

Remembering Slim's words, she shook off the feeling and slid into the soothing water. The water hugged her like a long-lost friend.

When Tara emerged from the bathroom an hour later, Karen was checking her hair and reapplying her lip gloss.

"Girl, I thought you'd given up on going out," Tara said, closing the bathroom door.

"I need to get some air, and it will give me peace of mind to check things out around here. Julio will kill me if I let something happen to his boo," Karen teased, lightening the mood.

"I was spooked earlier, but this spot is out of the way. I feel safe here. Julio used to call this spot our little secret. I'm going to lie down in a minute and try and get some sleep," Tara explained.

"I ain't going to be gone long. Get your cry out and get some sleep. You don't want to have bags under your eyes when you go see Julio on Sunday. Yo' shit is getting a little puffy," Karen said, looking at the swelling under Tara's eyes.

The two had always been there for each other, in every situation. Karen knew that she could depend on Tara, and her girl knew she could count on her to return the favor. They were ride or die. That's how they were schooled by the old vets in the street.

"I know, girl. I've got to man up and stop crying like a soft-ass bitch," Tara sang in her strongest voice.

"Now that's what I'm talking 'bout. They ain't never been able to keep us down. We just got to get reloaded. We got this," Karen shot back, pushing her shoulders back as she pimp-walked to the door.

Tara laughed and threw a pillow at her. It hit the door and fell to the floor just as Karen closed it and left. She wanted to cry, but she fought back the tears. She had to stop crying. She knew shit was fucked-up and she just wanted to stop thinking about it for a minute.

Tara reached for her medicine and snorted two fat lines into each nostril. She could feel her heart beat through her chest and she could hear each beat in her head.

She moved to the bed and lay flat on her back, staring at the starlike patterns on the ceiling, until they began to move to the heartbeats in her head.

Damn, I'm fucked up, she thought, curling up in the bed like a small child and pulling the covers over her eyes.

She closed her eyes tightly, willing herself to sleep. Her dad knew the system well. He kept the best lawyers on his team, and they kept judges in their pocket. If Julio's case was beatable, Slim would find a lawyer who could beat it.

Fuck, her mother would kill her if she didn't call her and let her know what was happening herself. By morning, the word would hit the streets that a soldier was down, and there would be ten different stories about what went down. Her high was lifting, so she called her mother.

Tara got comfortable in the bed and prepared for all the questions her mom would ask. The phone rang once and M&M's voice came through, loud and in charge.

"Hey, Mommy," Tara whispered after hearing her mother's voice. The sound of M&M's voice soothed her, and she felt a warm sense of peace.

"Tara, why you wait so long to call me? I talked to Slim and he filled me in on everything. I done told you about always trying to be all up in a man's place. You never want to lean on nobody. You should be here with your family," M&M pleaded, pacing around the huge king-size bed in her bedroom. She was so worried about her daughter and hoped she could talk her into coming home.

"I'm sorry for worrying you, Mom. I just needed to be somewhere quiet and think for a minute. I'm going to chill here for a minute. I'm sleepy as hell, but I'm cool here. I will call you tomorrow," Tara announced, turning off the light on the end table. The room got instantly still and she lay back and relaxed.

"All right, but I want to see you tomorrow, so I can see for myself that you are fine. Get some sleep. Your daddy got people all over this shit. The feds had to have somebody on the inside to get that close to Julio and his crew. Them boys was too careful," M&M shared.

"Ma, I'm sleepy. I will talk to you tomorrow," Tara whined, wanting to get off the phone and get some sleep.

"Good night."

Tara woke from her much-needed sleep, rested and ready to take control of all the things that were going wrong in her life. Her cell phone was blowing up. She had messages from everybody.

Everyone assured her that they were handling what they needed to handle. Tee told her that all his posse was rolling on the Black shit. Slim left a message saying his lawyer was sure he could get a bond for Julio. Santiago promised all the paper she needed to handle any and all business.

She placed her cell phone on the end table and got up; it was hard leaving the comfort of the cozy bed, but she wanted to get the day started. She fled her home so quickly the night before that she left behind so many things she needed.

After listening to the messages on her phone, she made up her mind that she was going home. She was a hustler, a fighter; she wasn't going to let the motherfuckin' feds or some young thug run her from her home.

Tara peeked in the second bedroom to the hotel suite; Karen was passed out on top of the comforter, sound asleep. She looked so peaceful that Tara decided not to disturb her.

After taking a quick shower and getting dressed, Tara wrote her a short note, explaining that she was going to run by the house, pick up a few things, and swing by to see her mother.

It was a beautiful day, the sun shining brightly. The sun practically blinded Tara as she reached in her purse for her sunglasses, then she walked to her car. Getting inside, the familiar smell from the Italian leather seats filled her nose. The smell reminded her of all she had to fight for. She quickly started the engine and pulled from the lot.

Little kids rode their bikes up and down the sidewalk as Tara pulled her car through her neighborhood. Everyone she passed seemed so happy and it made her smile. It was a fresh new day; things were looking up. She would think positive.

Tara began turning onto her street when she was stopped immediately by all the backed-up cars. The cars were bumper-to-bumper. Everyone was stopped and looking in the same direction . . . at her house.

DEA, ATF, Immigration, and Columbus police swarmed the house. It was like a circus in her yard. There were two camera crews interviewing detectives on the lawn as they broadcast live.

Tara's entire living room contents sat in the yard like it was nothing more than lawn furniture. The feds took pictures and tagged items. Tow trucks were parked in front of the house to haul away their cars.

Columbus police officers made trip after trip inside and back outside, carrying all Tara's designer pieces to a separate U-Haul truck. Expensive suits, dresses, and coats could be seen with price tags still hanging from them, being loaded onto the truck. Each piece carried by felt like a piece of Tara's life being carried away.

Tara watched from her car as a skinny black female officer carried an armload of pieces from the house. She could see the slip from her wedding dress dragging on the ground.

Her heart broke as hot tears filled her eyes and spilled down her face. She sat there and cried until the car behind her blew its horn for her to move on. She inched slowly down the street.

She returned to the safety of the hotel and spent the rest of the day getting high.

It was hard as hell for Tara to get it together so that she could go visit Julio for the first time since his arrest. She did not know if she could get through the visit without falling apart. How was she going to be able to see Julio and not touch him?

She wanted to tell him that the pain of being without him was killing her. She wanted to pull some Bonnie and Clyde shit and drive her car through the doors of the county jail and bust her baby out.

All kinds of crazy thoughts ran through her mind as she applied a thick coat of Julio's favorite lip gloss to her full lips. She wore a clingy silk floral dress with strappy high-heeled sandals.

Tara exited the car without bothering to check her hair. She'd just left the salon and she knew her hair was on point. This was confirmed by the stares she got when she entered the packed waiting room.

The line to sign in was snaked around four times and it reached the entrance. The small room was cramped and hot. Metal chairs with chipped paint were bolted to floor along the wall. Each one was occupied, and some held two people.

Old ladies, girlfriends, babies' mommas, and sad-faced children waited patiently in line for their turn to visit. Tara took her place in line with them. At the front of the line, behind a thick sheet of bulletproof glass, sat one deputy processing the entire line. The deputy never got in a hurry, and no one else came to help with the massive line.

When Tara finally reached the front, her feet were killing her and her dress stuck to her from sweating. Annoyed, she pulled her ID from her purse and stuck it through the slot in the thick glass.

The deputy moved at a snail's pace, checking computer screens and some list with a lot of writing again and again before he finally wrote Tara a visitor's pass.

"Get on the elevator and take it to the sixth floor. Show this pass to the deputy on duty when you get upstairs."

Tara took the visitor's pass the deputy was extending to her and followed his instructions onto the elevator and up to the sixth floor.

Julio waited patiently inside the small visiting cell. He'd been waiting in the cell for over an hour to see her. He pulled some strings and got the deputy to pull him from the dorm early for his visit.

He wanted to see Tara the minute she stepped from the elevator. He missed her desperately and he needed to see that she was okay. It killed him not being able to be on the streets protecting her. He was confident his soldiers had her back, but was more concerned about her mental state. Being without her was killing him; he could only imagine what it was doing to her.

He knew she was strong; she was cut from the same cloth as him. She could survive anything, but at what cost? Before his arrest, he sensed that her drug use was getting out of control. He prayed she wasn't using it as her crutch to get through this shit.

The elevator doors opened and Tara saw a row of small booths; in the second one from the left side stood Julio. He looked just as fine as he did the first time she saw him. His hands were pressed against the glass as if he could touch her. Tara stared in his eyes as she floated to the booth and picked up the phone to speak.

"Hi, baby," Tara purred, placing her hand against his hand through the glass.

Tara looked beautiful; she looked sexy as hell. She glided to the booth like a goddess. Julio studied every sway of her hips. His dick got instantly hard. He wanted to fuck her right then and there on the dirty visiting room floor.

"Damn, baby, you look good as fuck. I love you," Julio shouted into the phone, rubbing his dick.

"I love you too, *papi*," Tara sang to her man, putting on her best tough act.

"Turn around and let me see that ass. I missed that sexy body. Let me look at you for a minute. Turn around, *mami*," Julio ordered in a serious voice.

She wanted to please him any way she could. She stood before him and struck her sexiest pose and twirled around slowly.

"We can talk about all the bullshit in a minute. Right now, I just want to make love to my wife, mentally, with my eyes. Let me inside your head, baby," Julio instructed, leaning against the steel bars that confined him in the small holding cell. Her man was locked inside a small cage. He could see her through a small glass window. There were six identical cages along the wall of the room.

Tara stared back at him, watching as he licked his lips and placed his hand under his shirt and rubbed his sexy chest. She closed her eyes and she could feel him touching her. Waves of heat swept across her body and centered in between her thighs. Her hand instinctively slipped inside her panties.

The thought of him inside her caused her body to respond, and she squeezed her thighs together tightly and reached an orgasm. When she opened her eyes, he was staring back at her, smiling.

Julio reached his orgasm the moment she first closed her eyes. He quickly pulled a wad of toilet tissue from his shirt pocket and cleaned himself. She had that effect on him. The thought of her moved him. He watched as pleasure swept across her face, holding that picture in his mind as Tara opened her eyes.

"I will love you forever. I want to be with you forever. I

need you to hold us down out there," Julio told his wife. "You got to keep it together. I appreciate the shit you had your family do for my case, but my family got they own lawyers and they good. I'm getting some answers on how this shit happened. I don't want you worrying about this legal shit or nothing else.

"You can breathe easy on that Black shit too; I got somebody all over it. I just want you taking care of you until I come home," Julio ordered, getting serious now.

"Don't worry about me, baby. I got this. I'm fine. You're the best thing that ever happened to me, and I ain't going to fuck that up, trust me," Tara said, trying to convince herself of that fact as well as him.

Julio was being charged with five counts of conspiracy. He was sure he could beat those charges, but the feds weren't going to let him walk without him laying down for a minute on something.

He was prepared to give them a few years. Shit, he could do fed time with his eyes closed. He just needed to know that Tara was going to be there waiting for him when he raised from the belly of the beast.

The lovers shared their thoughts and soaked in each other's presence as long as possible. Against their wishes, the young, handsome deputy took his feet off the rusty steel desk and motioned for Julio to end the visit.

"Okay, Turner, I'm coming," Julio shouted, annoyed his visit had to come to an end.

"Promise me that whatever happens, you won't forget how much I love you; how good we are together. Promise me you will come home to me, Julio. Promise me. I need to know you will come home to me," Tara pleaded as tears streamed down her face.

"Nothing in this world or the next can keep me from

loving you and coming back to you. You're mine, always," Julio vowed, holding up his wedding ring finger and kissing the band.

The young deputy unlocked the cell and led Julio away to his dorm. He glanced over his shoulder at Tara the entire time. When he was just about out of her sight, he winked at her and blew her a kiss with his lips.

"Damn, your girl is fine," the young deputy complimented, leading Julio away.

The two friends spent weeks in the hotel room getting high and blocking out the world. They ordered room service for breakfast, lunch, and dinner. Some nights they would party at the hotel lounge and flirt with the white boys until the wee hours of the morning. They were spending money like there was no tomorrow.

Karen suggested they hit a lick at one of the malls in the area. She begged Tara to go back to work with her, but Tara wasn't ready for running up in them stores. Her nerves were shot to shit. All she needed was to fuck around and catch a case.

She needed to get her bank right, and that meant a trip to her mom's house. She knew she could count on M&M to help her out. She'd thought about calling Santiago and getting some paper from him, but she knew that was being selfish. Nobody knew how much money it would take to handle all the shit Julio needed handling. He was facing federal charges. If he was going to walk on that shit, it was going to take some cash.

She'd gotten up early that day, showered and dressed, and she was now on her way to the safety of her family. She left Karen a note explaining she was spending the day with her mother.

Tara pulled her car in her mother's driveway; she was

surprised to see that the only other car in front of the house belonged to her mother. She put her car in park and turned off the engine. She quickly got out of her car and approached the front door. It swung open, and M&M stood before her, dressed in a velour burgundy floor-length robe with gold buttons. Her mother looked like royalty standing before her.

"Hi, baby. I was just opening my curtains to let some light in on my plants and I saw you pull up," M&M said, hugging her daughter tightly while she kissed her cheeks.

Tara felt like a little girl wrapped in her mother's arms. She closed her eyes and enjoyed the moment before she let go and entered the house.

"It smells good in here. What you cooking?" Tara asked, following her mother from the living room.

"I was back in here making me some breakfast. Pour yourself some coffee. The biscuits should be done in a minute and we can eat," M&M explained, checking the oven.

"Where's everybody?" Tara questioned, sitting down at the kitchen table.

"Rabbit been rolling shotgun with Slim for the last few weeks. Things been so crazy in the streets that I ain't felt like being bothered with no bunch of company running in and out of here," M&M said with a worried look on her face.

"What's wrong, Ma? You look worried," Tara asked her mother, concerned by the look on her face.

"I'm worried to death about a lot of things; shit ain't like it used to be. You used to be able to trust people. You paid your dues and niggas respected that. They respected you and yours. Now these thirsty young thugs is just taking over with no honor or respect for the game."

"I know, Ma, the game has changed; it's a new day in the street. Shit fucked-up. I guess you heard about Roberto setting Julio and them up."

"Ya, I heard. Do Julio know what happened? I thought Roberto was his boy," M&M asked with a puzzled look on her face while she pulled the biscuits from the oven and placed them on the table next to the bacon and scrambled eggs.

"The dirty-ass feds had the nerve to put them all in a holding cell together. Carlito almost caught a murder case trying to get at that nigga. Carlito had to be isolated from the snitch.

"Julio laid low and let him feed him information. Roberto swears he didn't know Julio was going to be there that night. He claims they forced him to give them Carlito or he was going to be facing some stupid crazy time. He says he was trying to warn them that night, but they didn't catch on. I don't know who or what to believe. Julio feels the same way."

"You can't trust nobody but family. I want you to come home and stay with me until we have more answers. It won't be long before Slim get the answers he looking for and we know what we dealing with," M&M responded, sipping her hot black coffee.

"Ma, I know you want me here, but I need to stand on my own two feet right now. I got to do this for me. I have to deal with the fact that Julio might not be coming home for a while. I need to get him out of my system. I can't just come home and stay stuck. Let me do this my way," Tara pleaded with her mother, putting a warm, buttery biscuit in her mouth and savoring the taste.

"What do you need me to do for you? How can I help you? I want you to be strong. You have to be, to live the life we've chosen.

"I never wanted this life for you, Tara, but you craved it for yourself. It ain't easy losing something you want to hold on to so badly. You just got to trust that it will work itself out and what's meant to be will be. That's the only way I been able to be with your father this long."

"I feel you, Ma, I do, but it's gonna take me a minute to bounce back from this hurt. I ain't never loved anybody this hard before. I just need you to understand me and be here for me.

"I'm kind of short on paper right now. Can you help me out with the hotel while I decide what I'm going to do next?" Tara asked her mother as she watched her clear the kitchen table.

"You know I got you with some ends. I've got a suitcase full of pieces back there I was going to fence off to my new fence man. You can take those too and sell them in your spare time. They all fast movers, and you can get half price for everything in the bag. Just bring me a fourth and you can make the rest," M&M offered her daughter, trying to be helpful.

"I'll take them, but I probably won't get around to selling them until later in the week."

"That's fine; just bring me my paper when you sell them. Here, eat this last little bit of grits, there's no sense in me putting this little bit in the refrigerator. You need some meat on your bones. Have you been eating?"

"Ma, I been ordering room service and eating hotel food. I'm fine. I needed to lose a few pounds anyway."

"You don't need to lose nothing. Men like women with some meat on they bones. Why you think men walkin' off leaving women every day? They ain't got nothing to hold onto, that's why. How you think I kept the same man so long? I keeps him fed, happy, and I give him something to hold on to every day." M&M laughed as she wiped off the kitchen table.

"I'm going to run and get the pieces. You want me to get your purse too?" Tara asked, getting up from the table.

"Yeah, and bring the newspaper on my bed. My purse is sitting on the floor next to the bed."

Tara left the kitchen and headed to her mother's bedroom. The house seemed so peaceful. For a moment she thought about staying there and letting her parents pamper her and treat her like their baby.

She wasn't a baby, though; she needed to chill for a while and clear her head. The only way to do that was to get high and block out the world. *I won't be able to do that here*, she thought as she stood in the doorway to the bedroom before she closed the door quietly.

"Ma, I know you ain't put another new chair in your bedroom. It's starting to look like Mama Grace's house in here," Tara teased her mother, joining her in the living room.

"That's a five-thousand-dollar chair. I bought that chair and those three lamps by the closet door from that dope fiend, gay-ass Miss Sugar, last night for two hundred dollars. I wasn't about to pass up that deal. Even if I had to put the shit on the roof, I was getting it."

"Here's your paper and your purse. I ain't foolin' with you, Ma."

"You got to fool with me. I'm the only one that will get you told. I'm gon' let you do you; just don't lose you while you doing you," M&M taught, handing her a couple thousand dollars.

"I love you, Ma. I'll call you in a few days," Tara said, kissing her mother. She scooped up the suitcase and bounced from the house.

M&M stood and walked to the picture window and watched as her baby daughter hurried to her car. A chill swept across her soul. Her gut told her that her daughter was headed for a trouble she couldn't spare her from; she had to go through it to get to the other side of it. She whispered a prayer for her baby girl while she drove away.

Nineteen

Can You Handle It?

Tara sat at the small table at the Red Roof Inn and studied the clear sandwich bag that held the last of her precious crystal powder. She barely had an eight ball left inside the crumpled bag. She started out with two ki's of cocaine and now this was all she had left. She'd long since moved from the plush accommodations of the Marriott suites, and now the budget motels along Dublin Granville Road were her home. Now Tara lived from motel to motel. She stayed high, and the days drifted into each other.

Julio had Santiago stop paying the rent on her old apartment because she refused to stay there. She didn't feel safe in the apartment because no one could find Black. She'd been trying to reach Santiago for days, and he wasn't returning her calls.

"Girl, ain't no sense in studying that bag like you can wish the drugs back in the bag. The shit is gone, so get over it," Karen told Tara. "The way I see it is you either face the fact that the fantasy life is over and we got to get our hustle back on, or you can keep daydreaming," Karen said, spreading the dingy, ugly comforter over the double bed that sat side by side with its twin.

"I don't know what we gonna do. We're almost out of money and product, and the room rent is due too," Tara complained, getting up from the table.

"Can't you borrow some money from your mom and dad?" Karen suggested.

"That's not an option. I took a load of my mom's pieces to sell for her. I sold them and I didn't take her the money. I went by Alan's place yesterday and he told me my dad was looking for me and he's mad as hell," Tara explained, pacing back and forth over the worn carpet.

"Aw hell no, Tara. You know your mom don't play. I hope she don't think I was in on that shit. Damn, Tara, I don't want M and M mad at me," Karen whined nervously.

"Do you think I want her mad at me? It is what is it is, so stop whining and help me think," Tara ordered as she took the sandwich bag from her pocket and quickly took a one and one.

"Ain't shit to think about. We gonna have to put our girdles on and go back to work. You keep snorting that pow der; wasting most of it. If we cook it up and smoke it, we'd be able to make it last a lot longer," Karen announced, getting up and looking out the window.

Cooking the product would reduce it to its purest form taking it from cocaine to crack, and then they wouldn't have to use as much.

"I ain't fuckin' with no crack," Tara shot back.

"Cocaine is cocaine; smoked, snorted, it's still a drug. It's just purer when you cook it," Karen explained to her friend.

"How much you think we can make off this?" Tara asked, holding up the sandwich bag.

"Girl, we can make enough to sell and pay for the room

for the rest of the week, plus have some for ourselves to smoke," Karen answered, studying Tara for a response.

Tara thought about what her friend said. She was right; a drug was a drug. Crack couldn't be any worse than powder, and she'd been snorting the powder and she was fine. She was handling that shit as far as she was concerned, and didn't have a problem.

She wasn't quite ready to run back in and out of them stores boosting. Her nerves were shot, and if she could make some money and get high, it would give her more time to think about her next move. She needed time to get her head right before Julio's next visiting day on Sunday. She'd missed his last few visiting days, so busy getting high, and she promised herself that she'd make this one. Her cell phone had been turned off for a week now, and she knew he was going to be pissed when she saw him.

"Do you know how to cook it?" Tara asked Karen, sitting back down at the table.

"Hell yeah. Jay taught me that shit last year," Karen said, jumping up and getting her equipment from out of her purse.

Tara studied Karen closely as she skillfully pulled out everything she needed from her purse and began to cook the powder in a small glass vial. When Karen was done, she removed a yellowish, sticky, egg-shaped ball from the vial and laid it on the table to dry.

Once the ball was dry, Karen broke off a small piece and anxiously placed it on her crack pipe and lit it. Karen closed her eyes and inhaled deeply. She then handed the pipe to Tara.

Tara took the pipe and studied it closely. Her mind told her she was making a bad move, but her body willed her to do it, and so she did. The rush of the drug was like no other, like a mind-blowing orgasm that moved through her body like electricity. She slid from the chair and lay on the floor.

"Girl, you all right?" Karen questioned, jumping up and rushing to Tara's side.

"Hell yeah, I'm all right. That shit is good as hell," Tara said, laughing as she rolled around on the floor. Karen joined Tara on the floor and they both took another hit.

Twenty

Every Day I'm Hustlin'

Jay stood on the wooden balcony of his yellow duplex home looking up and down the street. Patience was not a strong suit of a smoker. Jay was not only Karen's baby brother, but he was a professional smoker. He was famous in the hood for being the best crack cooker in the city. He could cook up a perfect batch of cocaine, high or sober, day or night. Dope boys would come from miles around for Jay's services. They would get him straight with product for him to smoke, so he stayed high. There was always traffic in and out of Jay's spot. He was known by everybody in the hood as Cookin' Jay.

"I don't know what the hell is taking Rodge so long," Jay said to Tara as she joined him on the balcony. Rodge was a seventeen-year-old high school dropout with heart. Dropping out of high school was a big mistake, but he had too much pride to go back. He'd tried getting a job, but each time a good job came along, they always asked the same question: "Do you have a high school diploma?" So slinging crack was his claim to fame.

"You think you should call him again?" Tara asked as she sat down on the worn-out black leather sofa that sat against the wall.

"I already did, and he's not answering. I don't know why that boy got a cell phone; he never answers the thing," Jay complained, joining Tara on the couch as they both looked up and down the street.

It was a beautiful spring day and people were everywhere in the hood. Cars sped up and down the street as the pair studied each one.

"Jay, where the fuck is Rodge?" Karen yelled from inside the house.

"I wish I knew," Jay yelled back.

Just then, Rodge pulled the Ford Escort he'd rented from a crackhead onto Jay's street and parked. A person could get anything they needed with a pocketful of rocks. Smokers would rent out their car, house—shit, even they kids—for that shit.

Rodge's cousin had turned him on to slingin', and he was making a killing in the hood. He stayed busy. His phone was constantly blowin' up. As fast as Jay cooked up a sack for Rodge, it was gone. After he flipped this last package, Rodge planned to graduate to a half a bird. He went from buying eight balls to being ready to speak for a half a kilo of cocaine

"Here he comes," Tara announced, getting up and looking over the banister after spotting him.

Rodge got out of the car and waved up at Tara. He was a tall, dark-skinned, lanky kid with curly, jet-black hair. He was always flirting with Tara, and she used it to her advantage.

Tara could get Rodge to give her anything. He would stop what he was doing to service Tara. The bitch was fine, and she always kicked much game to a young buck.

Rodge never minded kickin' it with a vet. Plus, he figured if he kept sweating Tara, she would eventually holla at a brother.

"Karen, let Rodge in. Here he comes now," Jay ordered, getting up and rushing to get his pipe.

Tara grabbed her garbage bag full of pieces and removed the men's things she had inside. Tara made it a point of rolling up nothing but Nike gear when she and Karen hit Eastland Mall for the second time earlier that day. It was her first time back on the hustle, but boostin' was like riding a bike: once you learn, you never forget how to do it. She knew she could talk Rodge into taking everything, even if they weren't his size. Rodge was a mark, and she planned to use it to her advantage. He always bought everything and paid for it in high quality crack.

They each had two eight balls apiece, and they shared all they had with Jay.

The trio sat on the patio couch, high as fuck. They'd been smoking all day, and the sun was slowly going down in the hood. The sound of D'Angelo's sexy-smooth voice filled the air as Karen and Jay sang along to the music.

Rodge lay on the floor fast asleep, snoring, and Tara thought of their next move. "Hey, Jay, wake Rodge up and get us another hit on credit," Tara asked, getting up from her spot on the couch and standing over Jay.

"The little nigga want a piece of you, Tara. You ask him. He ain't gonna say no to yo' ass," Jay explained, staring at Tara.

"Okay, here's what I'm going to tell him: I'm going to ask him to give us a twenty piece. That I will pay him tomorrow as soon as I come from putting in work," she announced, looking at her friends, proud of her plan.

"If you tell him you gonna give him some of that, the little young boy will probably give you his whole sack," Karen teased, pointing between Tara's legs.

Tara got up and walked over to Rodge on the floor and shook him gently. He opened his eyes briefly and then closed them and went back to sleep. Tara sighed and shook him again.

"Hey, sexy, you ready to give a brother some of that?" Rodge asked, looking up at Tara as he rubbed his dick.

"Stop playin', boy," Tara ordered, slapping him on his leg.

"What's up, baby?" Rodge questioned sleepily.

"Let me get a twenty for all of us and I will pay you tomorrow when I come from working," Tara told the young dope boy. She stuck out her butt and licked her lips for added effect. Rodge's dick danced in his pants as he pictured himself on top of Tara getting his grind on. He wanted a piece of her bad.

"Rodge, you know Tara good for it. She gonna hit them stores up first thing in the morning and get you straight," Jay added.

Rodge pulled his sack from his jean pocket and carefully handed Tara three nice-sized rocks. "Here you go, boo. You owe me sixty tomorrow. I'll meet you over here to get my money," Rodge informed Tara, tying up the plastic bag and then stuffing it back in his pants pocket. He then pulled his arms through his T-shirt, wrapped his arms around himself, and curled up and went back to sleep.

Each of the smokers went to their separate corners and began smoking again. It did not take long before they were out of crack again.

Tara began cleaning out her purse, searching for some unknown discovery of crack. Karen bit her lip and cleaned her crack pipe while Jay devised yet another plan.

Jay sat on the white plastic lawn chair, studying Rodge's pants pocket until he could see just where the sack was located inside his jeans. He then left the room and returned quickly with a straightened-out wire coat hanger.

"Jay, what the fuck you doing?" Karen questioned her brother.

"I'm gonna rob this little nigga. He should know better than to get caught slippin' like this," Jay replied, bending a hook in the coat hanger.

"I ain't getting ready to be no part of this shit, Jay," Karen announced in a panic. She got up and went in the house.

"Wait, Jay, let's think about it first," Tara begged, moving around the porch nervously.

"Ain't shit to think about. We want to smoke and this little nigga laying here with a bag of rocks," Jay shot back.

"Okay, but whatever we smoke, I'm gonna pay him for tomorrow," Tara explained, studying Jay as Karen came back out onto the balcony.

Jay took the hanger and expertly fished the plastic bag from Rodge's pocket while the women watched intensely. When the bag was just about out, Rodge rolled over and stuck his hand deep in his pocket, pushing the bag back down inside.

"Damn!" Jay whispered, sitting back down on the couch.

All three of them stared at each other and began laughing. They laughed so hard and loud that they startled Rodge and he flipped over, removing his hand from his pants. The baggy came out with his hand all in one sweeping motion and flew across the balcony, landing in the corner. Rodge never even noticed it as he returned to his sleep.

Jay, Tara, and Karen could not believe their eyes. Tara quickly grabbed the bag from the corner and dished out two rocks apiece.

"This is all we're going to take. We're not going to smoke any more than we can pay for," Tara warned her friends with a very serious look on her face.

The three smoked until the wee hours of the morning before going back to sleep. Tara lay on one end of the couch, while Karen lay on the other. Jay slept peacefully inside.

Just before the sun came up, Rodge woke up and prepared to leave. Tara could hear him moving about, but she faked sleep. From the balcony porch, she could hear the front door close and Rodge walk to his car, then start the engine. Tara breathed a sigh of relief and went back to sleep as the sound of Rodge speeding up the street could be heard.

Later on that morning, Tara woke to the sound of kids playing on the sidewalk below. She wiped the sleep from her eyes and sat up on the couch. Karen was already awake and sitting up.

"Girl, I'm starving. We need to get something to eat. Let me go see what Jay's got in the fridge," Karen said, getting up and heading inside.

Tara sat on the porch and thought about the events of the night before. She knew she would have to make good on her promise to Rodge.

"Aw, hell no! Tara, come in here quick," Karen shouted from inside.

Tara ran inside as her eyes slowly adjusted to the darkness. The small living room was crammed but neat. Karen stood in front of a small twenty-six-inch black-and-white TV and listened closely to the anchorman.

"Known drug dealer and fugitive found shot to death in girlfriend's home," the anchorman said as a picture of

Black flashed across the screen. "Tina Robinson is being held and questioned in this case. It is believed that Tina is the sister of the victim's girlfriend. Police are also questioning Gloria Robinson in this case. This is believed to be a love triangle between two sisters. Coming up next on TV Ten news—" the anchorman could be heard saying as Karen turned off the TV.

Tara breathed deeply as Black's face danced before her. What a wasted life, she thought. She knew Black was the person who broke in their home that morning, and she knew with everything in her that he would have harmed her if he had found her hiding in the closet that day. But still, she could not help feeling sorry for the wasted life of another black male. Shit was getting real fucked-up in the game.

Tara walked back out onto the balcony and began to cry. She needed to change her life. She didn't want to end up like Black: a wasted life. She needed to stop smoking so much and get her life back on track. How in the hell did she get here? Sleeping on Jay's porch, smoking crack all night, and she hadn't been to see Julio in weeks. Her parents were so mad at her new lifestyle that they had all of their friends looking for her on the streets. Tara had to constantly move from place to place so she wouldn't run into anyone her family or Julio knew.

The last time she visited Julio, he questioned her so much about if she was or was not smoking that she could not take the pain and hurt she saw in his eyes. So she hadn't been back in a while. But this time, she would get a good night's sleep and go see her man.

Tara tightened the chocolate-colored, snakeskin belt to her $1100 Donna Karan pantsuit. She wore her best piece for her visit with Julio that day. It had been weeks since her last visit. Julio was furious with her. She hoped her appearance hid the fact that she was smoking, bad.

After waiting in the usual long-ass line at the county jail, Tara finally made it to the visiting room. She was confident she looked fine as hell. She knew once Julio saw her, he would forget he was mad at her.

Julio watched as Tara stepped from the elevator. He studied her up and down. Her appearance confirmed what he already knew: she was smoking. His wife was a crackhead. She was half her size, and she couldn't even look him in the eye.

Julio could feel a piece of his heart break. He felt helpless. He could control everything in the streets, but he couldn't control this. All his boys told him that she was smoking, but he didn't want to believe it.

Every time he questioned her about her smoking crack, she would beat him getting mad. She would cuss him out and hang up, knowing damn well it would take forever for him to call back. He would wait in the fuckin' phone lines for hours trying to reach her.

And worst of all, word on the street was she was kickin' it with a couple of young gangsters. How the fuck she just going to disrespect him? She was his fuckin' wife. He gave her his name. She was treating that shit like it didn't mean nothing.

Tara walked slowly to the small booth and picked up the phone on the wall. She wanted to die; the look in Julio's eyes said everything. She wanted to run from the room and never return.

The hurt in his eyes demanded that she stay. How did she begin to explain to him that she loved him deeply and being without him was killing her? How could she make him understand that being high on crack kept her from being consumed by the pain of him being gone?

"Hi, baby," Tara spoke quietly into the phone; she never took her eyes off of Julio.

"So, you finally found time to come see about a nigga?" Julio spat, staring Tara down.

Tara tried to fight back the tears that filled her eyes. "I'm sorry I haven't been to see you. It's been hard out here for me. I miss you so much," Tara tried to explain.

"Fuck, Tara, it's been hard in here for me. The only thing I asked you to do was take care of yourself. Do you know what worrying about you is doing to me in here? Do you? I got to depend on other bitches to hold a nigga down. What that shit look like and I got a wife? A wife, not no bitch I'm doing, a wife!" Julio shouted.

The deputy got up and walked to the holding cell and looked in. He could tell that the couple was having a serious conversation, so he left them alone with their problems.

"Julio, I know I hurt you. I'm sorry. I thought I could do this shit. I wanted to be strong for you," Tara cried, looking at him sincerely, hoping to reach him.

Julio's mind allowed him to drift to a place before all this madness. All he saw before him was the woman he loved, the woman he'd planned on spending the rest of his life with, being happy.

He wanted to break through the glass and hold her until she was safe and they were back at home.

"Tara, you need to get yourself some help. I've see women sell themselves, even their children, for that shit. You can't control it. Tara, do you see yourself? Everybody can tell you smoking," Julio pleaded with her.

"All you want to talk about is smoking. Damn," Tara shouted, annoyed. She hated all the questions, and she squirmed in the small visiting booth.

"Yo' ass still going for bad, ain't you?" Julio shot back. He was so angry with her for treating this shit like it wasn't nothing.

She was new to the drug. He knew where she was headed. It would either kill her or she'd end up in jail with him. He didn't want that for her, but he couldn't save her from where he was at. What she needed, he couldn't give her. So he decided to try tough love.

"I don't want a crackhead for a wife. When you decide you love me more than that shit, you holla at me. Until then, I'm cool on the visits. I got somebody that don't mind visiting a nigga," Julio spat as he banged on the bars to signal the deputy he was ready to return to his cell.

Tara watched through teary eyes as Julio walked from the room and never looked back. She was sure he would turn around at some point, but he did not. She took a few minutes to dry her eyes and straighten herself before she prepared to leave the jail.

Tara pushed the button for the elevator and it seemed to take forever. The ride down to the lobby seemed like an eternity. She wanted the hell out of there. She needed to get back to the hotel as soon as possible and smoke. That was her only escape from the madness of reality. A crackhead doesn't care if they are a crackhead when they are high on crack.

When the steel doors to the elevator opened, she came face-to-face with Candy and Julio's daughter.

Candy stared Tara up and down. The two rivals never spoke. Tara still scared Candy just a little bit. Candy used the opportunity to parade her baby momma status to the fullest.

"Word on the street was yo' ass was a crackhead, but I didn't believe that shit. Damn, you done fucked up now.

Julio ain't gon' never claim a crackhead for his woman. I knew it was just a matter of time before you was history," Candy spat, staring Tara up and down.

"You ghetto fabulous, stupid project chick, I will always be in his life. The nigga ain't gon' never be done with me. Oh, and did you forget I got his last name, you nothing bitch?" Tara shot back.

"I don't know why I'm even wasting my time talking to a crackhead. Fuck you."

Tara leaped at the back of Candy's head. She was grabbed from behind and led swiftly from the waiting room.

"Get your fuckin' hands off me. Get your fuckin' hands off me," Tara yelled, spinning around to see who grabbed her. She stared into the sexy green eyes of Scott.

"Calm down, baby girl. I'm just trying to keep you from catching a case at the jail," Scott whispered as he led her to his car. Once they were inside his truck, she began to cry.

"Good thing I was out here putting some money on my boys' books or a honey might have been laying it down for a minute on some petty shit." Scott said.

Scott pulled a fat one from the ashtray and lit it. He sucked in the smoke deeply and handed it to her. He watched her hands shake as she put the joint to her lips.

Damn, this fine-ass dime piece was going through some shit. One of his boys told him he'd seen her BMW in the hood at some questionable spots, but he didn't even entertain the thought that a vet like Tara was caught up.

Scott put his keys in the ignition and started the truck. He pulled from the parking lot of the county jail and headed for the freeway.

"Thanks for looking out for a sister," Tara offered once she calmed down and the jail was out of sight.

"How many times you done looked out for a brother;

you got that coming, boo," Scott said, reaching for her hand and holding it gently.

"Shit been crazy, Scott." Tara leaned back in the passenger seat and allowed it to hold her.

"I know. Let's just forget about it for a while and chill. You need to clear your head," he said, getting off the exit ramp to his house.

Tara sat back in the warm leather seat and thought about everything that just happened. Julio was done with her; she knew that bitch Candy would be laying in wait to move in. Fuck that bitch and fuck him. Why didn't he understand the pain was more then she could take? She needed her drugs. They were the only thing that eased the heartache.

She glanced out the window to see them pull into a carport in a large apartment complex. The apartments were brick with brightly painted green shutters. Everything looked clean and fresh. It calmed her.

"Where are we?" she asked, sitting up and looking at Scott.

"You need to relax. This is my spot, and you can crash here as long as you need to, no questions asked."

"Thanks. I really appreciate you looking out for me," Tara said, following him from the car into the apartment.

Scott's spot was surprisingly well decorated. She never took him to be the decorating type. The place was comfortable and manly. The living room was inviting, with brown and sea green furniture. A large bookshelf took up one whole wall. Tara was drawn to the books; she drifted to them.

All the books were by black authors, and there was shelf after shelf of books about the civil rights movement and slavery. She ran her fingers over the titles until she found one that caught her eye: *Convicted in the Womb* by Carl Upchurch

"That's a good one. I read it twice." Scott stood close be-hind her, peeking over her shoulder. She could smell the scent of his cologne; it tickled her nose.

"I didn't know you liked to read," Tara said, nervously moving away from him. She could feel his body heat and it made her uncomfortable.

"Like to read—shit, I love to read. I read all that shit. You got to school yourself or the motherfuckas will get over on you. Here, let me show you around. Bring your book," Scott instructed, taking her by the hand and lead-ing her upstairs.

His place was really nice. Tara was surprised by the warmth each room held. Once they reached the top of the stairs, a second side of him was revealed. The entire hallway was filled with African art.

"Wow, this is beautiful. Where did you get all these won-derful pieces of artwork?" Tara questioned, moving from piece to piece, examining each one carefully.

Scott sat down on the small hand-carved church pew that sat in the corner near the bathroom and enjoyed Tara's excitement over his collection.

"I've been collecting pieces for the last few years. I found this bench in an old secondhand store on Parsons Avenue. From the moment I saw it, I felt connected to it. It was like it was a part of me. I been trying to trace its his-tory, and that's led me to all these other pieces. A collec-tor in the short north told me it looked like some of Elijah Pierce's work," Scott shared with a serious look on his face.

Tara studied him while he spoke. The thug she knew was different, more mature than she remembered. He still had his swagger, but there was a man where a thug used to be. She joined him on the bench and listened to the ex-citement in his voice. He told her the story behind each of the pieces of art.

"I never would have thought my Harley-driving thug would be an art lover and a reader. Are you sure this is your place?" Tara joked, getting up and peeking in one of the closed doors.

"It's my place all right; I got a stack of bills with my name on them downstairs to prove it. A boy got to grow into a man sometime. It just took me a little longer." He laughed, opening up the door Tara was peeking in all the way.

"This is the master bedroom. The king lives in here."

The bedroom was huge: a king-size pedestal bed filled most of the room. African art accented everything; books littered the floor and both dressers. A full balcony could be seen through the sliding glass doors that took up much of the wall to the left of the bed.

"Your place is nice, Scott," Tara whispered, yawning.

"Come on, boo; let me show you the spare room. It's a cool spot with its own shower. You can freshen up and get some rest. You're straight here. We can talk about all the crazy shit that's been going down tomorrow."

The pair left his room and entered the guest room. The second bedroom was a lot smaller than the master suite but just as nice. A plush terrycloth bathrobe and slippers lay on the bed.

"All the bathroom items you need are in the closet next to the tub. Get some rest; we'll talk in the morning." He kissed her gently on her forehead and left, closing the door behind him.

Tara stood there stuck for a long while before collapsing on the bed. She lay there for what seemed like hours. She was mentally and physically drained. Her mind raced from Julio to Candy to Scott and back again.

She squeezed her eyes shut tightly. *Why won't the pain just stop? I need it to stop. Please, God, let it stop.*

She wrapped the terry bathrobe around her and then rolled up inside the comforter. She was so cold and empty; her body ached from all the pain. Staring up at the ceiling, she could hear Scott in the next room turn on the shower.

Did she need any more confusion in her life? Scott was the last person she expected to see today. He rushed in like a breath of fresh air. She could only imagine what would of happen if he hadn't been at the county today. The nigga was still fine as hell. He was doing good for his self.

Shit, she may have just found a new come up. She could kick it with him for a while. She didn't care how he was living like a square up in his cozy apartment; he was a dope boy through and through. He'd just mellowed out with his hustle.

The time she spent with him before Julio was all good. He was always a loving caregiver when they were together. She liked that in him. Not to mention the sex was good.

Tara rose from the bed. The room was dark. She felt her way to the light switch on the wall and turned on the light. She caught a glimpse of herself in the mirror on the dresser. She looked awful, her eyes were puffy and swollen and her hair was a mess. It stood straight up on her head. She looked like a clown; she couldn't help but laugh at herself.

Tara stared in the mirror. The taste of cocaine entered her brain. It flooded her body within seconds and she instantly began looking for her purse. Before her feet moved toward it, she remembered there were no drugs inside. She'd left her small stash with Karen. That shit was as good as gone by now and she knew it.

Fuck, what am I going to do? she thought, pacing the floor.

The sound of the water being turned off in the next room interrupted her thoughts. She would ask him for something. She knew he wouldn't want to give it to her, so she thought hard about what she was going to say to him. Each time she thought she had rehearsed her speech to perfection, she changed it. By four in the morning, she was so tired of thinking, she gave up.

She wasn't ready for all the drama that would come with asking Scott for dope, so she quietly called Karen on her cell phone. It took Tara a minute to convince Karen to come get her. She didn't even know where she was for sure.

"Girl, I'm just going to check one of his bills on the table downstairs for the address and then I'm bouncing. I remember passing a main street when we turned into the complex. I'll meet you up there. Once I get outside, I'll call you and let you know where I am," Tara instructed Karen.

"Yo' ass will ask a bitch anything. Damn, Tara, it's four in the morning. You better be glad I just came in my damn self. Call me back the minute you get outside. I'll be on my way," Karen ordered, hanging up the phone.

Tara crept from the bedroom and tiptoed through the hallway. She could hear music playing loudly from inside Scott's room. She paused outside his door and listened for the sound of any movement. All she heard was rap music, and she thought she heard faint snoring mixed in with the rap beat.

Her next moves were thought out carefully. She skillfully slipped from the hallway and down the stairs. Once she reached the bottom, she could see a lot easier. The light from the front porch flooded the foyer. On the table next to the door sat his mail.

Tara crept to the table and removed the letter on top. The crisp white envelope read: *Switch back to GEICO today and save BIG* in neon orange letters. Under the bold letters were his name and address.

Tara stuffed the envelope in her pocket and moved to the front door. *Please, please don't let him have an alarm system turned on.*

She thought hard about their arrival to his place and didn't remember seeing him set an alarm when they entered earlier. She took a deep breath, turned the lock, and then tried the gold doorknob. Turning the knob slowly, she pulled the front door open. She froze and waited for the sound of an alarm. No sound came, so she slipped from the house.

Twenty-one
Crackhead

Months passed and Tara's life was a mess. She was so strung out on crack that she was totally isolated from the real world and her family.

She woke that morning with the taste of rotten meat on her breath. Her eyes slowly adjusted to the darkness of the motel room. She'd been staying at this particular motel for about a month. There was so much constant drama in the hood that she made the decision to give the streets a break for a while. Every time she thought she'd found a dope boy she could kick it with, sit back on pause and smoke, the motherfucka would turn out to be a nutcase.

The last dope boy she fucked with messed around and got his feelings involved. He started thinking Tara was his woman for real. He thought he could tell her what to do. He was on some freaky shit all the time and he wanted Tara to go along with it. He kept trying to get her to go along with a threesome; she kept refusing. The day he came home with a video of a well-known crackhead prostitute sucking a dog's dick, she flipped. She bolted the minute the nigga wasn't looking.

Niggas in the streets were crazy and Tara wasn't trying to die for no crack. She knew how to stack her own paper, and she didn't need a nigga to give her shit for real. So she rolled solo; that way there was less drama.

Karen was her girl, but she lived for drama. Because she was so fine, niggas was always up in her grill and bitches were always trippin'. Shit was on whenever Karen was around. They'd been spending less and less time together.

The more she was alone, the more she enjoyed it. She could do anything she wanted, locked away in the cramped hotel room, getting high. Sometimes she'd get so high, her senses would be magnified. She would stand in front of the mirror and pick at the bumps on her face for so long her feet would get numb from standing in one spot. Other times, she would eat buckets of ice until her stomach hurt. Most every night she cried herself to sleep missing Julio.

Tara went days at a time without eating. The pure cocaine took her appetite. She would force herself to eat, which caused her to throw up a lot. When she was high, everything tasted like cardboard. Her weight loss was becoming very obvious.

She'd made it a point to pay Rodge back everything she owed him from that night over Jay's. She stayed in his good graces, and he would deliver to her anywhere.

Tara scanned the room, and her eyes locked in on her glass pipe, resting on the dresser. The events of the night before came into focus.

She'd been up all night smoking, and just before the sun came up, she got hungry. The only thing open that time of night was White Castle. Tara loved the cheap burgers, and she always managed to dig up just enough money to purchase her regular order.

She would spend almost her last dime on crack, but she kept enough money to get gas and something to eat. She never knew when she would need to make a run.

"Three cheeseburgers, an onion chip, and a large iced tea," Tara told the sixty-seven-year-old employee of the month with jet-black hair, who took her order at the drive-through window.

"Thank you kindly, sugar. Have a nice morning," the cheerful grandmother said.

Tara sped from the bright white building and headed back to the cramped room that she now called home.

She filled her stomach and returned to her spot at the small fake-wooden table with the hard red-and-purple matching chairs. She'd had a good day's work boostin' the day before and bought enough crack to last her for a couple of days with the money she made from selling her pieces.

She told herself when she first sat down at the table that she was going to make her drug last and she wouldn't be greedy. She had good intentions, but she didn't have good willpower. She stayed up all night smoking, and now she barely had a twenty rock on the table next to her pipe.

Tara skillfully broke the rock in half and placed the small yellowish piece of crack on the stem. She lit the drug and inhaled. The effect of the addictive drug was instant, and Tara was in the zone.

The room seemed bright, and everything looked magnified. She rose from her chair and staggered to the oversized mirror above the sink in the corner of the room. Tara stared at her reflection in the mirror and fixed her hair.

"Damn, my face is full of pimples," she said to herself as she began to pick at her face. She squeezed and picked at her face until her skin was bruised and sore.

Staggering back to the table, she retrieved her pipe and piled it up with the remaining pieces of crack. After inhaling the smoke into her lungs, she sat on the end of the bed and thought. She wanted more crack, but she only had about five dollars to her name.

She was tired, and she really didn't feel like driving far. She would have to put her girdle back on and go out. She would have to hit up one of the shopping malls close by. It was already late in the day; if she had any chance of getting in and out of the stores without any static, she'd better get moving.

Tara had all but worn out every spot in town. Most of the salespeople in her favorite stores knew her on sight. Most times, she spent hours trying to catch some new faces working in one of her regular spots before she could cop a few good pieces. She thought long and hard and then she mapped out a plan.

City Center was the closest mall to the motel, so Tara decided on that spot. She'd creep in the side door of The Limited, where they kept the expensive suits and dresses. If luck was on her side, she could be in and out in minutes without anyone noticing her.

Tara parked her car in the mall's enclosed parking garage. She checked her makeup in the rearview mirror before she exited the car. She didn't like going to work high, but it could not be helped. She needed some fast cash, and it was time to pay for her room again.

Satisfied that she looked fine, she swiftly made her way to the entrance of the mall. She was pleased to see that the parking garage was filled with cars. The more crowded the stores were, the easier she could be in and out without being noticed. Once inside, Tara blended in with the other mall shoppers.

The Limited was located on the third floor, close to the parking garage. Tara slid in the side door and quickly positioned herself behind the round display rack stuffed full with expensive suits. She glanced around the store to check the location of the sales staff. Lucky for Tara, all four salesclerks were busy waiting on customers. Tara skillfully selected five fashionable pantsuits from the rack and quickly ducked into the fitting rooms along the walls at the front of the store.

After trying two doors, Tara found one that was unlocked. *This must be my lucky day,* she thought, looking at all the merchandise someone had left inside the dressing room. She stuffed the five suits in her girdle and made room for seven of the silk dresses she'd stumbled upon in the dressing room. Her girdle was full, but she was confident that she looked cool enough to make it through the mall and back to her car. She checked herself one final time in the full-length mirror inside the dressing room before exiting.

The store had filled up even more with shoppers while Tara had been in the dressing room. People were everywhere. Two toddlers in matching purple short sets ran unsupervised in between the sales racks. Their mother chased them, but had no luck catching up with them. The teenaged sales clerk, dressed in skintight jeans and a T-shirt, did her best to come to the aid of the overworked mother as the toddlers knocked over a display table. Tara used this opportunity to make her exit.

Once out of the mall and safe inside her car, Tara removed her pieces from her girdle and placed them in one of the garbage bags she kept under the seat. Tara looked around the garage several times before she got out of the car and placed the garbage bag full of pieces in the trunk.

Hitting that quick lick gave Tara a rush. It had been so easy that she decided to make one more trip back in the store. She checked her reflection in the car window. She looked fine, but she could use a little lipstick. She quickly removed her tube of M•A•C Fetish lipstick from her purse and applied it to her lips.

Satisfied with her look, she headed back inside the mall. A handsome businessman in an expensive suit who was exiting the mall held the door for her as she entered. He gave her a friendly smile and swiftly made his way to the parking garage.

Back in the day, Tara would have used the brief exchange to collect a new phone number, but men were the last thing on her mind. She was focused on her plan, and there was no time for distractions.

Tara slipped back inside the side door of The Limited and repeated her earlier routine. Once inside the dressing room, she stuffed her girdle full of pieces and prepared to leave.

"Are you doing okay in there?" the store manager asked, knocking on the dressing room door.

"Yes, I'm fine," Tara shot back nervously.

Damn, where the fuck did she come from? Tara thought, glancing around the small dressing room. She grabbed two silk blouses and a pair of black dress slacks from the hook on the wall and opened the dressing room door. "These didn't work for me," she said, handing the garments to the store manger.

The two women locked eyes and froze for a moment. Tara recognized the store manager right away. It took the manager a few seconds longer to recognize Tara. The manager recognized the woman from the night a rack of leather coats disappeared on her shift.

"Would you like me to look for these in a different size for you?" the blond, short-haired, overweight manager asked Tara, taking the garments from her.

"No, thank you. I'm going to look around at a few other stores. I may be back later," Tara lied as she moved for the door.

"Good luck," the manager said, following her to the door.

Tara exited the store and tried her best to stay calm as she walked swiftly back to the parking garage. Once inside her car, a wave of relief flooded her body.

She backed her car from her parking space and moved to the exit ramp. She was so happy to be back in the safety of her car that she never noticed the store manager standing at the entrance to the mall, writing down her license plate number.

Twenty-two

Locked Up

"Trraayys!" Deputy Harris yelled, unlocking the door to dorm six.

Harris was a young black woman in her early twenties. She was a petite, cute girl who wore her hair cut short and close to her head. She prided herself in her appearance and made it a point to be fresh at all times.

She applied for the job at the Franklin County correctional facility because of the excellent pay, but the job had proven to be a source of entertainment and amusement for her as well. Deputy Harris loved hearing the creative street stories the women were always eager to tell. She would often spend the time after dinner making her rounds through the dorms, catching up on the latest gossip.

Every day was an adventure. The women and the stories were what she lived for. She was anxious to see what was going on in the dorm. Word had it they'd brought in some heavy hitters over the weekend along with some repeat visitors.

Hearing the sound of the squeaky wheels from the meal

cart, the women sprang from their places inside the dorm and headed for the door. The last meal of the day was seldom missed. Most of the meals served in the workhouse were unrecognizable and nasty, so the women stayed hungry up in the joint. Deputy Harris tried, whenever possible, to provide seconds to the pitiful crackheads and prostitutes that used the workhouse as a resting place before they headed back out onto the unforgiving streets.

"Deputy Harris, hook a sister up with some extras," a skinny crackhead said as she approached the doorway.

"Shorty, you know if I got it, you got it," Harris replied as she continued handing out the dinner trays. Her eyes scanned the door to see what new faces had arrived during the two days she'd been off. She was sharp on her feet and didn't miss much. She could peep a move by an inmate without having to think twice.

The two hookers at the back of the line thought she'd missed the pass-off of the contraband cigarettes. She didn't feel like dealing with the drama right then, but she'd handle it when she made her rounds later.

"Tara, is that you?" Harris gasped as she froze in her tracks. The woman standing at the door looked like Tara Moore somewhat, but the Tara Moore she knew was not a crackhead, and this woman definitely was.

The Tara she knew was always happy and laid-back. This Tara was sad and very visibly worried. Her drastic weight loss was a tell-all that she smoked crack . . . and lots of it.

"Hey, Harris, what's up?" Tara asked as she tried to avoid making eye contact with the deputy. Tara tried her best to act as if she hadn't noticed the shocked expression spread across Deputy Harris's face.

"I need to finish delivering trays, and then we need to talk," Harris announced in a concerned voice. "Take that contraband head scarf off your head before you come to this door," Deputy Harris continued as the other women made their way to the door to retrieve their meals. The skinny teenaged prostitute removed the ripped-up state sheet from her head and handed it to the deputy before getting her tray.

Tara took her tray and quickly reclaimed her seat with Cricket and Doretha, a gay couple she'd befriended her third night in the dorm. Cricket swore she knew Tara from the streets, and she tried her best to convince Tara of the same each time she woke from one of her crack comas. Tara slept straight through her first night in the dorm, and she barely remembered the second night.

Cricket was a tall, thin, light-skinned, gay girl. Her actions, conversation, and appearance were so much like a boy that Tara was constantly calling her "man." The girl was a fine-looking dyke.

"What day is commissary?" Tara asked Doretha as she silently hoped Scott kept his word and sent someone down to put some money on her books. She'd been arrested with $4.85 in her purse and a trunkful of pieces from City Center Mall.

She was only two exits from Scott's spot on Sixteenth Avenue when he called her and told her to meet him there anytime after seven that evening. He wanted her to kick it and spend some time with him that evening. He begged her to spend the day with him earlier, but she refused.

After she passed Scott's exit, Columbus's finest pulled her over. She was high as hell. It didn't help her case that her tags had been expired for over a year, either. The caked-up white-out over the original numbers looked like chipped paint. At that moment, she wished she had taken Scott up on his offer and exited the freeway to be with him.

The two of them spent two whole evenings naked in

bed after she finally made up her mind to call him a few weeks ago. Tara was surprised at how fast the old feelings they shared back in the day resurfaced.

Scott popping back into her life seemed to be just what she needed, although Tara didn't think she could ever feel anyone like she felt Julio. She'd wasted so much time trying her best to smoke away the pain her heart felt being without the love of her life.

She was so ashamed the day she ran back into Scott again, outside the Foot Locker at Eastland Mall.

Scott was dressed to kill as always, and his sexy gray eyes still pierced her soul. He still had a way of making her panties wet.

"Yo, Tara! Tara, slow up, baby girl. Is that you?" Scott yelled, catching up with her.

"Scott, what yo' sexy ass doing on the east side? You know you a north end nigga," Tara teased as the former lovers hugged.

"And you know this, but the east side was the only ones with a thirteen in the new Jordans, and I had to swoop me up a fresh pair. You know how we do," he said, patting his black-and-white Foot Locker bag.

"Where you running off to, baby girl? Can a brother get a minute?" he questioned, pulling her to a nearby bench. He wanted to question her about the night she ran out on him. He wanted her to know he understood where she was in her life right now. She looked so sweet and innocent standing before him, he just wanted to hold her.

"I was on my way to handle some business," Tara explained as she pushed the return receipts and cash deep into her jean pocket. Lazarus had just paid her six lovely twenties on two silk blouses she returned. Damn, she was glad she'd taken the extra time to make sure her appearance was right before she started her day.

She still took the time to look her best, even though she was spending more and more time smoking crack. She rarely left her motel room unless it was to hit a lick at some mall or make a crack run. She knew the people who really knew her personally would be able to tell she was smoking that shit.

Crack had become her lover and her friend. As long as she could feel the rush of the drug in her body, she didn't have to feel the pain of Julio being gone.

Tomorrow would mark a year he'd been in jail. He was now being held at the Pickaway County Jail in Circleville, Ohio, awaiting trial with the feds.

All she wanted to do was turn the hundred-dollar bill in her pocket into her precious drug, and post up in her room at the Red Roof Inn, get blowed, and not think about anything else in life.

"What you been up to? Where yo' fine ass being hiding?" Scott questioned as his cell phone started vibrating. He pulled his cell phone from his pocket, annoyed, and quickly checked the number.

"Here, Tara, take this number and get at me *tonight*. You hear me? I mean tonight. Don't let me have to hunt yo' ass down. You know I will. Yo' ass done walked back in a nigga's life and I plan on spending some time with you," he said, kissing her and handing her a professional-looking business card that read SOULJAH'S RECORDING STUDIO. He quickly got up to leave.

Tara watched him exit the mall and thought how fine he was and how bad she needed to just forget all the sad stuff. She looked at the number he gave her and stuffed it in her pocket with the money.

Tara called him that night, and the two of them ended

the night locked in a kiss on his king-size bed. The kiss freed her mind for a while. When he kissed her, she felt something. She hadn't felt anything with anybody in a long time. His kisses moved her.

"Tara, let me make love to you—real love, not that knockin' boots shit. Will you let me do that?"

"I need you to do that," Tara answered.

Scott was so gentle with her, the worries of the world slipped away. He wanted desperately to save her from herself. He lovingly undressed her completely; then he began kissing her naked body. He sucked at her left nipple before moving lower. She slowly parted her legs to allow him to please her more. What he really wanted was to be inside her. He climbed on top of her.

Tara lay beneath him, enjoying the pleasure he gave her body. He made love to her mind and her body. He stared into her eyes the whole time. Within minutes, the two of them came.

"Tara, I was young and dumb when I met you. A brother was trying to find his way in the streets, and you gave a nigga the time of day. I don't know what you been through and I don't want to know, but I need you to know that I'm here for you now. I won't go nowhere," Scott told her.

Tara's thoughts consumed her as she tried to make sense of her life. All she had was time to think, and she did, constantly.

"Girl, you just missed commissary. It was yesterday. Nikki, the girl in the gray pajamas, does two for ones and she shopped heavy yesterday. You want me to holla at her for you?" Cricket asked, wanting to please Tara. She knew who Tara's parents were, and she respected their position on the street. Cricket never knew when she would need to ask for a favor.

"No, I'm straight," Tara said, looking at the girl in the gray silk pajamas who lay across one of the only two single bunks in the overcrowded sleeping area that was packed full with women.

The girl named Nikki lay on the bed like she was royalty. There were two teenaged girls sitting on the floor beside her bunk, and they appeared to be hanging on to her every word. She'd never seen the girl before, but she knew she wasn't new to the game. Tara thought to herself, *Another coulda, shoulda, woulda session.*

"You gon' eat your mixed vegetables?" Doretha asked, eyeing Tara's tray.

"Yo' ass don't need no more vegetables. I swear I'm gone leave yo' ass if you mess around and get fat on a motherfucka," Cricket warned as she watched Doretha's double Dutch butt jiggle up and down as she walked to the door and placed their trays on the top of the stack of other dirty trays. The metal made a loud clanging sound as they settled into place on the floor, waiting to be picked up by the evening porters.

"Girl, I'm gonna take a shower. Watch the phones for me. I need to make a few calls when I get out," Tara explained to Cricket.

She hadn't bothered calling anyone other than Scott with her one free call. She knew when the police stopped her that she was booked. Tara was already on a probation bond from a case she'd caught at Kohl's department store.

Judge Nodine Miller told her, when she gave her the probation bond, that she better not appear in her courtroom again, for any reason, or she was on her way to the Ohio Reformatory for Women in Marysville.

Tara did her best not to think about her future. She could not wrap her mind around the possibility of going to prison. There had always been a way out. Her parents made sure of that for her. Julio made sure of that for her. But now she'd isolated herself from her family, and Julio was gone.

She crossed the cement floor of the dorm with a napkin-thin dingy gray towel and rock-hard bar of state soap in her hand, and headed for the shower. "Damn, shit in this bitch is still the same," she shook her head and said under her breath as she stared down the dykes in the dorm on her way to the showers.

There were so many young girls in the workhouse now. Most of the ones in the dorm were being used in one way or another by the old veterans who jailed for a living. There were dyke women that pimped new girls so hard, their family members and loved ones were putting money on their dyke girlfriends' books. Jail was one big hustle, just like the hood.

Tara placed her belongings on the three-foot-tall cement privacy wall as she undressed.

Although much thinner than usual, her body was still banging, and she soaked up her moment before she slipped into the metal shower.

These some dirty bitches up in this dorm. This shower is dirty as hell, she thought as she began washing herself with the hard bar of soap. She would have to lay down the cleaning laws first thing in the morning when the cleaning supplies were delivered.

Her mind quickly drifted to Julio. He was so far from her now, and it was all her fault. If she had not been so stubborn and hardheaded that night he was arrested, he would still be with her now and she wouldn't be locked up.

"Tara, stop trippin'," he'd begged her that night. *"Tara, stop trippin',"* she could hear him say.

Tara was startled from her daydream in the shower by the sound of Deputy Harris calling her name. "Tara! Tara!"

the deputy screamed over the sounds of the lukewarm water splashing against the metal shower walls. Tara peeked her head out the dingy shower curtain.

"Give me a second. I'm coming!" Tara yelled back, turning off the water and exiting the shower. She wrapped herself in her thin towel and walked to the orange steel door that confined the women in the dorm. "Why you yelling all loud, Harris? You see I'm in the shower. What you want?" Tara inquired angrily.

"Calm down, girl. Somebody just dropped off some clothes and put some money on your books. I knew you needed them, so I rushed them back here," Harris explained, handing Tara the brown paper bag with the belongings inside.

"Thanks, Harris. Good lookin' out," Tara offered in an apologizing voice.

"There's some pamphlets on the drug treatment classes we offer here on Tuesday evenings in the chapel. The lady who runs the group is a caring Christian, and a lot of women in here say she's helped them understand their addiction.

"I have some other rounds to make, and then I'll be back and we can talk some more," the caring deputy explained.

"That's cool. I need to make a few phone calls. Thanks for the info. I'm going to take a look at these pamphlets later on," Tara whispered sincerely as she slowly walked to her bunk.

She searched the brown bag, happy to see Scott had sent her all the things she asked for. It took a person that's done time to know just the right shit to get. Tara had everything she needed to get through the days ahead.

She was booked. She was on probation and out on bond, now on a new case. She wasn't going anywhere soon and she knew it.

She'd let Julio and her family down, and now she was most likely on her way to prison. She was tough, and she knew she'd do her best to survive the unknown.

Crack kept her mind in a fog most of the time, so she didn't have time to think about how fucked-up her life really was right now. She'd just spent the last few days in the work-house in a drug-induced deep sleep. Now the fog was lifting and she could think clearly. There was so much to think about. How was she going to fix this? Where did she start?

Her body was so tired from the all-night smoking sessions on the streets. Her ritual was the same daily. She'd get up around four in the afternoon and dress in one of the few work outfits she had with her, and then head to the nearest mall to hit a quick lick. She would be in and out of the mall within a couple of hours. She knew good shit, and it didn't take her long to pick up some fast movers and be out and then push the pieces on the street.

Her first stop after that was always at a cool spot where she could get her drug. Then she would post up in her motel room and get her head right. Some nights she would sit in the same cheap hotel chair and smoke for so long her ass would go numb.

She was like a zombie in the way she moved through the days of her life. Nothing mattered. She only woke up because her body was programmed to do so on its own. There were some days when she stayed in the motel room and cried the entire day away. She would cry until her body ached, and then she would drift off to sleep. This had been going on for months; she was either asleep or high.

Julio was her reason for living. They had been inseparable, and fate tore them apart. Now the separation was killing her. She hadn't been back to visit him since the day she ran into Candy.

Tara got dressed in the black two-piece silk pajama set

Scott sent her and put on the matching robe with the terry towel lining. She felt better already. The material hugged her body and comforted her. For a brief moment, she felt like her old self.

"Tara, there's a free phone out here," Cricket informed her. "You better get out here and get it. I can't keep these thirsty bitches off it for much longer. I ain't trying to go to the hole over laying a bitch out in this motherfucka. These young girls are always testing a thoroughbred. What the fuck is up?" Cricket questioned, walking back and forth from the dayroom to the sleeping area, daring anyone to speak.

Two hookers who were sleeping soundly woke from their sleep, moaned, rolled over, and went right back to sleep.

"Cricket, hold that noise down. I'm coming," Tara ordered.

She could feel the stares of Nikki and the two young girls Nikki had been talking to as she crossed the room. All of them were shocked to see that Tara was so obviously smoking crack.

No one judged her; they all knew how unforgiving the streets were, and sometimes a bitch was forced to self-medicate to deal with the pain. Nobody judged another bitch's story in jail. The only thing that was nearly unforgivable was harming a child.

She'd caught Nikki staring at her several times that evening. She needed to find out who this chick was and why she was so interested in her every move. That would have to wait, though; she wanted to give Scott a call and thank him for looking out.

Tara was glad to have reconnected with Scott, but she wished the timing would have been different. The two of them were always coming in and out of each other's lives at the wrong time. He'd provided her a needed moment of escape. She knew he cared about her, and she felt safe in his arms. Scott filled a need in her body and took her mind off the pain, but her heart still longed for Julio.

After dialing Scott's number, Tara listened to the automated commands and waited for Scott's voice to answer.

"Yo! Yo! What's up, shorty?" Scott questioned cheerfully in the phone, trying to gauge her mood.

"I'm chillin'," Tara answered back.

"I been waiting for you to call me. Damn, you had a nigga posted by the phone trying to see what's up. I called a lawyer and he checked on getting you out on bond, but your judge got you on lock," he explained, wishing he had better news for her.

He wanted to help her so bad. From the first time he met her, he always wanted to comfort her. She was always so hard for a female. He respected that. They were the ones who survived and made a difference for the rest of the niggas like him. Sisters were the real tough ones. They were the ones who gave peace to niggas like him.

"Thanks for trying. I appreciate that. I owe you. It may be a minute before I can pay you, though," Tara joked, trying to lighten the moment.

"You know I'll take my pay in some of that good pussy you sitting on," Scott teased back as he got comfortable on his bed. His mind told him they could have had a future at a different time. All he could do now, though, was be there for her and send up a few prayers. He hadn't thought about praying in years, but something told him Tara needed some help that he couldn't give her.

"I'm gonna hold you to that deal. I want my pay," she laughed, remembering their nights together. "I'm going to go. Thanks again for everything. You've always been there for me. A sister needs a man like you in their corner," Tara complimented as she prepared to hang up.

There was a lot more she wanted to say to him, but she

didn't want to lead him on. She knew the pain of waiting for someone who the system controlled. She didn't wish that pain on anybody, and was just glad to know that she had a true friend in her corner. She wanted to make sure he knew that she was grateful for his friendship, but her heart belonged to Julio.

"Tara, call me anytime. I'm out here running these streets, trying to stack some chips, so if you don't get me the first time, call back until you get me. If you have to lay it down, I got you," Scott explained.

"I will, Scott. Thanks for everything. I'll call you in a few days. Bye," Tara said softly as she tried to fight back her tears.

The waste of what she'd done to her life weighed heavy on her heart. She wanted to fix all the things she'd broken, but where did . . . how did she start? She'd taken chances her whole life. So many people held the power over her happiness. Somehow she needed to find the answers to all these questions.

Tara was tired of thinking. The thinking brought way to much pain. Damn, if she just had a hit of crack, the fog would lift and she could escape the thoughts in her head. She'd think about all that tomorrow. She couldn't face it right then.

Tara hung up the phone and spun around. "Let's get the party started up in this punk-ass dorm. Doretha, deal the cards. I'm going to show y'all how to really play cards," Tara said, laughing as she danced back to the picnic bench and joined the gay couple at the table.

"You got a partner, Tara?" Cricket asked while she cleaned off the table from dinner.

"No, but I'll get one," she answered back. Tara went in the sleep area and announced to the room, "Anybody want to play bid whist?"

"I'll play," Nikki responded, getting up from her bed and putting on her state-issued flip-flops. The two women stared at each other for a moment and both returned to the dayroom together.

There was something familiar about the girl Nikki. Tara felt a connection to her that she could not explain.

They began the card game and won every hand together. Before long, the pair were interacting with each other like old friends. Tara learned that Nikki was being held by the feds on serious drug charges. The poor girl was facing life, and this was her first time ever being locked up. She asked questions about jail and the procedures like a kid on the first day of school. Tara could tell that she was scared but intelligent.

Nikki was a pretty girl with long brown hair. She had a potato-shaped face with bright eyes. Even stripped down and no makeup, Tara could tell she could hold her own in a roomful of models.

After hours of playing cards, they finally took a break. "I need to get me something to eat," Nikki said, getting up from the table. "You want anything, Tara?" she offered.

"Yeah, girl, bring me something sweet," Tara said, getting up to stretch her legs.

"Come with me to my bunk. I got all kinds of stuff and I don't know what you like," Nikki explained.

Tara followed her to her bunk and looked around. Nikki had set up shop in the workhouse. The girl had everything she needed to be comfortable. She knew she wasn't going anywhere soon.

Nikki noticed Tara checking out her stacks of books.

"I love to read. It clears my head. I've been reading some really good self-help books lately. Have you heard of T.D. Jakes?" Nikki asked Tara as she handed her a stack of books. Tara took the books and carefully read the synopsis of each one.

One stuck out like a sore thumb: *Woman, Thou Art Loosed!* by Bishop T.D. Jakes. It felt as if the book was speaking to Tara. The words rang in her head like music. She could feel a pulling in her stomach, and she knew she had to read this book.

"Can I read this one?" Tara asked softly.

"Yes, just remember to use a book marker so the pages don't get messed up. I'm funny about my books. I like to keep them nice," Nikki explained.

Tara barely paid her any attention as she walked, zombie-like, back to her bunk and curled up with the book, forgetting all about her snack. *Woman, Thou Art Loosed!* The words rang in Tara's soul as a wave of peace swept across her.

She stayed up all night reading the book, and by daybreak she had finished. Somewhere during the night, she began taking notes on a small piece of paper. She had so many questions she needed answers to.

Tara slid from the top bunk and put on her state tan flip-flops. The dorm was peaceful and quiet; only a few women were awake for the day. The deputies had already made their morning rounds and turned on the TV and phones. A young, college-looking white girl, who was brought in the night before, sat on the floor, crying into the phone, begging someone on the other end to please come bail her out.

Tara picked up the phone and thought hard before dialing the number. She could hear the voice on the other end loudly saying, "Hello, hello." Tara almost hung up, but then she spoke.

"Reverend Hairston, this is Tara," she said softly into the phone.

"Tara, how are you? I've been praying for you," Reverend Hairston said.

"I'm okay. I just wanted to ask you a question," Tara whispered, leaning against the wall.

"What is it, Tara?" Reverend Hairston questioned sincerely as he prayed silently.

"Is my life beyond repair?" Tara asked, crying.

"Tara, honey, nobody's life is beyond repair. Sometimes God has to snatch us out of the way to get our attention. God can take a negative situation and turn it into a blessing. I am believing God, that He will use this time to turn your life into a blessing for yourself and others. Trust Him and let Him use you," Reverend Hairston spoke into the phone, words of healing for Tara's soul.

"I don't know how to start to change my life," Tara confessed as she slid to the floor and sat down.

"You don't need to do anything but read your Bible and pray, and God will give you the answers you need. Use this time to seek God. You can come to know Him in a very real way. Ask Him to save you and believe that He will, and He will. Now let me pray with you," the Reverend said.

"Dear Heavenly Father, we thank you for your blessings, your mercy and your love. We worship you and praise you for all you've done. You've been so good. We thank you for keeping us. We realize we could have been dead, but you saw fit to spare our lives and we say thank you.

"Father, I ask that you watch over my sister. Show her your glory. Take this valley in her life and give her a mountaintop experience. Allow her to come to know you in a very real way. She needs you to walk with her and to hold her hand. Go with her, stand by her, protect and guide her life. Father, show her who you created her to be, allow her to come through as pure gold.

"We are standing on your promises. We know that all

things work together for good to them that love the Lord. We love you, Lord Jesus. These and all blessings we ask in the precious name of Jesus. Amen."

When Tara finally hung up the phone, she'd asked Reverend Hairston every question on the wrinkled piece of paper, and somehow everything seemed like it would be okay. Her answers had been found in prayer. Her answers had been found in God.

"Tara, how long you been up?" Nikki asked, sitting down at the picnic table in the dayroom in her terry towel robe with her hair tied up in a homemade head scarf.

"I haven't been to sleep, Nikki. I stayed up all night reading the book you gave me, and it has changed my life. I just finished talking to my pastor, and he prayed for me, and I really feel like things are going to be all right," Tara shared with her new friend, joining her on the bench.

"When I read the book, it did the same thing for me. I've had my family send me every book Bishop Jakes has written. I'm on my third one now. It's called *Can You Stand to be Blessed?* You want to read it with me?" Nikki questioned, glad to be able to have someone she could talk to about religion.

"I want to read everything you have by the bishop. He's my cat. He has a way of talking to your heart.

"I got some letters in the mail. I'm going to read them and then take a nap, Nikki. I'll check out the books later," Tara explained, leaving the room and heading for her bunk.

She lay on her bunk and slowly pulled three letters from Julio from under her pillow. She studied his handwriting; it made her feel close to him to look at the words he created on the paper with the pen.

Her heart ached for him. Her body craved him. Julio was the love of her life. But she now realized that she had to love herself more. She now put her trust in God and believed He would fix all the things that were wrong in their relationship.

Tara lay down on the bed and read all three letters carefully. Julio was so angry with her for so many things. He was so hurt by her drug use. He felt deserted by her. In the first letter, he told her that he wanted a divorce and he wanted his name back.

In the second letter, he wrote ten pages explaining how he had niggas in the street reporting on her every move. He was aware of all the times she cheated on him. He called her every ho in the book.

By the third letter, some of his anger started to fade. He had stopped calling her names, and he even asked how she was holding up.

Although it hurt her deeply to read the words he wrote, his pain healed her. She understood his anger; it was how he dealt with his pain. Tara even understood when he told her in one of the letters that Candy had been coming to see him regularly. He went on to tell her Candy had proven to be a true friend to him. He would then talk about how bad he needed her and she wasn't there. This would then make him mad, and the curse words in Spanish would follow.

She knew beneath the harsh words was a man that was hurting just as badly as she had been all these months. He was alone going through hell; the drugs never allowed her to look at his pain. When she was high, all she thought about was herself. She was glad Candy was there for him when she couldn't be.

Tara pulled her yellow legal pad from underneath her mattress as she searched the edge of the rusty steel bed rail for her pencil. She closed her eyes for a moment and thought of the love they shared.

After ending the letter, she folded it neatly and kissed it

gently. She sent a piece of her heart with every word on the page. She placed the important letter in the white legal envelope and sealed it.

Tara pulled the latest letter from Julio out one last time and read it over and over again. Studying his words on the legal paper made her feel close to him. She hoped he could feel her in her letter. She spoke from her heart, and that was real.

She carefully put the letters in a neat pile and placed them under her pillow, and did the only thing she now knew how to do . . . she prayed.

Nikki stood at the door with the other inmates, waiting on the deputy to let in the women coming back from court. Nikki could see Tara through the small square window in the steel door, and she smiled. Tara smiled back through the door at her friend. Nikki could not read Tara's mood.

Tara stood at the door, still a little stunned by Judge Miller's sentence. She'd told herself that she would be okay with whatever the sentence was, that it was God's will for her life, but she was still taken by surprise by the sentence.

"I sentence you to three years at the Ohio Reformatory for Women in Marysville. Hopefully this will allow you time to think about your actions and begin to turn your life around," Judge Miller said with a serious face. Tara could still hear the words echoing in her ears.

As the steel door opened, the women rushed to meet the ladies as they slowly walked inside. Tara announced to everyone, "Three years," and sat down on the rusty metal bench.

The women sighed, and the jailhouse lawyers began telling her how she could take time off her sentence once she got to Marysville. Some of the women tried to comfort her by telling her how much better things were there. Tara listened out of respect before going to her bunk to lie down.

"You all right? Do you want to talk?" Nikki whispered, peeking up at Tara from beside the bunk bed.

"I'm cool, Nikki; I'm just sleepy, that's all," Tara lied, pulling the scratchy wool blanket over her as she lay down and closed her eyes.

"You still want to have Bible study later?" Nikki questioned. The Bible study classes Tara started were good for the dorm. Most of the women attended, and the dorm was more peaceful. Women can be hell locked in a small space together.

The women all looked forward to Tara's weekly Bible study classes. Both Tara's and Nikki's lives were being changed daily by the T.D. Jakes books they read together.

The two of them had become fast friends. Each woman thanked God for providing a shoulder to lean on. They both were anxious to share their newfound peace with the other women.

Tara was a natural teacher. She had a gift for explaining the confusing Bible verses to the women. Most of them had never stepped foot in a church, and they had so many questions.

"Yeah, but let's wait until after dinner. I'm going to take a nap. Wake me up so I can make a few calls before the trays come," Tara instructed her friend.

"All right. There are four more girls who want to have Bible study with us. In a minute the whole dorm will be in on our Bible studies," Nikki said proudly, walking back to her bunk.

Tara lay there thinking about what Nikki said. She looked around the room at all the women. Jail was a strange place;

she never would have believed she would come to know God in a personal way in jail. If anyone had told her that a year ago, she would not have believed them.

Tara used her time in the workhouse to seek answers for what was wrong with her life. The Bible, NA meetings, and the other books she read allowed her the chance to heal, and she used every chance she got to share her healing with the other women.

There were so many broken women in jail, so many woman lost like she was, and she wanted to share with them the peace she'd found.

She was surprised by how little most of them knew about God. She was grateful for all the times Mama Grace had dragged them to church when she was young. The seeds that were planted way back then allowed her to freely trust God. Tara was disappointed by the sentence, but she trusted that God would guide her through the next three years.

It was hard for her to call home and talk with family; she hated disappointing them. She knew they wanted much more for her life. The pain of watching your child go off to jail was killing M&M. Tara heard the pain in her mother's and her father's voices every time she spoke to them on the phone.

The last time she spoke to her mother, M&M told her that Karen was in rehab and doing well. Tara was happy for her friend. She wished she could speak to her and let her know she was proud of her.

Julio had been sentenced to five years fed time. She knew she'd let him down, so she never got mad when he began writing her angry letters. She was just glad he was writing her. Underneath all the words, she knew he still loved her, and she held on to that love.

She drifted off to sleep and thought of him.

After dinner, Tara prepared for Bible study. Nikki stood by the cement wall and talked on the phone quietly. Tara could tell by the look on Nikki's face something was wrong.

She wiped off the table and placed her yellow legal tablet and Bible in the center of the table and sat down. Several other women with their Bibles in hand joined her.

Cricket and Doretha approached the table and started to sit down. "Aw, come on, Tara, with that Bible study shit. We want to play cards," Cricket complained, looking at the table.

"We won't be that long, and then you can have the table," Tara offered Cricket.

"We want to play now, not later," Cricket shot back. The two women stared each other down before Cricket spoke. "All right, but you only have an hour."

Doretha stared at the floor the whole time.

Tara could hear Cricket say to Doretha as she walked away, "I'm sick as fuck of the preacher and the pastor and all this church shit."

Deputy Harris unlocked the door and walked in the dorm. She looked around the dorm at the women and removed the contraband head scarves from two girls on the phone by the door.

"Ladies, Sheriff Karnes has approved for you to go outside for one hour this evening. If you want to go, you need to be ready in ten minutes. I'll be back to get you. And don't even think about coming out this dorm with no contraband on your heads. Bring me that rag in your pocket, Audrey," the deputy ordered Cricket, calling her by her government name.

"Damn, Harris, you don't miss shit. Give me a break. I just got this one the way I like it," Cricket complained, handing the ripped-up T-shirt to Deputy Harris.

"I'll be back in ten minutes to get you, so be ready," Harris instructed, closing the door and locking it.

The women moved quickly around the door and prepared for the unexpected treat of going outside. Of all Tara's days in the workhouse, the women had never been allowed to go outside.

The women waited anxiously by the door and speculated about why they were being allowed the chance to go outside. Everyone had their own theory.

Once outside, the women hovered in a group together. Nobody knew what to do first. It was a beautiful, warm, sunny day and the warmth from the sun washed over them all. Tara was approaching two months in the county jail, and it was a welcomed treat to be somewhere other than the confinement of the dorm.

The women were allowed to occupy a small enclosed area that was designed for the inmates to exercise. For whatever reason, it was rarely used for what it was intended, so the grass was unusually green and soft. Some of the women took off their shoes and walked barefoot through the grass. Others sat down and enjoyed the softness of it. They were all like children on Christmas morning with a new toy.

"Tara, I really need you to pray with me. My family is trippin'. Every time I think I can do this time, I get some more bad news. Can you pray with me?" Nikki pleaded with her.

Nikki was so sick of her family arguing over *her* money. She would call home to check on her son, and the whole phone call would be wasted with her mom and sister on both lines arguing about her money, and they always wanted her to choose sides. She'd given both of them access to her bank accounts, and they were going through her money like crazy.

Two women nearby heard their conversation and spoke up and said, "We need you to pray with us also. I go to court tomorrow, and I don't know what my judge is going to do," one of the women explained.

"Children's Services is trying to take my kids from my mother," the other woman added, circling around Tara.

Tara joined hands with Nikki and the woman on the other side of her. The woman who had to go to court grabbed hands with Nikki. Women began walking up from everywhere around the yard and joined in the prayer. Cricket slowly walked toward the prayer circle and joined hands with Doretha and a pregnant teenage girl.

Tara looked at the sincere desperation in the women's faces, and her mind drifted to the Prince of Peace Holiness Church. *"If God's been good to you, then you ought to stand up on your feet and say, 'Thank you.'"* Tara could see Reverend Hairston running around the pulpit as the church broke into a shout.

"Dear Heavenly Father," Tara began to pray, "we are truly grateful to you for sparing our lives. We give you honor and we give you praise. Please forgive us for all the things we've done wrong. We stand before you so desperately. We can't make this journey without you. There are so many things we can't control, and we need you to work on them for us. So many of us need you to watch over our loved ones until we can be with them again." Tara prayed as the sun shined brightly on the women in the yard at the Franklin County Correctional Center.

Just as she was about to move her lips to continue her prayer, a loud voice interrupted her thoughts.

"Ladies, ladies, break up that organized circle," the white-shirted sergeant ordered, rushing toward Tara with six deputies backing him up.

The women quickly broke up their prayer circle and

scattered around the yard. None of them wanted to get caught up in any drama, especially when they were trying to do the right thing.

Tara continued praying silently. She prayed for all the women's needs, and she prayed for herself. She refused to allow the deputies to come between her and her relationship with God. She was so grateful to Him for her newfound peace. She felt a peace which surpassed all understanding. She knew the only way she would be able to get through prison would be to hold onto that peace for dear life. And that's exactly what she intended to do. Amen!

MESSAGE FROM THE AUTHOR

I was taken to church at an early age by my grandmother; my connection to my spiritual foundation began at an early age; however, I was unable to escape the influences of my exposure to street life by my parents.

My life was changed forever when I met and married a Dominican drug dealer. I was swept off my feet and into the fast lane. I found myself caught up in the street life and addicted to drugs. I ended up serving three years at the Ohio Reformatory for Women and Franklin Pre-Release Center.

During my incarceration, I did much soul-searching. It was while I was awaiting my incarceration that I met Vickie Stringer, now founder and CEO of Triple Crown Publications, who gave me a book entitled *Woman, Thou Art Loosed!* by T.D. Jakes. Profoundly affected by the novel, I began to reconnect with my spiritual foundation and embark on the road to recovery.

After much hard work and dedication upon my release from prison, I became a general manager and manager trainer at two of the leading national athletic shoe chains (Lady Foot Locker and Foot Action USA), where I received awards for best sales leadership of the year, best profit turnaround, best sales gain, best sales percent, and best audit control. These accomplishments, coupled with the drive to succeed in all of my endeavors, led me to the position of office manager and marketing and publicity manager of Triple Crown Publications, the pioneer and leading publisher of hip-hop literature.

I believe strongly in giving back. I have worked hands-on with several reentry and prison programs and currently serve as a life coach for the Bonds Beyond Bars Program sponsored by the Girl Scouts Seal of Ohio Council. I am a proud board member of both the Flintridge Community Development Board and the Franklin Pre-Release Citizens Advisory Board. I also serve on the Juvenile Community Planning Initiative, focusing on disproportionate minority contact.

I am currently the program director for Revival Development Corporation, where I am able to touch the lives of at-risk youth in Columbus, Ohio, daily. Without a doubt, I know that we have an obligation to make a difference in the world. When we look at our communities, the magnitude of the problems our neighborhoods face becomes overwhelming; however, we cannot be discouraged by this. If we reach out and touch the lives in front of us then, day by day, we empower each other and the world changes.

In writing this book, I believe that God will use my story to let the world know that your life is not beyond repair. Each day we have a fresh opportunity to get it right; to discover our purpose and who God created us to be. Somebody's blessing is waiting on you.

Pray for me as I begin working on my second novel.